W9-BDH-880

NOSE

for trouble

DORANNA DURGIN

W🌐RLDWIDE®

TORONTO • NEW YORK • LONDON
AMSTERDAM • PARIS • SYDNEY • HAMBURG
STOCKHOLM • ATHENS • TOKYO • MILAN
MADRID • WARSAW • BUDAPEST • AUCKLAND

NOSE FOR TROUBLE

A Worldwide Mystery/February 2007

First published by Five Star Publishing in conjunction with Tekno Books and Ed Gorman.

ISBN-13: 978-0-373-26592-3
ISBN-10:   0-373-26592-1

Printed in U.S.A.

Dedicated to Suzanne Thomas and her Cedar Ridge
Beagles, and especially for the little fellow who joined
my crew as this book headed for the home stretch,
Cedar Ridge DoubleOSeven.

With thanks along the way to Jim Maciulla, DVM,
Julie Czerneda (boy does she read fast), Ferragus for
believing in Dale and Sully from the start, Lucienne for
seeing it through, and Jennifer for cheering along this
ride of dirt-road bumpiness.

ONE

New home sweet home.

Dale Kinsall sat in the comfortably full parking lot of the Foothills Veterinary Clinic and let recent changes roll over him. Steamroller, even. The surrounding view was no longer of flat Midwest dairy cow fields and long white barns bordered with trees, verdant grass, and road ditches thick with cattails. Instead he found himself amidst drought-dry high desert, with the San Francisco Peaks directly behind him, ponderosa pines lining the road and climbing up the base of the Peaks, and natural volcanic cinders waiting to crunch beneath his feet. Massive cinder hills dotted the landscape, some with signs of old mining operations. The dry air still made his sinuses recoil in shock when he drew a deep breath. Late spring in Flagstaff, Arizona.

And I have only myself to blame.

Well, and maybe the fire.

A cold wet nose gently bumped the back of his arm. Dale realized he'd never quite removed his hand from the stick shift, as though perhaps he might throw the Subaru Forester in gear and burn rubber out of there, spitting gravel—*cinders*—from the tires. Thirty-four and suddenly life didn't seem so predictable anymore. Maybe it was a lesson he should have learned earlier.

Bump.

He glanced back over his shoulder to discover the obvious:

Sully had again escaped from his soft-sided travel case. Cedar Ridge Sully, escape beagle extraordinaire. And Sully looked at Dale with an expression totally devoid of guilt. In fact, with the slightest crease above those chocolate brown eyes and long floppy ears pulled forward to frame his soft face in Flying Nun mode, there was quite clearly—and as usual—only one thing on Sully's mind.

when do we eat?

"Never," Dale muttered at him, but not without a gentle tug on one of those ears to make the beagle smile. A cat-toting woman navigated the doors out of the clinic, doing a creditable job of hanging onto the Silly Putty cat as she maneuvered past the young man and gawky young setter on the way in. Dale looked out at the building again, long and low and brown with no indication of the extensive facilities hidden in the back. Two benches flanked the doorway under a porch overhang, and drought-limp landscaping bordered the front between no-nonsense painted 4x4 porch posts. And then there was the sign. Freshly painted at the bottom of the Foothills clinic sign was *Dale Kinsall, DVM*. "There we are," Dale told Sully. Another customer, this one carrying a tiny goat, entered the clinic while Dale watched. Larger animals would go around back—they tended plenty of stock, horses most of all. "And we might as well go in and start making it feel like home."

He slipped a collar over Sully's head as the beagle invited himself to clamber into a front seat already occupied by the carelessly overstuffed boxes Dale was reasonably sure belonged at his new desk. He'd gotten a little hasty during the final stages of packing and only hoped he wouldn't open any office boxes to the sight of old laundry or grade school mementos.

Balancing between the boxes on the seat and the cooler stuffed into the passenger leg area, Sully gave Dale a startled, unhappy look. His expression went from amiable to the unmistakable down-turned quirk of lip and droop of ear, dog caught by an abrupt *i don't feel so good* and Dale didn't hesitate; he fumbled with his seatbelt, freed himself, and escaped from the Forester just in time to haul Sully out and—

hu-hu-hu-rrrrup!!

"Wonderful. What is that, pine needles? Really great way to christen the clinic, Sully. You might have just peed on something." But Sully excelled at droop-eared forlorn sorrow, and Dale sighed and gave the young dog a pat, glad to remember the short hose at the corner of the building. He had no intention of leaving the entry walk…well, sullied.

The silent pun cheered him, and abruptly the changes and the challenges ahead didn't seem so overwhelming. He pulled the hose free from its casual coil on the ground and turned it on, sluicing the walkway clean and then sluicing Sully's face clean with no regard to the beagle's horrified expression.

He heard the footsteps of someone's purposeful approach and looked up with a smile ready—

"This isn't your day!" The newcomer stood between two parked cars with a bike by his side and an outraged expression on his face.

"Er," Dale said, using all the intelligence he could muster and soaking his shoes before he remembered to release the hose sprayer handle. At second blink he realized this newcomer had detoured from his journey along Highway 89 to deliver his declaration. Dale hunted for something more meaningful to say in response but only repeated himself, this time less certainly. "Er…"

The man flung an accusing finger at the bold numbers attached to the side of the clinic. "You're odd!"

One of us certainly is, Dale thought, and offered a weak smile. "Okay," he said, hoping that might make the man go away. He didn't *look* like an unbalanced person as he stood beside the Forester; in fact, in his nifty biking outfit and clean-shaven face under a neon helmet, he looked like a habitually active, functioning individual.

But the man didn't act like he was going to go away, so Dale returned the hose to its corner, squishing audibly, and shut off the water. Sully was conspicuously quiet on his leash, either still feeling a little ill—not likely, given his cast-iron constitution—or wary of the man's demeanor. For his own part Dale thought it was a good time to escape into the clinic, and rued the fact that his car door still hung open, waiting for attention. Sure enough, as soon as he returned within range, the man said sharply, "Rules are made for a reason, you know."

"Yes, of course," Dale said, pretending he didn't feel the narrow-eyed scrutiny of the man's hard blue gaze. Maybe this was typical of his new home. Maybe he'd just have to get used to casual encounters of the baffling kind. In this case, it seemed a quick retreat was the way to go. He gave the scowling fellow a *we're all friends here* kind of smile and turned away from the SUV—

—and *whoomp!* ran solidly into someone—a female someone—who'd just come storming out of the clinic at high speed. Sully startled off to the end of his leash while Dale grabbed the woman to keep them from both going down and then hastily readjusted his grip to keep himself from getting arrested. She jerked back and they tried twice to go around one another in the same direction, until she drew back in exasperation to glare at him.

At second thought there was more than just glare there; her lower lip and chin had a slight tremble to it, making her look much more vulnerable than he suspected she would have preferred, especially to judge by the part of her that was indeed still glaring—her eyes, nearly black eyes. Her heart-shaped face had the distinctive features and complexion he was quickly coming to recognize as Navajo, but she was a smaller-boned package overall. She wore a collared tee embroidered with *Laura Nakai, DVM* and *Pine Country Clinic* and she filled it out very nicely indeed.

Heel, Dale told himself, realizing that he'd collided with a colleague, albeit one who worked in the clinic across the city.

But it was a very small city. It was to Dale's mind little more than a long, narrow town, pulled out like thick taffy with lumps of commercialism and residences on either end and a strip of old Route 66 hotels where the middle was thinned by the encroachment of Mt. Elden, the shorter mountain of the Peaks. The other end of it was a bigger lump, heavy with the university community. The Foothills Clinic—and now Dale—resided outside Flagstaff proper in the small almost-town of West Winona. That this woman worked on the other end of it all still pretty much put her in his backyard.

He gave her the best smile he could muster with his feet squishing and the sounds of the strange accusatory man departing behind him and Sully tugging gently on his leash, rooting around behind the wilted plantings in front of the clinic. "I'm sorry," he said, running a hand through hair too recently cut to actually fall over his eyes. Black and thick and *please, God, let it stay that way,* it generally grew too quickly to keep in hand and the habit never went away. "I was distracted."

Her glare faded long enough for her to take in his wet shoes, the rapidly drying walkway, his SUV crammed to the ceiling with boxes and the kind of objects that enter a car only to move from point A to point B. A favorite desk lamp squashed up against the side window of the cargo area, a sheaf of loose papers crept for escape, and a very visible old stuffed elephant he suddenly wished he'd packed in the middle instead of at the very visible edges. "So I see," she said, and then her glance rested on the man who cycled away from the parking lot with

WN-WN stamped on the back of his shirt. The woman's face cleared somewhat, though her distraction remained evident. "Ah," she said. "You ran into Win-Win."

He followed her gaze to the fast retreating cyclist and wondered what that was supposed to mean. "Did I?" he said, and then upon short reflection added, "He called me odd. Which is probably true, but it's an awful personal thing to say to someone in a parking lot." Sully, still mostly immersed in small shrubs and groundcover, pulled the leash; Dale gave it a gentle pull in return. "Sully," he said, but Sully only gave the tilt of head and ear that meant he heard, but…

busy.

The woman gave a short laugh, though it still had the edge she'd brought with her out of the clinic. "Not *you*, the building." She gestured at the street number on the clinic sign. *7977*. "Someone from Waste Not-Water Not caught you hosing things down on the wrong day. You know, even days, odd days. Don't you read the paper?"

"Not yet," he admitted, but not willing to also admit just how baffling he found her words. Nor did he have to, for Sully had realized that Dale was in conversation and that he was somehow not the focus of it; he came trotting out of the bushes with his tail held high and his recently sluiced face and chest entirely smeared with the fine dusty high desert soil. Dale gave an inward groan.

But Sully wasn't through. He came, he saw, he liked—and he put his tail in gear and flung himself on the woman as though he'd never had a moment's training otherwise, smearing muddy paw prints down her jeans.

"Sully!" Dale said in his *doom voice,* horrified. He bent down to capture twenty-plus pounds of wagging—and then the world went gray and whirling, betraying him entirely, and he kept right on going down. With much shock, he found himself on hands and knees while Sully commenced nuzzling and bumping and worrying.

Laura Nakai came to the rescue. Gently but firmly, she pushed Sully away, securing his leash around one of the clinic's porch posts. She pressed down on Dale's shoulder when he started to gather his feet under him. "Sit," she said, so he did, instantly feeling the water soak through the seat of his jeans. *It just gets better...* But the Forester and the parking lot and even Laura Nakai still whirled around him in dizzying swoops, so he propped his forearms on his knees and closed his eyes. She said, "You're new to the area, aren't you?"

Through clenched teeth, he asked, "What gave it away?"

"Besides the packed vehicle and the general ignorance?" she responded, digging in her leather backpack-purse as she crouched beside him. "The altitude sickness. Do you have a headache? And I'll bet you haven't had anything to drink all day."

"No!" he said, startled. His eyes flew open, but quickly shut again. "I'm not—I don't—"

"I meant water." Real amusement in her voice this time, she put a sports-bottle in his hand and nudged upward. "Drink. It's tea, but it's wet and cold."

He drank. The instant it hit his mouth he realized how thirsty he was, and how many boxes he'd lugged to and fro that morning without remembering to drink a drop. *It's the desert, dummy. Dumb, dumb, dumb...*

She might as well have been reading his mind. "People forget. Flagstaff isn't a furnace like Phoenix, but it's just as dry; you have no idea how much you sweat out. Get yourself a sports bottle and keep it full. As for the altitude...you'll adjust."

He groaned without thinking, and she gave his shoulder a pat, but even then he felt her amusement. Small women seemed

to find it amusing when a big man did girlie things. Like
fainting, for instance.

I *didn't* faint.

Just almost.

OH WOE.

   dale's sick. me too but who cares, that was whole moments
ago. dale! don't be on the ground! don't look so pale, it's not
right! i can't reach you because the woman tied me, that's not
right either. beagle woo-oooh! beagle woo-oooh!

   they're ignoring me. i'd like a drink too, but—oh, he looks
better already. maybe it was that loud man. i'd like to chase his
bike, i would. but the woman is nice. she smells good, an open
smell…she likes dogs. i would trust her. she's not happy
though. dale missed it, too busy falling down. not the breathing thing, that makes noise. another thing.

   untie me? someone untie me? i'm left out! beagle bark!

"CUTE DOG," said Laura Nakai, sitting back on her heels as
Dale took another drink. "Nice to see a well-bred beagle. Do
you show him?"

   Dale found he could focus on her, though the world had a
far-away feeling. He took a deep, surreptitious breath, testing
for tightness in his chest or the faint burn of irritated lungs. Odd
how quickly that had become habit again. *The climate will
help.* Or so everyone said.

   She'd quirked an eyebrow at him, waiting.

   "Uh," he said, feeling stupid. "I meant to. Life…got in the
way. Maybe now that I'm here."

   Sully barked again, a woebegone sound. *me!*

   "Yeah, yeah," Dale told him. "We know you're there. You've
made quite an impression on us all today."

   "Try agility competition. He looks like he already keeps you on the run," she said dryly, closing her little backpack and gathering herself to stand up; she glanced over her shoulder at the clinic door, and her fine features tightened. "I've got to go. Keep the tea, and *drink* it. If you know someone who can drive you home, call them. And take it easy for a few days."

"Thank you," he said, trying to imagine if he could possibly feel more humbled. "I actually work here. Or I will. So I'll be okay."

"You—" She abruptly closed her mouth, and it thinned slightly in a response he couldn't understand. Her deep brown eyes latched on to him, really *looking* at him, and her expression didn't improve any in the process. Dale had never felt taller or gawkier, in spite of the fact that he'd finally filled out to his height lo these many years ago. He'd definitely never felt less dignified.

His tentative offering of a smile didn't do any good. She thrust herself to her feet and said tightly, "Good luck," as she strode swiftly for the small hatchback hunkered down at the end of the parking row.

Dale watched her go, dazed in every brain cell. The little car jerked into reverse, swung a quick backwards turn, and accelerated up the short steep incline up to the highway, barely hesitating before darting onto the road itself. Behind Dale, Sully gave a puzzled little whine.

"Yeah," Dale said. "Me, too."

TWO

DALE LINGERED CROSS-LEGGED on the walkway, drinking tea and looking at the Peaks, the dry terrain, and the pines surrounding the cinder-crunchy parking lot. Thinking. Behind him, lining the front of the clinic, two wooden benches stood guard; he could be sitting in one of them. Although that meant getting up, and if he was getting up, he'd just as well sit in the car—even if it did suddenly seem further away than he'd remembered. So for another long moment he sat, until he determined that the hot little poke of pain in his butt was from one of Flagstaff's ubiquitous cinders grinding its way into his pocket area. Just about then Sully worked his leash loose and marched over to climb into Dale's lap with no doubt that the lap was indeed there just for him.

mine.

Mud and all.

"All right, then," Dale said, and lifted Sully, climbing to his feet. Carefully. The world stayed upright and so did he; he counted the process a success. He wiped his muddy hands on the navy blue of his loose T-shirt. Not exactly washboard, that stomach, but enough lean muscle to be reassuring—at least until he realized what he'd done, and tried ineffectively to brush the mud away. *Quit while you're ahead,* he told himself, and did. He returned to the Forester to embark on a search for the towel he knew would be there, somewhere, simply because one did not go off with Sully in a car and not have a towel. And also because Dale had a sneaking affection for *Hitchhiker's Guide to the Galaxy,* and thus knew better than to go anywhere without a towel.

He spread the towel and plunked his wet posterior behind the wheel, two parking spots down from the entryway and feeling anonymous enough. The strong spring sunshine offset the cool temperature and even won the fight; sitting here sipping tea and consuming blue corn tortilla chips seemed like just the right level of ambition for the moment. Sully sat on the floor at his feet. He gave Dale his *big brown eyes* look.

"You're drooling," Dale told him. He bit a chip in half and gave Sully the other half. Sully inhaled it and sat there looking like he'd never gotten anything at all and wasn't life a cruel trick?

Dale was by no means immune to this expression, but found himself too distracted to offer it proper homage. Laura Nakai. She'd been upset...obviously a woman of strong feelings, much as she hid them. He thought he'd like to bump into her again. On purpose. And then he remembered her words. "Don't I read the paper," he muttered, pretty much about the same time he recalled that he did actually *have* a copy of the paper—yesterday's or the day before's—sitting on the front passenger seat. Somewhere. Under boxes. Gingerly, he lifted a box and felt around for it. From the corner of his eye he caught Sully lifting his nose toward the bag of chips between Dale's knees and without turning, he said, "Don't even think about it."

poop. Sully settled back on his haunches and made a resentful face until he forgot to.

"It's here somewhere," Dale said, fingers reaching and searching. They scrabbled across slick newspaper and pounced in triumph. He didn't quite have the room to grasp the paper between fingers and thumb, but he edged his hand sideways and trapped the layers of newsprint between his index and middle fingers, tug-tug-tugging—

Victory retreated as the paper ripped, leaving Dale with a third of the front page, most of which was taken up by a picture of the dramatically receded shoreline at Lake Mary and the newly exposed detritus. "Who'd throw a computer away in a lake?" he wondered, taking another slug of tea. He passed a chip to Sully, let the dog take a bite, and absently put the rest of it in his mouth. "Or a washing machine drum? That's a hefty little package to wrestle around."

whatever. Sully kept his eyes glued to the chips bag.

"Here we go. Level Two water restrictions. Odd-numbered street addresses should water Tuesday, Thursday and Saturday." He glanced at the clinic address again: *7977.* "I guess we're odd at that. And on a Wednesday. Excellent planning, to move out here in the middle of…" he looked more closely at the paper and quoted, *"…Arizona's worst recorded drought."* He shoved the chips out of Sully's reach and spread the partial paper over the steering wheel, looking for more information. All he got was a truncated story written in self-consciously grim text. "Hmm, murder over by the university. Second one this year. Only the second! Now *that's* a number I could grow to like. Victim was one John Heflinger." Except after that tidbit, the paper deckled off into nothingness, leaving everything but half a headline and a few torn sentences; no details whatsoever.

A USPS Jeep pulled up in the spot Laura Nakai had so recently vacated; Sully immediately alerted. The mail was the mail was the mail, and every mail truck deserved extra attention.

Dale absently crossed his ankles, making a cage of his legs. "I don't think so," he informed the beagle, taking another swig of tea. He thought maybe if he drank it all, and *maybe* if he had a few more chips in lieu of actual food, he'd still be okay to unload what he'd brought. And Dr. Hogue was expecting him today, albeit not at any particular time.

One of the clinic workers, resplendent in scrubs with dog breeds printed all over it and short-shorn wire bristle hair sticking up where she'd shoved her fingers through it, came out as the mailman went in. She sat down on one of the benches flanking the entry and gave him an amiable wave. "Hey, Hank."

"Hey, Dru," he said back, just as amiable, balancing several packages atop the stack of mail he carried. "Those things'll kill you, you know."

"Yep." Her voice was cheerful enough, her words muffled. Dale glanced over at the click of a lighter and discovered an older woman. She probably thought of herself as "mature," but P.C. or not, that many wrinkles meant *older* to Dale, as did the dumpy shapelessness beneath the scrubs, the kind of shapelessness where some things fall and some things square up and they kind of meet in the middle. But her arms showed muscle and her eyes, as they caught Dale watching her over the cigarette-lighting ritual of flame and cupped hands, had a hard glint that made Dale think he wouldn't want to tangle with her even if she did look old enough to be his mother. Older.

At her gaze he looked hastily back to his chunk of paper, embarrassed to be caught staring. He didn't recall meeting her when he'd flown in for his interview, but there were a number of the vet techs and support staff he hadn't yet met.

Sully perked up, alerting Dale to the reappearance of Hank the mail carrier. Unfettered by packages, Hank proved to be a lanky forty-something, balding on top and making up for it with thin, graying shoulder-length hair. A hard round little potbelly pushed at his shirt buttons, exacerbated by his slouching posture. Hank's attention seemed aimed at the truck now lurching its way into the entry drive and down the brief but steeply angled hill to the parking lot itself. A homemade camper topped the truck bed, swaying alarmingly with the give of the vehicle's tired shocks.

Bright country-look curtains peered out from the edges of the little window on the side; the camper shell itself was painted with unreadable gingham lettering, a few sheep, and a token fence section. The entire thing was so overwhelmingly *cute* that Dale wanted to run and hide. Hank evidently felt the same way, given the wary look on his face.

But Dru ignored the newcomer and said to Hank, "Hey, that dead fellow. Weird, him being staked like that. I mean, *uhh!*—" and she thumped herself in the chest "staked for real."

Dale felt his eyes widen; he flipped his partial paper over, looking for any mention of stakes or staking.

Hank said, "*Big* stake, too—one of those tree stakes. Pinned him right through to the ground. And it was *his*—he was out planting some tree."

Dale found nothing in the paper but stared at it with determination as though it had suddenly become fascinating. *Only the second murder of the year,* that was nice. A grisly, creative murder… SOP around here? He wasn't sure he wanted to know. And half a weather report with many little pictures of clear skies and the obvious effort someone had made to avoid repetition barely served to distract him from Dru's next words.

"Makes ya wonder if he saw it coming," she said. "I mean, it musta taken a sledge. And whoever did it woulda had to stood up over him—so was he awake? Or did the guy kill 'im, then stake 'im?" She lowered her tones into drama level. "And no one heard anything but a barking dog…"

Dale stared rather desperately at the weather section, too startled by her casually brutal assessment to hide his reaction, not wanting to be caught eavesdropping any more than he'd wanted to be caught staring and definitely not wanting to hear this at all. In the background, the newly arrived truck's door opened, closing with that dull sound of something not quite latched. Closed again several times until the driver was satisfied. *Wednesday: Sunny. Thursday: Bright and clear. Friday: Sunny and clear. Saturday: Clear and pleasant.* As far as he could tell, they might as well have used a rubber stamp. They certainly weren't fooling anyone.

"They don't know the cause of death—they haven't done the autopsy yet," Hank said wisely. More truck door activity filled the background. Someone was very busy doing *something*. "Or if they have, they aren't admitting it."

"Probably because it's too horrible." Dru seemed to get a certain satisfaction from that thought. "Probably the guy saw it coming. Flat on his back, too scared to move—" She flung her arms wide and lifted her feet from the cement porch floor in what Dale thought of as a *Dead 'Possum* pose, cigarette smoke trailing through the air like skywriting. Two day-old dead smoking 'possum by the side of the road pose. "And *wham!*, here comes the stake."

"You been trapped with that disinfectant stuff again?" Hank asked, sounding amused. But before she could respond, his eyes went wide. "I knew it!" he said, looking around rather wildly; his eyes lit on the empty bench opposite Dru and he leaped up onto it.

The scrabble of many tiny toenails made things clearer; Dale turned in his seat to spot the frenetic arrival of a flock… herd…pack…of tiny dogs. Not quite Chihuahuas, not quite anything else. They all had medium, frosted black-over-white coats, big bug eyes, and prick ears. They strained eagerly against their tangle of leashes, towing along a busty helmet-coiffed bottle-blond wearing an *I love my dog* sweatshirt. The leashes proved too much for her; she dropped several.

"Ahh, nooo," Hank groaned, cringing, and Dale prepared himself to rescue the beleaguered mail carrier as the little dogs launched their…

Attack?

"Awww!" Hank said in dismay, shooing ineffectively at the small creatures. "Awww, c'mon now!" They scaled the bench with no discernible effort and latched on to him, gripping his ankles tightly between their spindly little forelegs as their backs hunched up and went to work in an unmistakable, socially unacceptable motion.

Biting was definitely not what they had in mind.

Dale let out a sudden snort of laughter, desperately muffled. At his feet, Sully growled in a baffled way, then slunk to the furthest recesses of the available floorboard space, embarrassed for his fellow dog.

Dru made no attempt to hide her snorting guffaws. "Could be worse, Hank!"

"Every time I come here—!" he sputtered, dislodging one of the creatures.

"Don't hurt them!" the woman cried, gathering leashes and tugging ineffectively.

"Hurt *them!*" Hank said. "A guy's gotta have some pride, lady!" He jumped over the arm of the bench, awkward but successful; the leashed dogs jerked back and ping-ponged off the ground, eagerly bouncing up to follow while the woman bombarded them with cries for obedience that made Sully pull his ears forward but had no effect whatsoever on the leaping, yapping little dogs. Hank made it to the Jeep and dove inside; the engine ground to life, whining a little at the sudden reverse and escape velocity.

Dru watched without making any attempt to help gather the dogs, not even a little shift of her weight to indicate she might be thinking about it. Finally the country-themed woman propped the door open with her foot and dragged the tiny dogs into the clinic.

Now Dale made no pretense of not watching. Staring. Gawking, even.

Dru looked over at him with a twinkle of wicked humor in her eye but a deadpan expression. "There's a reason we call him Humping Hank," she said. "But don't tell *him* that."

"What," Dale said, hunting words as he turned slightly to face her, letting one long leg rest on the ground, "What *were* those—"

"Teacup Huskies," Dru said wisely, watching him through a slanted gaze. Still definitely wicked. "She breeds them."

"But…" he said. *No such thing.* Never had been…probably never would be. Alaskan Klee Kai, yes…but these dogs weren't even close.

"Oh, we know," she said, easily able to fill in his unspoken objection. She flicked ash to land just beside her foot. "But we don't tell *her* that, either. Someone gave her two of 'em and told her that's what they were, and off she went, breeding 'em. Just your basic punting dog, if you ask me." She pantomimed the action, flinging more ash.

"I see," he said carefully.

"Welcome to the zoo," she told him, and grinned, no question about the wickedness this time.

"Excuse me?"

"You're the new doc, aren't cha? Seen your picture, so just in case you thought you were sitting there all incognito, you weren't. Grab a box and let's go. Sure am glad to see you haven't got one of the fat sausage-shaped ones, which is what I figured it for when I heard you had one."

Much more faintly, he repeated, "Excuse me?" and resisted an urge to check his zipper.

"Beagles!" she said, standing to grind her cigarette butt under the ball of her foot. She bent over to prod it, making sure there was no spark of life left, and then toed it under the bench. "Don't get your knickers in a twist, I sweep 'em up the end of every shift."

"No," he said, turning hastily away to acquire the box from the passenger seat. "Not twisting. Not me."

In the end, he took the box, the tea and the chips. He had a feeling he might need whatever faint sustenance they provided. And of course he took the dog. Not fat or sausage-shaped. And thank goodness for that.

THOSE WEREN'T DOGS. can't convince me. stubborn, stubborn. but the man…the one who brings things…i liked him. i'd like to—

not polite. dale would yell. big beagle sigh. all right then, in we go. nose to ground, sniffsniffsniff…ooh, what's this? smoky stinky thing with red lip stuff on it.

i think i'll eat it.

DRU WAITED UNTIL DALE had pushed his way through the double door airlock that served to confine errant pets more than it buffered the climate. Inside was the reception room he'd seen last month during the interview process. A neat set of shelves sat in the corner with displays and brochures for specialized food and joint supplements. A long padded bench seat lined the walls on either side below posters featuring dog breeds and animal obesity warnings with examples of skinny, just right, and belly-drags-the-ground, a bulletin board with animal adoption requests…pretty much just as he remembered it. Not so different from his old practice.

The receptionist wrangled with the teacup husky woman. She and her milling charges filled the entry area and spilled into the waiting room, while the other owner/animal combinations pulled back to the very edges of the room, obviously not sure whether to be appalled or amused. The stout receptionist plucked a pen out of her toweringly complex hairdo and pointed at a spot in the schedule book, shoving aside the recently delivered stack of mail. "You see? Your appointment was for an hour ago. We'll be glad to work you in now, but—"

Something set off the little faux huskies—the first started with a *yip-yip-yii-iii* in its little soprano voice and the others gleefully took up the cry. Resolutely, the receptionist raised her voice, continuing without a hitch. "But it's going to be at least half an hour."

"But I'm sure I wrote the appointment down correctly—"

Dru looked back over her shoulder, rolled her eyes for Dale's benefit. He gave her a shrug of a smile, shifting the box in his arms while Sully tested the limits of the leash, nosing every inch of the shiny linoleum tile floor.

The receptionist abruptly smacked her hand against the counter, shocking the howling doglets to silence. The owner looked on in startled offense, but the receptionist—a deeply black woman with *Sherenne* on her nametag and brassy blonde streaks in her hair—merely gave her a sweet smile and said, "I'm sorry there was a mix-up. But you can see we're very busy today. Until I get my Tardis, there's nothing I can do about the wait. We'll fit you in as soon as we possibly can."

The woman narrowed her eyes slightly, evidently stuck on the pop-culture reference to the time-travel device and pretty sure she'd been insulted in there somewhere.

Dale was pretty sure she'd been insulted in there somewhere, too.

"If that's the best you can do, then," the woman said, still looking suspicious. It didn't match her cute sweatshirt at all. "Although I have to say I expect more when I'm bringing you this much business." She stalked into the waiting area, creating even more customer-to-the-wall shrinkage as the little dogs cheerfully greeted everything within reach without regard to the hissing and growling and scrambling they inspired.

"Coast is clear," Dru said, waving Dale onward. "Hey, Sheri, you met the new doc?"

Sheri looked up from the much-maligned schedule with evident surprise, her eyes widening slightly as she tipped her head up to regard all of Dale. She smiled a slow smile. "Dr. Kinsall," she said. "It *is* a pleasure."

He gave her a little wave with the fingers that curled around the edge of the box. "Hey," he said, marginally aware of the vibes of interest suddenly emanating from the waiting room. "Nice to meet you."

"Mmm," she said, and raised a naturally arched eyebrow. "Just so you know, I'm the one with all the power around here. The woman with the schedule, you know." She didn't quite wink, but it lurked around her eye.

"No question about it," he said. Sully's gently waving tail bumped his leg; she'd passed the Sully-test, it seemed.

Dru said, "So is it true your last clinic burned to the ground?"

Utter silence fell over the waiting room; the curiosity grew from moderate to palpable. The hair up Dale's arms tightened; he felt his mouth drop open slightly and could do nothing about it. The box suddenly got much heavier. He rested the front edge on the high counter.

Dru continued with cheerful obliviousness. "And that you crisped your lungs up trying to save the animals?"

Sheri's eyes widened slightly; she looked from the breath-lessly expectant waiting room occupants to Dale. Even the little dog pack fell silent.

Dale floundered. He hunted for his cue-card answer, the one that never failed to fail him.

Sheri gave a forced little laugh. "Woman, there's just no telling what's gonna come out of your mouth—"

Dale looked at that steely little glint in Dru's eyes and said,

"More or less." And then he shrugged at her surprise, seeing she hadn't really believed it at all, hadn't expected any hint of confirmation. He could have just said *no* and gotten away with it. "Maybe less than more. How about I put this box somewhere?"

"And I know just the place," Sheri said somewhat fiercely, glaring at Dru. "Don't forget I schedule *you*, too."

Dru shrugged, entirely unaffected. "These things get around," she said. "Tell it all up front, then no one's got anything to talk about. Gimme the box, I know where your office is. You can go back for seconds." She took the box from him without waiting for his response and headed for the door to the working part of the clinic.

Dale gave his empty hands a bemused look. "A spontaneous press release," he said. "I can't imagine why I never thought of that."

Sheri picked up on the dry tone of his voice. "You never mind her. Cleaning those kennel runs and stalls give her too much time to think."

"She's the *kennel* help?" he said, and glanced at the waiting room occupants. They were trying to pretend they weren't listening, but not with any success. He lowered his voice. "That's hard work! She must be old enough to be someone's grandmother."

"Twelve someones. Doesn't seem to slow her down. And actually, the *Flagstaff Post* probably *will* be in touch. You're big news around here."

Big news is one of the things he'd come here to get away from.

Get real, Kinsall. It's not about you, it's about the clinic. So he nodded and said, "Thanks for the heads-up," as Sully's front feet came to rest slightly against his knee; when Dale looked down he made it clear his hound nose had discovered the dog treats sitting on the counter and that this therefore made him entitled to one. Dale obliged.

Sheri looked over the counter and said, "Oh! Cute!" and earned herself some serious wagging as Sully agreed. Sully. Dale should have left him in the Forester until he finished hauling boxes. Just more proof that his dehydrated brain wasn't quite thinking straight. Or possibly at all. He said, "How about I just pop him in one of the patient crates until I can get the office set up?"

"Fine by me," she said. "And I am, as I mentioned, the woman with all the power."

"Not to be taken lightly," Dale agreed, glad for a reason to remove himself from view of the still-riveted waiting room audience. But as he turned to leave, through the glass of the doors he caught a glimpse of a man approaching, staggering under an awkward load. Dale plucked Sully up and deposited him on the counter in front of Sheri. "Hang on to him."

She looked at him open-mouthed, then snapped it closed as Sully took advantage of the arrangement to taste her lip-gloss. "Watch out for that," Dale told her with a quick grin, then pulled the doors open one after another, to meet the man just beyond the porch.

No wonder the man staggered. In the makeshift stretcher of a bloodied blanket lay the limp form of a big Dane mix, a champagne-colored dog with darker mottling—a dog that was meant to be lanky, but not…

Not emaciated. Dale winced. Not meant to have bones jutting out against tight skin, fat non-existent and muscle nearly so. He grabbed the trailing ends of the blanket, taking a large part of the load.

The man saw Dale's reaction. Between gasping breaths he said, "Not…my…dog. Rescue."

"Just in time." Or maybe not. Dale bumped the first door

open with his hip, then the second. Sheri kept her Sully-assaulted mouth clamped shut, but her eyebrows went sky-high; she thumbed a switch by the computer and a doorbell noise sounded audibly in the back. Dale would have preferred to take the dog straight back and start work—*Ringer's, blood work, warming pads, Nutri-Cal, electrolytes, radiographs to check for cancer or other causative internal problems*—but the truth was he didn't know which areas were open or where the supplies were kept, and the staff would be so confused they'd just lose whatever time he'd gained. Not to mention he was hardly the only vet here. This one was out of his hands.

"Found her…a little while ago," the man said, beginning to catch his breath now that he had help and they'd paused by the desk. He was a naturally gaunt fellow, thin enough so it looked like he could use some help right along with the dog. But although the beard over his lean cheeks was more scraggle than design, both he and his clothes were clean, and—the acid test—his teeth were white and obviously familiar with dental tools. "I thought she was dead at first, but somehow she's not." He lifted a knee under the dog to take some of the awkward weight.

Dale gave the dog a hard look, shifting his grip on the stained blanket. She didn't look at him; she didn't look at anything. Her dull stare remained unfocused, the exposed flesh of her flews, pale. Her short, fine coat looked dull and scruffy. He wished he had a hand free to stroke her head. "It takes a lot of neglect to get an animal into this state."

"She's not from my neighborhood," the man said, embarrassed. For not finding her sooner, Dale surmised. "I was checking out a job today—I'm a contractor—and I saw her. I, er, liberated her."

"Don't tell me that part," Dale said quickly, getting the strong impression there was something more to it…more even than simple trespass. Breaking and entering, cutting collar or chain…he didn't want to know troublesome answers to any of the questions police might ask if it came to that. "I'll assume she was on public property." He looked at the messy blanket. "Is she hurt?" Three scrub-dressed people hustled out of the back, appropriated the dog and stretcher, and hustled away again.

"I'll be back for her history," the shortest of them called over her shoulder on the way out.

"I can't give them much," the man said sadly, looking at his now empty hands. "The poor thing." He took a breath, seemed to realize he hadn't answered Dale's question. "Oh. No, she's not hurt, just starved nearly to death."

A woman in the waiting room clutched her cat carrier more tightly to her ample bosom and squinted at the man through outdated owl-eye glasses. "That dog lives only two doors down from the man who was murdered last night," she said, and her shrill voice cut through all the other conversation and animal mutterings. "I sneak her food and water all the time."

"Not *enough*," the man said, with a surprising vehemence.

"I don't know you. What were you doing on my street, skulking around people's yards? And here we've just had a murder!"

"Manners!" Sheri snapped, but the woman only held the cat carrier more tightly yet and glared at her target.

The man ignored Sheri with equal glare factor. "I wasn't," he said. "The dog must have gotten loose, and more power to her. Besides, I was at the city trail use forum last night."

Startled, Dale hunted for words, distracted by his growing unease with this man, the sudden conviction that the man lied…but about *what,* Dale wasn't sure. Sully offered an abruptly sharp bark at the rising volume of the conversation. *Excitement!*

Dale gave him one of those looks, which did the trick.

Silence. Though when he tried it on the waiting room, it had no apparent effect.

Somewhat defensively, the woman said, "But there's blood on the blanket."

The man blinked at her, and for a moment Dale thought they were going to have war. Then the rescuer seemed to regain some of his composure, as if he'd suddenly decided this woman didn't matter anyway. "That's old. I pick up strays when I can, get them to the rescue league. Couple days ago I found one in the road…but he'd been hit by a car, never made it to the clinic." He moved past Dale to the end of the counter, craning to see through the small window in the door that led to the back. "I hope *she* makes it."

"It'll be close," Dale said, with a very tactile memory of his hands closing down on clammy, tacky blanket. He said to the man, "I wish I could give you more optimistic news."

The man looked at Dale's wet shoes, muddied jeans, and moving-day T-shirt. "You're one of them? The vets here?"

Dale blinked back. "I guess…I am."

The man scored the waiting room assembly a withering look, transferring it briefly to Dale. "Then take care of her!" he said, and stomped out of the clinic.

Dale looked at Sheri and Sheri looked at Dale. After a moment, she gave him a shrug. He wasn't sure what it meant, other than she intended to go back to work. She lifted Sully's twenty pounds with the ease of a woman accustomed to lifting a child and held him out over the counter.

Sully hung limply, his ears hanging even lower, used to this particular grip only when Dale was holding him over a tub with every effort to have the least possible contact. *woe. bath?*

Dale was reaching for him when the treatment room doors swung open again; the shortest tech reappeared, flashing metal piercings topped by spiky hair. She held the nasty blanket in a careless grip, realized its owner had abdicated, and tossed it one-handed at Dale. "All yours," she said, with no apparent recognition of Dale as one of her vet employers.

He caught it without thinking and then made a face at it. Sheri twisted her mouth in temporary resignation, letting Sully's feet touch down on the counter top. He wagged his tail with hope, but kept it down between his hocks just in case.

"Where—" Dale started.

"All the way down the hall," Sheri said. "Ought to be a pile of stuff there by the door. Jorge sorts it out."

"Jorge?"

"Dru's kennel help. Always looking for a buck. So some of the stuff he keeps. If he thinks we can use it here, he holds it back." She put a thoughtful finger against her full lower lip, one colored with an intense red that probably had a name like Crimson Passion or Run Away, You Fool! "Come to think of it, he's been using your office as…hmm, let's call it 'intermediate storage.'"

"Well, that'll change," Dale said, turning to head down the hall. Something in her lack of response stopped him, and he looked back to say in a voice more uncertain than he meant it to be, "It will. Won't it?"

And Sheri just shrugged.

BUSY. WOW. fresh blood on that blanket, makes me wanna chase something. fresh people hair, makes me wanna roll, roll, roll! and this is our new not-home home? it has people, dogs… mouth kisses! gotta wag. they like dale. gotta wag. and what's this? papers, they smell like the one who brings things.

i think I'll eat them.

THREE

"DOGHOUSE," DALE SAID, stretching to stash a box on the very top of his office shelves the day after his astonishingly hectic introduction to the clinic. The extension of his torso tickled his lungs, and, hands full, he turned his head to cough, automatically polite. *Mustn't offend the file cabinets.* Also automatically, he froze a moment, waiting to see if the irritation would worsen, and did a quick mental check of his rescue inhaler, Big Blue. *Top desk drawer.*

boring. Sully yawned loudly and curled up on his snuggly pillow of an office bed. Trust a hound to put things into perspective, even a little hound.

Dale decided to leave the inhaler for now and took a healthy swig of water instead. Learning, finally, to drink up the moment he felt thirsty. Still learning to use the current sports bottle without dribbling down his shirt—today, an old hooded sweatshirt that was about to come through at the elbows, making it just about time to cut off the sleeves. He brushed futilely at the dark trail down his chest and stomach and decided to be grateful the top hadn't popped off.

It wouldn't have been the first time.

Another gulp and he took a deep and satisfying breath. *All right, then.* But he sat against the edge of the utilitarian metal desk—now his—anyway, looking around the room. As with any vet's office, priority had gone to the treatment areas. This little room with its heavily shaded window, dusty off-the-rack plastic blinds, and duct-taped desk chair had been crammed in at the end of the building, opposite the public entrance. Until his arrival, it had been—aside from Jorge's junk purgatory—used as filing storage. Several stacks of ancient files remained in the corner, awaiting the official stamp of rejection and providing a teetering base for a desiccated spider plant. "Thoughtful," Dale told Sully. "A pre-killed office plant for the man with the brown thumb. And no, you may not chew it. It's the principle of the thing."

Sully gave a soft snore.

Dale glanced over at him with a smallest of satisfied smiles. He'd get a new chair, possibly a new desk—one with drawers that opened. And all that junk cleaned out of the corner—was that the Dane's bloody blanket? Yuck. He took it back out to the end of the hallway and returned to survey the results. Sleeping dog in the corner, the bookshelves half-filled, the file cabinets waiting archived personal research and new administrative material...once he found his diploma and unpacked his photographs, the place would be entirely his. There was even a closet, into which he'd thrown a rain slicker. After a lifetime in the Midwest where rain was just rain, Dale couldn't wait to see the monsoon storms everyone took for granted around here.

If we get one this year. To judge by the grim expressions he saw on every face when the subject of the drought came up, he might wait a while before he saw an active monsoon.

"Then again, who knows," he told Sully, earning a half-opened eye. "They weren't expecting that murder, either." A final gulp of water, a final dribble, and he knelt at the big box beside the desk and flipped open the top, his thoughts drawn back to the covered porch along the back of his box-filled house and how it made the perfect shelter and wind-break for the doghouse he contemplated.

"Just a little one," he told Sully. "Snug and warm. Besides, it's not like you're going to spend all that much time out there. It's just in case." Expecting to see reference books within the box, he stared a blank moment at the top of a thousand-piece puzzle box, the image of a German castle nestled among drooping pines on its own mountain top. Aunt Cily had given this one to him not long after he'd come to live with them. Little boy needing distraction from the loss of his family, and needing something to do that wouldn't kick up his newly asthmatic lungs, an asthma not yet under stable control.

Some of his puzzles were just puzzles. Some of them were memories—good and bad all tied together. He remembered clearly the look on Aunt Cily's face as she handed him this particular box, her own pain at the loss of a sister, her hopes that the gift would ease the struggles of a young boy trying to adjust to too many things at once.

It would have helped if they'd told me what happened.

Sully lifted his head as Dale removed the puzzle, finding beneath it a crumpled handful of age-softened red bandanas, a cheese grater, and then the expected reference books. The box in his hand tilted, offering the familiar sound of shifting puzzle pieces...although these days, more challenging than the puzzles themselves were Dale's efforts to keep Sully from instantly vacuuming up any fallen pieces and mouthing them with the satisfaction of a six year-old battling a piece of bubble gum too big for his mouth. Even now, he watched with his head cocked, ears lifted forward. *mine?*

"Not a chance," Dale told him. "It's going back home, all thousand pieces of it." He put it in the box of similar mis-packed items, filling it just beyond capacity. "I'll be right back—assuming no one tries to snag me about the reception at the RoundUp." It seemed they all wanted to make sure he remembered, as if he had the slightest chance of forgetting, especially not with the RoundUp Café right next door. "Stay put, sleepyhead."

NOT SO ASLEEP i don't scent old dale clothes. dale always says red for these…i don't know "red." scent of dale's hair, how to resist? soft yellowish cloth, a nice size. sly mouth! happy mouth! mine now, scent of dale's hair and skin so strong. gotta wag. i think i'll roll on it. take it back to my bed—mine!—and sleep, oh happy nose.

until we eat.

A WOMAN RUSHED INTO the Foothills waiting room as Dale came at it from the other side, through the treatment areas and past the X-ray machine. She spared him not a glance, staggering under the limp burden of her bearded collie. Past the brochures on parasites, past the sales display of dental care items, and right up to the receptionist's counter, where she displaced the startled owner of an indignantly hissing cat. "She just collapsed—she's only a few years old!"

The nearest vet tech—Isaac, was it?—left a substantial basset hound on the weigh-in scales with its surprised owner and slipped in to take the beardie, ably relieving the dismayed owner of her pet.

Dale, standing with the box of mis-packed trinkets in hand, had an instant of hesitation—but Dr. Hogue conferred with a regular patient and Brad Stanfill, his established junior partner, was next door at the RoundUp Café grabbing an herbal tea break. Sheri gave him an expectant look and said, "You waiting for an invitation?"

Dale dumped the box on the counter and shoved up the sleeves of the old gray Cornell sweatshirt, glancing at Sheri. "Records?"

"Not one of ours," she said, meaning not a regular patient. That she knew right off the top of her head took him back. *Small town life, boy. Get used to it.*

"Draw blood," Dale said to the tech on her way through the swinging door, behind which lay the triage room with its brushed steel tables and crate-lined wall. "I want a full panel plus glucose, BUN and creatinine, and I want stats waiting when I get in there."

"On it," she said; she was a short plump woman who seemed to think he should have known they would handle it. Maybe he should have…but he wasn't taking any chances.

The receptionist shoved a clipboard across the counter with a blank patient history sheet on it. He scrawled quick notes, nudging information out of the dazed owner. *Female. Megan. Three. Just back from a dog show. Not eating well over the last week, sporadic vomiting, spells of trembling, regular vet has treated her for GI irritation, just took blood the day before but doesn't have the results and is closed on this afternoon. Legs just went out from under her while—*

"I was clipping her nails. She hates it, but she's good for me."

Dale stopped writing at that, looked at the woman…something teased at the edge of his mind—

The swinging door popped open, and the plump tech stuck her head out. "Doctor—" she started, and stopped there, clearly having forgotten his name. They were even; he had no idea of hers.

But he knew what that look meant. *The dog's crashing.* He jammed the clipboard back at the receptionist. "I want to see it when you're done," he said, and pushed through the door. Someone thrust a lab coat his way; he took it, shoving his arms through the sleeves. Too small.

"I'm barely getting a pulse," said the woman, and memory finally placed her as the new tech hired when he'd come aboard. Jade. She had short, spiky hair, bleached. And a discreet nose ring. "She's bradycardic, dehydrated, and underweight. Not to mention looking worse by the moment."

"You've got the blood?" He moved to the dog, put a gentle hand on her thin, trembling side. "Thatta girl, Megan."

"In a mo." Isaac, a big silent fellow with a mournful hound

face and glasses too small for his curving arch of a nose, stood by with a vial and needle.

The woman retrieved a pair of battery-powered Laube clippers from the cart beside the shelf where she'd been rummaging, pulled the dog's foreleg straight and carefully shaved a waterfall of silvery hair. "All yours," she said to Isaac, brushing away the loose strands and wrapping her hand around the dog's elbow to pop the vein up.

Isaac stooped over the dog's leg, muttering, "Hard to get a vein...nothing here—" But a moment later stood back and gave the third tech room to whip a couple rounds of stretchy Vetrap around the catheter.

An idea bloomed. "Add cortisol to that blood panel," Dale said suddenly. "Push electrolytes. And I want to see her sodium/potassium ASAP."

But he already knew. The lab results might be days away, courier to Phoenix and back—but potassium would be off the scale, sodium barely there. He was willing to bet undiagnosed Addison's disease had sent Megan spiraling toward death.

At his back, the doors swung open, accompanied by Dr. Hogue's heavy tread. "I'm not retired just yet," he said—a light comment that didn't quite hide his irritation.

"Addison's," Dale said, moving aside so Dr. Hogue could make himself the more commanding presence. Nothing to do at the moment, anyway, with the IV in place and the techs efficiently taping the catheter into security on Megan's foreleg. Nothing but, "We need to get pred on board. And do we have Florinef?"

"Florinef," Dr. Hogue grunted, breezing a hand along the very top of his stiffly brush-cut hair—a style strategy that nearly hid the thin spots, but not from someone of Dale's height. "Expensive stuff. Diagnosed Addison's?"

"This would be first DX," Dale said. "History and symptoms

fit; if I'm right she can't wait for the labs." Not for the pred and the supportive care, in any event.

Dr. Hogue grunted, and then he nodded. "I'll talk to the owner."

Dale squelched his impulsive offer to take care of the conversation. Dr. Hogue was too used to running the place, and Dale…Dale didn't actually even work here yet. In fact, he had a box of his personal things sitting on the counter within reach of Sheri, and a beagle left unsupervised in his chaos of an office.

It was still hard to leave. It was always hard to leave with a crisis unresolved, still feeling like Dale's responsibility. Dr. Hogue noticed his hesitation and glanced over, steely blue eyes piercing over the reading glasses perched on his nose.

Dale gave him a wry smile, trusting the older man to understand the tug of such a case, and left through the swinging doors, not quite prepared when he found himself dumped back out in the reception area. Megan's human mother rushed up to him, even as he saw Sheri reaching into his abandoned box. Resolutely, he turned his attention to Megan's mother and said, "Dr. Hogue is with her now. I don't really have anything to tell you, except she's in the best of hands."

Tears had already allowed the woman's make-up to wander freely over her face. "Does she have a chance?" she whispered.

"I'm concerned about her," Dale said. "But as I said, she's in good hands. I'm sure Dr. Hogue will be out to speak to you as soon as he can." He didn't know this woman; didn't know the subtle cultural ways of his new home, across the country from the old. Dairy cows and corn swapped for beef on the range and honest-to-goodness cowboys. But he dropped a gentle hand on her shoulder anyway and was glad to see she seemed to take strength from it instead of offense. "You did well to get her here," he said, and meant it. "You've already got blood work in process, and now we can provide support until we're certain what caused her collapse."

That did it; her shoulders straightened and Dale let his hand drop away. The rest was up to Dr. Hogue.

Now there's a change. A year ago, would he have walked out of that treatment room? Had he actually learned something in recent months?

Probably not. Dale watched the woman reclaim her seat in the reception area, so familiar with the undercurrents of a waiting room with emergency care in play. Owners emotionally distraught, unconcerned with their public emotions and their migrating make-up. Other owners with their pets clutched tightly to hand, worried about an animal they didn't even know, guiltily grateful it wasn't their own.

A rustling noise caught his attention; puzzle pieces shifting, and papers shifting after that. He turned back to the counter to catch Sheri with a gleeful expression, rummaging. Shameless and rummaging, for she didn't stop when she caught his eye. "Lessee here," she said. "A puzzle, for all those free moments in the office. And here, a potato peeler. An old dog collar, can't say as that don't belong here. And clippings about—ooh, about the fire!"

Dale dispensed with niceties and took two long steps to snatch the box away from her. "These," he said, dignity wounded, "are the things that are leaving."

"Well, good, because we don't have no time around here for any honking big puzzles." Sheri absently checked the back of her elaborate and perfectly coiffed hairdo and the pearls studded along the curve of it. Dale took it as a sign of retreat or possibly belated embarrassment—except she went on to say, "If you've got any small ones, though, we could maybe stand to build some of those."

"I'll see what I can do." He rested the box against his hip and headed for the door.

"But those clippings were too old to be from last year—"

She followed him around the inner right angle of the counter, entirely undeterred.

"They were, weren't they?" He made it through the door, counting himself lucky she didn't walk right through the counter on his heels. "So was the potato peeler, if we're counting."

He made it to the little SUV without incident, considering himself lucky. *Dale Kinsall, what on earth have you gotten yourself into?*

And no part of him had an answer, but he couldn't help but lean back against the Forester and grin at the sky, and he stayed there with the high altitude sun on his face until he was sure the grin wouldn't sneak back out while he was trying to look stern for Sheri's benefit, and then he headed back to the office. *His* office.

Sheri conspired to be deeply busy, filing paperwork, cleaning her personal counter area of everything but her coffee mug and the little cloth doll that now bore a toothpick in its chest and a small toe tag with the name *John,* barely legible, penned on it.

Stern. Very stern.

DALE REACHED his office door and stopped short, recognizing in that moment his restlessness and distraction. Moving, Megan…the way packing and unpacking seemed to have stirred up the very things he'd meant to leave behind.

Time for a walk. If nothing else, to stretch his legs, though Dru the kennel granny had reminded him of the drought-enforced national forest land closure just this morning—and then obligingly told him the next best thing, just half a mile away off 89.

Dale found Sully on his bed in the corner, being *heavy* and to all appearances exactly how Dale had left him…except for the mysterious appearance of the bright red bandana under his head and shoulder. "Did you satisfy your fetish?" he asked Sully, who didn't respond aside from the faint flick of an eyebrow that meant he'd looked Dale's way from his curled-up position. Still being heavy, which to Sully's way of thinking meant his solid little black and rich brown self couldn't be seen. Not even the white flashings that covered his muzzle and ran up between his eyes in a wide blaze, or the white of his chest and legs. So no one would notice if he'd stolen a bandana, and no one would think to ask him to leave Dale's office.

"I see you anyway," Dale told him, and picked up the leash and collar sitting on his desk. Sully leaped to his feet, ears flagged forward, bandana and heaviness and even his silly fetish for the scent of human hair—especially Dale's hair—forgotten. "You know," Dale informed him, holding out the leash snap, "only the one edge of that bandana had any contact with my hair."

enough. Sully stood lightly against Dale's knee and presented his head for the slip chain collar, after which he did his little *walkwalkwalk* dance, tail high and waving with the authority of being quite certain they were indeed going out to ramble.

But Dale redirected him away from the lobby and off in the other direction. The back door: for grieving owners, contagious pets, and a vet who couldn't face a waiting room poised for news of Megan.

From the Forester, he grabbed a water bottle with a belt clip, and spent a few moments trying to convince it to secure to the waistband of his jeans. After uncertain success, he swapped Sully's leash and slip collar for a flat collar and Flexi Lead, and headed briskly out of the parking lot as if he knew where he was going.

An odd feeling, to be walking along a four-lane road, especially one traveled seldom enough to allow him a quick jog across all four lanes when he saw Elden Trail Road on the opposite side—just as Dru had described it, a dusty one-lane dirt road backing a pine-nestled subdivision on one side and national forest on the other. He couldn't walk in it, but beside it…the next best thing for a man new to the area who still hadn't breathed in enough scent of warm ponderosa pines, become accustomed to the baby-powder fine dust of every step, or come to terms with the way a crisp air temperature meant nothing against the heat of high-altitude sun. Dale's skin said it must be eighty degrees Fahrenheit; the thermometer at the clinic had said sixty-eight. He decided to buy himself a good hat at the first opportunity and meanwhile tread the edge of the shadows from the looming pines to his right. Sully trotted along at the full sixteen-foot extension of the Flexi-lead, weaving back and forth over the road to cover twice as much ground as Dale and panting happily.

Don't forget the water. Especially with the pleasantly brisk pace he'd set, happy to be exploring his new home, happy even to feel the prickle of sweat at his waistband and the back of his neck. "Hold up," he told Sully, and Sully returned to him in that same pleased trot, allowing the Flexi-lead to retract; Dale applied the locking thumb brake to keep it six feet and stuck the Flexi casing under his foot to fumble at the small of his back for the water bottle. "You want some?"

Sully took a few obligatory laps from Dale's cupped hand and lifted his head, distracted by something in the forest underbrush.

"Relax," Dale said. "It's probably someone's cat. We're hardly in the wilds." In fact, he saw clear signs of recent forest thinning, preparation for the prescribed burns he'd read about. And to their right he gazed upon a row of backyards as suburban as any, even if they comprised a small niche of suburbia thrust upon this fringe area of Flagstaff and West

Winona. Struggling grass covered the lawns, and the trees were as much horticultural as native. The only thing to strike his eye as unusual was the way the houses varied from small ranches to the occasional looming structure of Southwest character. No boxes all in a row for *this* neighborhood. "No varmints there, either," he told Sully. Just a lone dog, looking chained but from this distance, hard to tell. A basic shepherd/Lab mix behind one of the less-groomed homes, lean and tufting with retained undercoat.

But as Dale tipped his head back to take a swig of water—*dribble*—and consider that maybe it wasn't him at all, maybe it was this particular set of water bottles, the chained dog spotted them and commenced to bark. Sully, to whom all the world was a friend, barked a return greeting—

And bolted.

He jerked the Flexi casing from under Dale's foot in that moment when Dale leaned back at his most precarious, and before he could do so much as shout Sully's name, the foot went out from under him and he landed—of course—on his ass in the dirt. Dust puffed up around him; he coughed sharply. As he scrambled to his feet and got the coughing out of his system, he realized Sully had ended up not with his new potential best friend, but in the yard beyond, barking with significance. *bawh!*

No telling what he'd gotten into; Dale saw only the waving white tip of Sully's tail. And no point in trying to bellow a recall. Sully—in all his adolescent scent-hound glory—would never even hear his voice. Nothing for Dale to do but jog on and berate himself for carelessness, hoping whatever had lured Sully turned out to be stationary.

A moment later and he took back that wish. With dust in his lungs and a faint familiar tightness in his chest, Dale could do nothing but put on speed when he saw the human-sized form sprawled near a small planting of bushes against the back property line. He thought *heart attack* and *stroke* and *are there poisonous snakes up this high?*, but when he cut across the chained dog's yard to jump a low planter box that made up the last obstacle between himself and the face-down man—for by the breadth of those beefy shoulders and the extremely flat bottom, a man it was—Dale found nothing to confirm his suspicions one way or the other. Sully danced at his arrival, offering a pleased *ba-woul!*...right before he dropped his shoulder to rub on the man's head and hair—in his world, such a posture was an offering for his benefit.

"Sully!" Dale's aghast and unprecedented tone stopped the beagle short; he backed away with an uncertain expression and Dale told him, "Just sit. And *stay!*" as he put a cautious hand on the man's arm.

Warm. Warm and pliable. Dale put both hands on the man's back and shook him slightly. "Can you hear me?" he asked, adhering to old CPR training. He gave the man a more assertive shake. *"Can you hear me?"*

No response. Was the man's hand just a little cooler than it had been, distinctly cooler than his torso? "Aw, hell," Dale muttered, knowing there'd be no happy day at the end of all this no matter what he did. He did a quick check—no torso movement, no breathing...no pulse of the carotid under his fingers. He rolled the man over, tipped his head back, and gave him two quick breaths. Then he found the tip of the breastbone and applied himself to CPR, knowing he couldn't do it long, not with the hint of a wheeze he'd breathed into this man's lungs and the sharp urge to cough he'd been fighting. CPR, one-two-three...and then he stopped. Had he heard...

Gurgling?

Tentatively, he jostled the man. Sully cocked his head, targeting the sound.

Definitely a gurgle.

Slowly, Dale leaned over the man and applied another CPR compression, this time watching the slack mouth.

Water appeared as he pushed, slipped back down the man's throat when Dale eased the pressure.

What the—

Dead. Dead and drowned, in the middle of a dusty, drought-stricken lawn.

Suddenly Dale noticed the details. That his own pants were wet at the knees, that his hand bled from a sharp-edged cut. The discovery led him to find the broken drinking glass beside the dead man, broken so recently that the ice cubes rested on top of brownish grass. And though dark dampness seeped into this corner of the yard and droplets of water hung from the fresh plantings Dale had vaulted to get here, a quick glance found the hose coiled neatly by the faucet at the back of the house.

Most oddly of all, paw prints littered the dirt of the sparse grass. Dog tracks, all smaller than Sully's, and—now that Dale had discovered them—far too many to count.

The man himself was middle-aged, with a comb-over that hadn't lasted whatever indignities he'd suffered before Dale arrived. The blood smearing his short-sleeved zipper-front shirt had come from Dale; aside from his disturbed comb-over and general dampness, the man appeared surprisingly tidy. Even his canvas sneakers gleamed whitely, a trick Dale already knew to be nearly impossible with the earth so dry. The man's slack features rested on an egg-shaped head with a paucity of chin and generosity of forehead, and nothing about them indicated why he had ended his life in this place, in this way.

Cell phone. Dale hoped he had his, and straightened at the hip so he could dig in his front pocket for the slim, barely-there device that was somehow a phone. "911," he told Sully, and dialed it. *Wait there,* they told him, as if he'd simply continue on with his walk. As if he could, with the way his chest tightened down on him and his rescue inhaler in his desk drawer. Big Blue. *Hadn't thought about the irritating dust. Hadn't intended to run.* Still, things had been better than that lately.

He didn't tell them the man had drowned; he wasn't about to be the first to say it out loud.

So he waited. He glanced up and down the backyards, finding himself still alone; not a neighbor in sight. No shouting children in the distance or mild rumble of a car engine. Dale sat back on his heels, allowing Sully to climb into his lap; Sully aimed an intent tongue under Dale's chin and the side of his neck while Dale eyed the backyards and considered if he'd work his way through this particular asthma attack—sometimes he could, if exercise had triggered the thing—or if he was in trouble. He noticed, belatedly, the rising wind gusting against his back and the way it made the trees groan. And then he looked again at the—

The body.

"Welcome to northern Arizona," he said out loud, hearing and hating the wheeze behind those words.

Sully licked his neck, and the sound of sirens rose above the sound of the wind.

FOUR

DALE KNEW THE ASTHMA DRILL. All the old habits, restored. Maintain a resting position. Think calming thoughts. Take medication. *Not here. Oops.* Wait and see if there would be any improvement. No.

No, indeed. And why was that? Realization struck; Dale wanted to thump his own forehead. *Because, you idiot, your regular daily inhaler's been empty for a week.*

No true way to tell the inhaler was empty of medication without counting days; it puffed out a fine strong serving of air regardless. And nothing like a move across the country to throw your habits off. Like refills. Stress, acclimation…all those things he wasn't quite used to monitoring again.

Not that finding a body could be considered stressful.

Dale looked at the man again, unable to help the bubble of unease that Sully was still trying to lick away.

I've seen death. I've caused death. Euthanized pets, with or without the owner present. Sometimes the hardest part of the job…sometimes the most merciful.

Not the same. He wasn't sure if it was harder or easier…but definitely not the same.

He wished the man's watery blue eyes hadn't been half-open.

Within moments—and yet not nearly soon enough—he saw the flash of bubble lights, just barely visible beyond the house. A shadow gave away the presence of an officer, coming up beside the house in a wary posture. The dog in the next yard barked fiercely a few moments and gave up.

Dale raised a hand, watching the foreshortened shadow hesitate as the man's hat and the peering part of his face became visible at the edge of the house. Then it reflected the motion of a gun being holstered.

Dale couldn't remember ever feeling more exposed.

The figure moved out from beside the house and turned out to be a woman. She crossed the lawn with long strides, her lanky form offering more efficiency than grace; her khaki shirt, forest green pants, and the various accouterments on her Batwoman Utility Belt served to totally obscure the scant curves she possessed. Sully waited until she was nearly upon them, and then gave a warning bark as deep as anything he'd ever voiced. *my dale!*

She stopped where she was, looking not the least intimidated. "Deputy Rena Wells," she said. "You made the call?"

He held up his cell phone in response, feeling his chest close around him; he hunched slightly in response.

She frowned, giving him an unnervingly perceptive look from pale brown eyes. "You okay?"

"Asthma." Dale tried not to look as apologetic as he felt, knowing this was his own damn fault. He tried to look confident and matter-of-fact. "I need to go get—"

She gave a short shake of her head. "I can't let you leave; there's an investigator on the way. I'll call an ambulance for you."

Dale made a strangled noise not entirely asthma-produced. "Let me call someone," he said, making it a suggestion. Someone at the clinic, only moments away by car…

As if there was anyone at the gossip-happy clinic who wouldn't offer every detail of his request at the first possible opportunity. He'd talked to Hogue about the asthma during his interview, of course … but he hadn't intended it to be common knowledge. He'd intended to get it back under control again.

Nice start. But even as Deputy Wells gave a thoughtful nod, a name popped into his head. *Dru.* Brash, opinionated, grand-motherly Dru. He had the sense she'd be glad to conspire with him, to come to the rescue at the same time she learned secrets no one else here knew. It was only an impulsive feeling…but Dale trusted such things. He turned the phone on and hit the already-programmed auto-dial for the clinic.

"Foothills Clinic," Sheri said, sounding remarkably business-like and professional.

"It's Dale." He struggled to keep his voice as normal as possible. He somehow didn't say, *It's Dale and I'm at a murder scene in the throes of exercise-induced bronchospasm that's not going to go away because I screwed up my meds.* Probably because he didn't have the breath for it.

"Dale?" she repeated blankly. He could almost picture her playing with the little cloth doll. It had acquired a penned-in face the last he saw it, big wide eyes and a mouth in an "oh" of horror. One woman's attempt to deal with the incomprehen-sibly awful by turning it into the bizarre.

"Dale Kinsall," he said, shortly this time. "Let me talk to Dru."

"Oh, *Doctor* Dale. You want to what?" Disbelief colored her tone. "Where are you? You sound funny."

A minor explosion of yapping filled the background; Sheri's connection crackled slightly as she tended to something at the reception desk. A moment later Hank the mail carrier's voice came through very clearly. "Aww!" he said. "Aww, leggo!"

Dale didn't wait for Sheri to give him her full attention again; he grabbed it. "Dru," he said. *"Now."*

She sounded wounded. "All righty then, Mr. Doctor. You'll have to hold."

"Hurry," Dale told her, but got no response other than the soft, regular clicking of the hold line.

Deputy Wells frowned at him, her fingers tapping a thoughtful beat against the leather of her wide belt. "I'm gonna call an ambulance," she said, and her hand abandoned her belt to move for the small radio mike clipped to her shoulder.

Dale held up a desperate finger, forestalling her long enough for Dru to come on the line and snap, "Yeah?" From the muffled barking and the clatter of kibble dropping into metal, she was in the food prep area and not hesitating a bit in her duties.

"Dru, this is Dale. Dr. Kinsall. I need your help and I need it to be just between you and me."

He could sense her immediate interest; the clanging and kibble pouring came to a stop. "Why?"

"Later." The words came dearly now, and his breath wheezed audibly both on the way in and on the way out. If he didn't get this under control fast, he'd end up in an ambulance, all right. Controlled and stable, he never got this bad. But since the fire, he hadn't quite gotten to "stable." Most of the time the asthma was a little problem, and responsive to his medications. But it remained brittle and still sometimes tipped from mild to Big Trouble before he even knew it. "Top desk drawer, blue inhaler. Bring it out—" And that's where he ran out of words.

Wells didn't hesitate. She took the phone, glancing up at the dirt road as if to assess its usefulness. "This is Deputy Wells of the Coconino Sheriff's Department. We're down Elden Trail Road. Can you do as Dr. Kinsall asked?" Her face flickered with surprise; Dale could only imagine Dru's response. Wells glanced back down at Dale, frowned, and said, "Hurry."

Great. I love a good first impression. Numbly, Dale took his phone back. By this time Sully had abandoned his pretense of being tough and now assaulted Dale with his worry, his tail wagging low between his hocks, his ears flattened, his brows furrowed. *daledaledale?*

"She's got about one more minute," Wells said, jamming her hat down more firmly on her head as a gust of wind sought to flip it away. "Then I'm putting in the call."

Dale didn't have any argument left. Nor did he look up when Sully alerted to an inaudible sound, or when that sound turned to the rumble of a motorcycle. Motorcycle. *Should have known.*

The bike drove up the road and stopped just behind Dale, and a moment later Dru, not wasting time or fuss with the body, the deputy, or Sully's greetings, trotted down the hill with Dale's inhaler in her hand and a garishly red and pink motorcycle helmet on her head. She crouched to take up Dale's hand, shook the inhaler hard, and firmly press it—in the correct orientation—into his hand, and then she eyed him until he met her gaze, apparently satisfying herself that he could deal with the inhaler on his own.

Breathe out. Press down on inhaler. Breathe in slowly. Times four.

As if he were the one dictating his breathing at all. Didn't matter; he'd get some of it and in another four minutes he could do it all over again. He glanced at his watch—digital, and this was one of the reasons why.

Dru put her hands on her hips and said, "You didn't have a spacer on that," in what could only be considered an accusing voice.

He raised an eyebrow at her.

She waved it off. "I've worked my way through raising two generations. You think this is new to me?"

"Will he be all right, then?" Wells cast an anxious eye on Dru's proximity to the sprawling body.

Dru shrugged elaborately. "I'm not the one to ask. And while you're at it, ask him how he got himself into this state. A six-year-old, I can understand."

Ouch.

Sully felt the censure; he put himself between Dale and Dru. *hey!*

Uncertainty flickered over her spare but nicely boned features; Wells came to a decision. "I'm going to ask you to move back up to the road."

Dru crossed her arms. "What's gonna cause more tracks? Me walking to the road and then back down here if our unprepared vet doesn't start breathing, or me just standing here waiting?"

A hint of desperation tightened Well's mouth while Dale couldn't help but admire Dru's logic. He glanced at his watch, fighting the onset of familiar desperation.

"Another minute," Dru said, and though her words were characteristically short, her voice held understanding.

"Vet?" Wells pulled a small notepad from her breast pocket and flipping it over. "Military training, then?"

They all glanced at the body.

Dale finally managed a word of his own. "Veterinarian."

Wells almost looked disappointed.

"Now," Dru said, and Dale shook the inhaler, using it while Sully lifted his nose, got a whiff of the medication, and disembarked Dale's lap to sneeze.

Wells seemed a little frantic. "Careful, don't let him get into the scene—"

Too late for that. But, sympathetic, Dale handed the Flexi-lead up to Dru. She took it, turning it over in her hand as she guided Sully to her side—the opposite side from the body. Uncertainly, he sat, not taking his eyes from Dale. "There's blood on this thing."

Wells gave an obvious look at the body, where blood—Dale's—also smeared the dead man's neat shirt. Dale held out his hand for her inspection, distracted. *Was that last breath a little easier?* He managed to say, "The glass…thought he was alive. Tried CPR…got into…the glass."

"Are you feeling better?" Wells crouched to look at him, much as Dru had done moments before. Unlike Dru, she stayed there a moment, silent and watching, while her trained gaze wandered his face, checked out the corded muscles of his neck and the slight hunch of his shoulders—finally, truly relaxing a little as the beta2 agonist of the inhaler did its job—and ended up back on his face.

"You could take a picture." Dru's voice held a wicked delight at the suggestion.

Sure enough, Wells stood up, blushing. "Soon as you're able, we'll go back up to the road. We need to get away from the scene—all of us."

Dale's limbs had that heavy feeling, the one that said his body had been shuffling all the available oxygen to his brain and to the muscles that had worked so hard to bring in air. But he didn't want to be here a moment longer than necessary.

Dru saw his intent. "One more time," she said, referring to the inhaler. "I'm thinking you're lucky I got here when I did. And if you're going to start hacking and spitting, you just remember to do it downwind."

"The crime scene!" Wells said in horror.

Why he found that funny, Dale couldn't really say. But he found himself choking on laughter, enough so he had to wave Wells away even as Dru's complacent voice reached him. "That's better, all right. Sounds like hell, of course. And your four minutes are up, Mister Dr. Dale. Suck it up and let's get further away from this dead fellow. Is that *water* in his mouth?"

Dale took his allotted four puffs, closed his eyes to blank his mind a moment and let the drug work, and…

Finally. Real breathing. Still a little wheezy, and plenty of gunk production waiting to be coughed loose. But…real breathing. He shifted back, ready to get to his feet.

At that, Wells put a hand under his elbow, displaying more strength than he'd expected. And Dru, not to be outdone, took the other arm—displaying all the strength he'd pretty much expected. They went up the slight berm to the road and Dru pulled him over by the motorcycle. He glanced at it, for the first time taking an interest in such extraneous things. Blue and white BMW logo, a sturdy but modest road bike with enough scuff to show some age and enough gleam to show habitual care. The round headlight nestled in a small fairing and windshield, and twin kickstands kept it standing straight.

"Can't get 'em like this anymore." Dru touched a handgrip/clutch with as much tenderness as Dale had ever seen on her. "'76 BMW R90. Probably last longer than I do in the end." And then she looked over at him, reassumed her gruff expression, and said, "Sit down. I've got a first aid kit in the saddlebags. I'll take care of that hand."

Wells wandered off down the road, carried on a conversation with her shoulder, and came back looking not entirely pleased, giving Dale just enough time to cave to Dru's prodding questions and confess to the forgotten inhaler refill. Wells said, "The detective will be here soon."

"Ought to be here *now*." Dru pulled the first aid kit from the saddlebag and took Dale's hand with a competent grip. Now that the cut had some attention, it turned painful; he winced in spite of himself and was surprised when Dru's attentions immediately gentled—for all her expression did not.

Underlying concern bubbled to the surface of Dale's thoughts. "You didn't tell—"

"No one knows who didn't already know." Dru smeared a line of cool antibiotic ointment across the heel of Dale's palm. "Don't see why it's such a big deal, but that's your concern."

Because it makes people ask questions. Because he was tired of thinking about the answers to those questions. "Sheri—"

"Nosy as usual. And bossy." Dru's lips twitched with a suppressed smile and Dale had a sudden twinge of alarm. "I told her your little beagle had pooped on the trail and you hadn't brought any pick-up bags."

Dale blinked. "She believed it?" Suddenly the notion of walking into the clinic and declaring not only his underlying asthma but also his distracted failure to refill his prescription didn't seem like such a bad thing.

The twitch turned into a bona-fide grin, entrenching her smile lines into her normally faint, square jowls. "No. But she knows if I feed her a line like that, she's not going to get anything else out of me. I'm a granny—the two things I do best are puttin' on plasters and keeping secrets. Whether you stand up to her questioning is your own problem." She patted a large square Band-Aid over Dale's hand. "I think you'll live."

Not a great choice of words. They both looked over at the dead man, drowned in a drought in the middle of his failing lawn. Wells looked at the dead man, too, her fingers tapping against her belt. "Now that you're here," she told Dru, "you'd better stay here till the detective clears you. He may want to take samples."

"Poo," Dru said. "I'm going to MyWay to get that prescription refill. They know me. They'll hand it over." She directed her piercing blue gaze at Dale. "That *is* where you get it?"

Numbly, letting Sully climb back in his lap without much notice, Dale nodded—and felt lucky to have chosen her approved pharmacy at her approved grocery store. Then again, it was the only grocery store within convenient reach of West Winona…he'd moved here long enough before starting in at the clinic to learn that much.

"How about tonight?" she said, breaking into his bemused thoughts. "You have a late phase?"

"Usually." Half a day later or so, a less severe follow-up bout. "But I'm covered."

She gave him a darkly contemplative look, and he thought for a moment she would demand an explanation—that he had short term steroids on hand, because sometimes he still needed them. *Sometimes.* Things *would* get better, though. They had, the last time.

He didn't want to think about how long it had taken.

Wells frowned at Dru. "You need to be available to us."

"I'll be back." She said it negligently as she packed up her first-aid kit. She wheeled the bike down the road and a polite starting distance away before she turned it around, as if aware that given the slight chance, Wells might get official about insisting. As she threw her leg over the saddle and flipped the second kickstand up with her foot, she said, "Back in a flash! Tell your cronies not to pull me over and I'll be back even sooner!"

Sully barked fiercely at the bike as the engine revved and Dru guided it past them. *loud! bad loud!*

Dale sighed—grateful that he could—and scruffed up the top of Sully's head. "You should have stayed with me. We'd be back at the clinic by now, none the wiser."

Wells looked at Dru's receding taillight and then at the forlorn body in its forlorn yard. "He's gonna give me grief," she muttered.

"It was less intrusive than EMTs," Dale suggested, crossing his legs as if sitting in the middle of a dirt road was his preferred resting position, and turning Big Blue over and over in his hand was preferred entertainment. Sully settled himself more comfortably and turned his attention to Wells as if expecting her to do something entertaining.

"He's still gonna…" she said, and trailed off into pensive, looking beyond the houses as if she could sense the detective's arrival.

Dale rested his cheek on the top of Sully's dusty hound head and wondered what the dead man's life had been like.

DALE LAP. MINE. life is good. dale making the scary noises, not good. do i smell fire? no. no fire. just hot pines. and dead man. and people scent, dog scent, bubbly drink in the grass scent. more dog scent…all over the dead man. sigh. chin on dale's knee, this is good. the impatient woman watches.

maybe she'll have food.

YES, I MOVED the body, I thought he was still alive. Yes, my dog romped around the area; that's how I found the body in the first place. Yes, he was on a leash, but I fumbled it. Yes, I bled on the shirt. I didn't realize I'd been cut, and I was trying to save his life. No, I don't know this man. George Corcoran? No, I don't even know this area. Yet. Yes, I work around here. Or I will. Do you want to come to my welcome-aboard reception?

Dale pushed aside a half-eaten prepackaged rice bowl and massaged his tired eyes, unable to keep the words from running through his mind…again. All the questions, all the answers. And all while the evidence technician went to work around George Corcoran's body, taking pictures of this, samples of that, notes about everything. Dru returned as promised with Dale's new daily canister, told them quite shortly that she'd seen nothing, stayed out of the yard and spat downwind of the body—this last with a wink at Dale—and then provided her contact information before roaring back off down the road.

Eventually Rena Wells drove Dale back to the clinic and he

got in the Forester, gave heartfelt thanks for the blessedly short nature of his commute, and returned to a house that wasn't quite his yet. On paper, yes. But not yet *home*.

Home was still Ohio, with those flat green fields and deciduous forests, tornado warnings and…

And family. Aunt Cily, who was the most practical and least silly person he knew, a warm soul wrapped up in a thoughtful, considering outer shell. And Uncle Bud, the only one who called her Cecilia and who years earlier had gruffly instructed Dale simply to call him "Bud."

Dale realized that Sully was whining. Probably *had* been whining for quite some time. A glance showed him just what he knew he'd see: Sully, sitting alertly at the Line of Doom where the carpeted living room area of the great room changed to the Saltillo tile of the dining room. To Dale's back stood the three and a half-foot high back wall dividing the kitchen and dining room; before him sprawled the living room, carpeted except for the tile hearth of the fireplace. Boxes loomed everywhere he looked, proving to him just how much he'd managed to accumulate over the years. Well, once he got the shelves up in the puzzle room, things would improve. Half these boxes belonged there and the rest could hang out there while he sorted and arranged and probably tossed half of what he'd brought, suddenly realizing that, like Ohio, it was no longer part of his life.

In Ohio, Sully had been denied his fast-blooming begging career with the Line of Doom, the clear demarcation between the eat-in kitchen and the hallway of the little old farmhouse Dale had owned—or at least, that he had shared with the bank. The flung-open floor plan of this southwestern house denied them easy solutions, so the line of carpet-to-tile had done the trick. The new Line of Doom.

Sully whined again, far enough from the table to meet Dale's eyes over top of it, possibly to see the plastic bowl Dale had just pushed aside. Big, brown *please* eyes, *pleasepleaseoh-please*…

Dale glanced down at Sully's toes. As expected, two toenails on one foot extended onto the tile. Dale cleared his throat, a meaningful if juicier sound than he'd meant it to be; his lungs were still full of gunk.

Without so much as blinking, Sully pulled his foot back. He was every bit as appealing as he meant to be.

Dale made a sudden strangled noise—a deliberately strangled noise, one of defeat—and Sully jumped to his feet, stout brushy tail wagging and this time quite careful to stay behind the line. "You win," Dale told him, putting the bowl on the floor. "Your sheer force of personality takes the day. And I ate most of it anyway. Okay, it's yours."

Okay was what Sully had been waiting for; he scrabbled across the tile and gobbled down the rice, gleefully shoving the bowl across the tile and against the backwall until Dale took mercy and put out a foot to stop its journey.

Call home. That's what he needed to do. Just a casual call, a *how are you* call.

Except Aunt Cily would know. "What's wrong?" she'd ask, and if he answered she'd fret and if he didn't answer she'd fret…and he knew how much she hoped for him from this move. A new home, away from old baggage. And into the clear air, relatively free of pollution and pollens. To call so soon after arrival with the asthma cough interrupting his words and the irritation of the day's attack roughing up his voice…

That would require some real fretting.

So…

Maybe tomorrow.

"Just you and me, Sully," he said.

eating. busy.

"And tomorrow we're covering overflow for the morning."

Walk-ins, emergencies…whatever. "Tomorrow afternoon, it's back to sorting out the office. And listen up, Sully. No finding any bodies tomorrow."

Sully worked hard at polishing rice atoms from the gleaming black plastic. *whatever.*

DALE ARRIVED AT the clinic early the next day, relishing the Power of the Key. No matter the time or day, the clinic was his to wander. Wander it he did, taking the opportunity to listen to the silence and the sound of his sneakers meeting the linoleum tile floor, occasional squeak and all. His foray into the back kennel area broke that silence; the peace turned abruptly to mayhem. Even that made him smile, especially when Sully quivered in indignant response.

The dogs in the patient crates reacted with less interest, and the cats ignored them altogether. The bunny hid under his towel, which Dale took to be an improvement from the previous day's failure to care. The rescued Dane curled in her huge bottom crate, already looking like a different dog—hydrated, fed, even cleaned up a little. The beardie, too, looked brighter, definitely benefiting from the prednisone and supportive IVs. Her regular vet should have the labs back today…

The triage and treatment area…spotless. Everything in its place. In one area, the diagnostics—a Vetscan blood analyzer—pricey but oh-so-nice. A bin of heartworm antigen test kits, ready for the spring rush. A centrifuge, tidier in size than the model Dale had used in Ohio. Microscope, of course. In the adjacent section of counter, an autoclave and latex glove storage. Boring natural in color; Dale would have to see about getting in some purple ones.

Dale considered it all, wondering if things could be rearranged to allow for a second table. Then he moved on to the pet exam rooms—two of them—also spotless. The reception area showed signs of wear and stain. He sat in one of the chairs, rearranged long legs a few times, and made a face. Maybe they could add a few more chairs.

Behind the four-foot reception counter ran a lower work desk outfitted with penholders, forms, a computer station, and credit card swiper. If he recalled correctly, Kundita-the-petite, East Indian of feature and accent, handled most of the billing. He remembered her mostly for her efficient silence in the background of Sheri's efficient noisiness. In the back corner a standing station allowed for on-the-fly prescription drug work, and another part-timer kept her personal things in that area.

Sheri kept the biggest workspace, up against the wall at the end of the short arm of the counter "L." A glance showed Dale a picture of a little boy—son, or nephew?—all smiles, with skin lighter than Sheri's but still richly brown, and a head full of ringlets. And there was the cloth doll, of course. Today it had little trousers, the toothpick had been removed, and the inked-in features were smeared as though its head had somehow gotten soaked in water. It had a new toe tag. *George.*

Hmm.

On the wall to the left of Sheri's closed laptop, she'd cleared her whiteboard of personal notes and written neatly:

NOSE FOR TROUBLE 8

Dale considered it a moment and decided that sooner or later—and probably all too soon—he'd learn what that meant. For now…the boxes.

In his office, Dale replaced Big Blue in the desk drawer, deciding not to admit to himself that he needed to have two of the inhalers—one for work and one for home. He dove into the boxes instead, also not thinking about the other things the previous day had presented to him.

The dull, lifeless eyes of George Corcoran.

The paw prints, the broken glass, the gurgle of water in dead lungs. He felt that same responsibility that weighed on him during a clinic crisis, that same sense of things undone…a familiar feeling. It went beyond today, seemed somehow to have been there forever. The responsibility to see it through.

But George Corcoran was already dead. And the county sheriff's department was doing its job. Dale wasn't involved. *You just found him. That's all.*

The unfortunate thing about unpacking, he realized, was that it left one's mind free to think. To puzzle over what he'd seen, and to realize, suddenly, that he'd be ducking questions about it all day. He checked his watch, decided Dru's morning part-timer would be here any moment now to start cleaning kennels, and decided he might as well face facts. There was no running away from yesterday, even if he was still pretty much deter-mined to run away from the days not so long before. On the other hand, questions about yesterday might well shift everyone's interest away from the Ohio fire. The one where everyone called him a hero and he felt only guilt and failure. Dru might well keep his secret about the asthma attack, but she hadn't promised to stop with her blunt questions about the Ohio rumors.

Someone entered through the back door, headed straight for the kennels in an audible teen shamble, and immediately turned the radio up to window-shattering volume—presumably to hear the rock music over the barking.

Sully lifted his head, his ears flat against his skull.

"No kidding," Dale said. "Give him a moment. Maybe it's just a kick start to his day." He shelved a handful of books using the vague system that seemed to make sense only to Dale himself, approximating the positions of *Small Animal Surgery* and *Textbook of Veterinary Diagnostic Radiology,* and then gave much thought to ear plugs while he emptied the rest of the box. A glance at Sully revealed doggy misery. *Enough is enough.* Dale strode out to the kennel area, where he found signs of someone at work on the outside runs—an open door, and the doggy boarders all closed in, their exit doors locked. The dogs themselves paced and whined and barked at nothing in particular, restless and unhappy.

The radio perched high on a shelf above the broom and mop storage. Dale turned it off and waited.

Within moments a kid came through the door, looking annoyed, his mouth forming what Dale easily perceived to be a crude word. T-shirt under worn flannel shirt—these high desert early mornings remained crisp no matter the pleasant nature of the afternoons—and equally worn, baggy jeans. Untied laces flopped at his high-top sneakers, and a carelessly held industrial-size pooper-scooper dangled at his side. He stopped short when he saw Dale, hesitating between *who are you* belligerence and the inevitable conclusion that this new authority figure belonged here.

Dale didn't give him the chance to work it through. He pointed at the radio and said with implacable simplicity, *"No."*

"Aw, c'mon." The kid—a bleached blond with chunks of lime patching his hair—had a face full of the righteous disbelief only a teenager could project. "There's no one here but me."

"I'm here."

The kid gave him a contemptuous eye. "I don't know you."

"Dru calls me Mr. Dr. Dale, but you can call me *sir.*" Dale crossed his arms, supposing that he'd be more imposing with his white coat on instead of the red and gray OSU T-shirt he intended to trade for scrubs before the clinic opened. Not long from now, in fact. "And I'll often be here this early. Even if I wasn't, *they're* here." He pointed at the kenneled dogs, all of whom were settling nicely. Then he smiled. "If that's not enough, then…I'll just have to tell Dru how loud you've been playing the radio."

"No! No, man, don't do that." The kid waved his hands in front of him, forgetting he had the pooper-scooper. It hit the nearest kennel run and clattered to the floor; he bent to pick it up without hesitating in his reassurances as he raised his voice over the scatter of offended barks. "It's not such a big deal. You want the radio off, it's off."

"Uh huh." Dale would be convinced when the next few days brought silence. "So you cleanup in the morning? What's your name?"

"Jorge," the kid said warily, clearly believing no good could come from this conversation. He pronounced it with hard H sounds instead of soft Gs. A small ring pierced his brow, winking in the combination of fluorescent and natural light.

"Jorge. What else do you do around here?"

"Dru's my boss."

It wasn't what Dale had asked, so he leaned against the mop cabinet with a casual shoulder and waited.

Jorge looked like he wanted to mutter a curse and didn't dare; no doubt the misdirection ploy often worked. In truth, Dale wasn't intensely curious about the kid's duties, except to learn the rhythms of his own clinic. And except that a nagging inner voice told him that this kid was capable of bringing trouble into the clinic with him, and after some hard experience, Dale was highly attuned to trouble. Jorge pointed at the small room Dale had traversed to reach the kennel, the feed room with its bins and bags and the laundry area. "I wash the bedding," he said. "And I wash the bowls."

Dale suspected that Dru would say there was more to it than that, and sooner or later he'd figure out the division of labor; for now he was pleased enough to learn the kid wasn't doling out dog food. And as for his indefinable uneasy feeling…time would tell. It wasn't like Dale had a problem with kids in general, or kids working at the clinic. He'd actually been a teenager once himself, he was pretty sure of it. More than that, a teen with a job at the local clinic.

"I gotta finish up," the kid said. "I've got to make it to school."

"I'll see you tomorrow then," Dale told him. He had his own duties to tend…and if his still-ringing ears weren't mistaken, the first of the other staffers had just arrived.

FIVE

SURE ENOUGH, Brad Stanfill strolled into the triage room just as Dale passed it, and Dale followed him in. They'd never had much of a chance to talk; Dale still struggled to get a sense of whether Brad had wanted Dale's new position.

But Brad greeted him with a sleepy smile and a lift of his tea-stained travel mug with a garish Montezuma's Castle logo, no sign of any potential lingering resentment. Hadn't wanted it, hadn't gone for it. "Here's to caffeine," he said, looking like he needed it—though Dale had observed that he always had that heavy-lidded look. His sandy brown forelock kept slipping over his eye, which added to the impression—along with the habitual slouch of his slight frame. "Not that I've *got* any caffeine, but all the more reason to toast it." He took a sip of the tea and admitted, "My wife has a thing about it. Herbal tea and bottled water. Every now and then I sneak in some chocolate milk."

Dale had a sudden urge to confess to the Lucky Charms in his cupboard, but successfully fought it down. Brad in the meantime moved on to suppose he might bring his own dog in for the day if he didn't actually have three of them, and if his wife didn't run a small business out of their home so they had human company all day anyway, but Dale's little beagle certainly seemed to enjoy the office routine and behaved himself to boot, didn't he?

Brad Stanfill clearly didn't need caffeine, sleepy expression or not. Dale waited for a break in the conversation, and—after a few near misses—found himself in the middle of Brad's commentary about the not-too-distant community Environmental Fair and the clinic's contribution to the free spay and neuter certificates.

"Dr. Hogue has always participated—"

Dale finally dashed headlong into the space between two words. "Sounds like a good idea to me—I'm in." Dale tugged at his T-shirt and headed for the swinging door exit at the same time. "Gotta go change—I'm batting overflow today."

Escape!

Maybe it was nerves. Maybe Brad Stanfill wasn't always set on fast-forward. Maybe he'd been as uncertain as Dale about their first extended private encounter.

One could hope.

As he made his cowardly flight out of triage and past the reception area, the phone rang. Dale reached over the counter to grab it. "Olentangy Vet—I mean, Foothills Clinic."

"Just checking," said a man's voice. It wasn't friendly. "Watch yourself." And hung up. Loudly.

Dale slowly hung up the phone. Had that been for him? Or the clinic?

Not the clinic. Not again.

It didn't feel random, not with a murder filling the day before. It felt like he should rush off to ask questions, to understand who would make such a phone call and how it connected with him finding—

It doesn't, he told himself. *Leave it alone.*

Movement by the inner door of the airlock entry caught his eye, breaking through his thoughts. In the small window of the wooden door, a frizzy head and set of owlish eyeglasses appeared, then sank beneath the level of the glass. A moment to reset the jumping posture, and the head reappeared…disappeared. Another moment and a hand appeared in its stead, waving enthusiastically.

Spotted.

Pretty much like a deer in headlights, but spotted nonetheless.

Dale glanced at his watch. The first appointment wasn't due for fifteen minutes, and Sheri should be here any moment. Let someone in before Sheri arrived to take charge? Not a chance.

He fled to his office.

There he greeted Sully, exchanged a few howl-whispers of conversation, and headed for the file cabinet to dig out a scrub shirt from the top drawer. He'd learned to hide them; other people didn't mind grabbing an oversize shirt, but it'd only taken one time of going shirtless beneath his carefully buttoned lab coat to remind him it didn't work the other way around and he'd better be prepared.

His hand, groping behind a collection of empty file folders, found only space and cool metal. Slowly, he closed the drawer and turned to lean his back against the file cabinet. "They got me," he said to Sully. "Already!"

Sully heaved a great sigh of commiseration, chin on his paws and brown eyes following Dale's every move.

At least this time he had the T-shirt. Far from professional, but better than faking it beneath the lab coat.

On second thought—

He scooped up his lab coat and strode back to Sheri's station, expecting to find her there by now and not disappointed; she bent double to stash her voluminous purse in some hidden niche, presenting him with a perfect view of her ample panty line.

In the reception area, a short, frizzy-haired woman leaned over a chair, brushing it off. The view was bottoms up everywhere he turned. But then the client righted herself and sat down beside a cardboard cat carrier, only to spot him in the process. She flung an accusing finger at him. "You!"

Best defense: a good offense. Or even a bad offense. By then Sheri straightened, too, and as soon as she caught Dale's eye he pointed a much more restrained finger in her direction and said, "You!"

Possibly no one in this office had used that voice on her before. "Me?" she said, her eyebrows rocketing halfway up her high forehead.

"You," he confirmed. "You're the one with all the power around here; you told me so yourself."

The surprise changed to something that was part defensiveness, part cockiness. She crossed her arms over her own scrub top, a white material with riotous paw prints. Her hair held the exact same style of the day before, down to the pattern of little seed pearls riding the waves. "What of it?"

"You're now in charge of my scrubs. I'll bring them in; you keep them."

All her attitude melted away, whatever it had been to start with. "Oh." She waved a hand at him, limp with its lack of concern. "That." And she bent over to her mysterious niche to return to her rummaging.

"Yes," Dale said, somewhat stung, "that." As he tried to think of some safe way to tell her he didn't want to talk to her butt and would she stand up and at least listen to him, Brad Stanfill sauntered out of the office, tea in hand.

"Decided against changing?" he asked.

"He wouldn't let me in!" The woman stood, determined to have her say. "He saw me, I know he did."

"You were early," Sheri said, severely muffled.

"But he was *here*."

"And you were *early*." Sheri popped back above the counter to glare at the woman and then smiled sweetly at Dale, right before she threw him a wad of suspiciously familiar material. "Already done," she said. "I rescued this from someone who will remain nameless. You just keep your scrubs with me from now on, Dr. Dale."

"You're the new vet?" the woman said. "Nice way to start, by snubbing your customers."

Feeling the balance of reality shifting around him, Dale indicated Sheri. "She's the one who runs this place," he said. "If you were me, would you have stepped on her toes?"

Sheri lifted an imperious brow at the woman.

Miffed but left with no reasonable argument in the face of Sheri's clear dominance of all, the woman settled back in her chair. But her expression quickly shifted to triumph. "I'm not early *now*." She tapped her watch with a rough fingernail. Come to notice it, her hands were rough in general, scratched with everything from fresh wounds to peeling scabs. "*Now* it's time for Feta's appointment. With Dr. Brad."

"Feta?" Dale murmured between unmoving lips, only loud enough for Sheri's ears.

Sheri leaned forward, not the least bit inconspicuous. "Feta. As in cheese. As in, you don't wanna know how bad this cat smells up close and personal."

Ah. Dale gave a pleasant smile as Dr. Brad picked up the patient paperwork from the tiered file holder on the wall and motioned for the woman to precede him into the first exam room. She picked up the cat carrier with some effort and headed past reception. A deep growling noise issued from within the carrier; as it neared Dale it gave a great hiss and suddenly jerked, a nearly successful leap for freedom and bloody mayhem.

As Dale jumped back, he thought he saw a look of sly satisfaction on the woman's face. She disappeared into the weighing area and from there to the exam room.

Dale looked at Sheri askance. "Brad's going to handle that thing?"

"It's not a bad cat, once you have it in a good scruff grip." Sheri sat down and flipped up the lid on her laptop, all efficiency as she prepared for the day. But then she looked up with a wicked grin. "It's getting hold of the thing in the first place that's the hard part."

Dale considered the ratty state of the cardboard carrier and wondered if they had any duct tape on hand. He didn't even want to think about an escaped Feta.

The phone rang; Dale's hand collided with Sheri's as they both reached for it. She gave him an imperious eye and he retreated, but a moment later he wished he hadn't. Sheri's friendly greeting to the caller quickly slipped to surprise, and she took the phone away from her ear to give it a *look*.

"Huh," she said, replacing it in the cradle. "Someone's got an attitude problem this morning."

Dale closed his eyes; felt a muscle in his jaw twitch.

For the first time, he heard Sheri sound uncertain. "Dr. Dale—?"

But Brad Stanfill interrupted, emerging from the exam room. Escaping, more likely, and slipping out a door barely opened and then quickly closed. "She lost her grip," he said.

"I saw that," Dale told him, thinking of the owlish glasses and frizzy hair as they'd appeared in the door glass.

"No, I mean literally. None of the techs will touch that cat. They all knew he was coming in today—you notice there's no one to be seen? They'd rather get dinged for being late. So she's got to hold him until I can trank him, and then we can get on with things."

Sheri held up the appointment book for Dale's benefit, her long, manicured fingernail tapping at the appointment in question. "You see how I never book anyone right on her heels? Learned better. Other people don't like the smell. Or the—"

From inside the room, the woman shrieked an angry curse. Seconds later, the cat shrieked back.

"—or the screaming," Sheri finished.

"She's got him," Brad said with satisfaction.

"And he got her," Sheri muttered.

Brad hitched up the lapels of his lab coat, a man prepared to face off with danger. "And he's even de-clawed. Now quick, let's talk about finding dead people. That beagle must have a nose for trouble!"

Of course he'd heard. Who wouldn't have heard? Dale was surprised he hadn't been thoroughly grilled on the whole incident within moments of setting foot in the clinic, regardless of the time and lack of other occupants. He was surprised Sheri hadn't left him a note, grilling him in absentia.

"Ah *ha*," Sheri said, standing up so suddenly that her wheeled office chair went scooting out behind her. She grabbed the dry-erase marker with a flourish, scrubbed vigorously at the whiteboard with the flat of her fist, and scribbled:

NOSE FOR TROUBLE 9

"Kinda surprised I didn't get you yesterday," she told Brad. "Now go trank that cat before she loses hold of it."

"Yes'm," he said, amiable as ever. Maybe one had to be, in order to fit in here. High-energy talker to get a word in edgewise, low-key mood so it didn't matter when you couldn't…

Dale wasn't sure where that left him. Too intense, he thought.

"I'm running a pool," Sheri said. "You want in? It's for how many times someone says 'nose for trouble' before the week is out."

"Four days," Dale mused. "Could be a lot of them."

"I can count that high," she told him, lofty. "And while I've got you here, you can tell me everything that happened. Dru wouldn't say a word, other than muttering about how some guy had taken a bath. Everything I know, I got from the news—and that's just not *right*."

Inspired, Dale held up the scrub shirt. "Gotta change," he said. "Never know when we might get a walk-in coming right through that—"

On the other hand, some things were getting predictable.

They heard the rumble of the pickup truck first—a big diesel that pulled up and didn't cut off, somehow imbuing the motor with the sound of impatience. Sheri glanced down at her schedule and shrugged.

Dale got a glimpse of a man through the small door window, enough to strike a familiar chord before the door opened and he faced the same person who'd brought in the emaciated Dane only days earlier. Lean to the point of hollow-cheeked, clean-shaven this time… Dale hastily shrugged into his lab coat, eyeing the harness-restrained dog. Another rescue?

It fit the part—a lean, dingo-colored adolescent shepherd/Lab mix, shedding undercoat tufting out at its haunches and ruff. All the same, it had the look of a dog recently brushed, as if the tufting had been much worse. But there was no disguising the smell. Dirty dog…and somewhere, a dirty and infected wound. A short length of chain hung from its neck.

Quick initial assessment conducted, Dale looked up to meet the man's gaze, discovering a surprising amount of defensiveness there. "I rescued him," the man said. "Will you take him?"

"The shelter—" Sheri started.

"Don't talk to me about the shelter." The man started to glower at her, seemed to think better of it. "Look at his neck. You'll see why I brought him in."

Outside, the truck engine revved slightly; the man shifted uneasily—but said nothing as Dale crouched, gave the dog an instant to understand and accept that Dale intended to touch him, and carefully lifted the dog's chin to get a look at the matted ruff. "Aw, hell," he muttered, remembering after he'd said it that such a reaction wasn't part of his professional demeanor. At least the waiting room was empty; he glanced at Sheri, who shrugged slightly as if to say she hadn't heard him at all. She also stood up to lean over the counter, trying to see what had upset him.

Dale tipped the dog's head the other way so she could see the too-small chain around its neck, and how it had pinched the growing dog's neck over time to create a gaping, infected wound, while in some spots the skin had grown right over the chain. He wouldn't have a good idea of the actual damage until Isaac got here and took clippers to the dog's neck.

Sheri sat back heavily in her chair, lips tight and a flush making her dark cheeks even darker.

The man seemed gratified by their reaction. He relaxed and looked at Dale as one might look upon a conspiring friend— although, oddly, Dale found his new expression almost more off-putting than his original brusque approach. "Can you take him, then?"

Another glance at Sheri. She said, "We've got an arrangement with the local rescue group. Paws for Cause."

Another thing about which he needed to learn. Dale nodded to the man, who'd taken an instant to glance over his shoulder at another rev of the truck engine.

"Someone's impatient," Sheri muttered. "What's your name, mister? We'll keep the harness and leash aside for you. Especially if you're going to be regular with this sort of thing. 'Cause you don't come to this clinic, do you?"

Many people would have looked abashed; this man just shook his head. "I work on the other side of town and use Pine Country Clinic. Name's Ledbetter. I've got to go…but I'll be back for the leash. And if Paws for Cause doesn't come through on the vet bills, I'll try to help out." He handed the leash to Dale and turned to go, but as his hand touched the doorknob, he looked back. "That Dane…did she make it?"

"Come and see," Dale invited, absently stroking the rescued dog's head and ears.

Ledbetter gave a short shake of his head and a grim little smile. "I'll take that as a yes. And by the way, I'm sure you have to report this dog to animal control, so I'm glad to tell you there were no tags on that chain. I found the dog wandering along 89 just north of here. I wouldn't be surprised if the owners didn't bother to hunt for it—or for that matter, if it's actually had any shots."

At that pronouncement, he left, not allowing them time for any more questions.

Dale could see why. He fingered the sharp, cut end of the chain, careful not to tug on the dog's wound, and held it up where Sheri could see.

"Wandering, my sweet Aunt Lulu's ass," she said. "He *liberated* it. Just like that Dane. We'll call him 'Slice.'"

"He said his name was—"

"Not that strange man. The dog. Slice."

Dale looked at her askance. "I'm not sure, but I think that's sick."

Sheri gave a satisfied nod. "Probably," she said. "So's the whole situation. Including that man Ledbetter." ·

He found himself strangely relieved to hear her voice the words. "He's a bit odd, isn't he?"

"Odd, schmod. He's out and out strange. He went from acting like Mr. Sneer to all of a sudden we're best friends. Don't get me wrong—he done good in rescuing that dog. However he did it. Animal control would have taken it away from any home that did this to it, anyway. But that doesn't make him not strange, 'cause he is."

And new to Sheri as well as to Dale, or she wouldn't have had to ask his name.

Dale sighed, patted the dog, and stood up. "I'll take this

fellow in the back. As soon as Isaac gets here—it's Isaac this morning, right?—send him in. I'll get started."

"Not too proud to do the techie work, are we?" Sheri said. She gave the whiteboard and its *nose for trouble* count a significant glance. "Or is it just that you think you can get away without giving up the goods on yesterday's adventure?"

"Well," Dale said, as thoughtfully as possible...treading a careful line. The dog whined, nervously tugging first one direction then another, and showing no apparent familiarity with the leash whatsoever. "I'm actually figuring I'll talk about that if and when I want to. It was a bad scene, Sheri. I'm not savoring it."

It took her aback; it couldn't help but take her aback. And he thought he saw a smart-ass answer forming on her lips...except she hesitated, and then nodded. "Yeah," she said. "Okay. But if you're gonna spill any juicy details...spill 'em here first."

"Because you're the one who does the schedule, right?"

She seemed relieved he'd returned their conversation to their established standard. "That's exactly right. By the way, we've got a camera in the triage room. It's up behind all the Vetrap, in a box. Digital and everything—Isaac knows how to use it. Just bring it to me when you're done and I'll get the pictures in our system."

And if they ever found the dog's owners, those pictures would become evidence.

"All right, dog," Dale said. "Time to turn you into a cover model. A model in a state of neuroleptanalgesia, but I'm sure your handsome nature will show through."

"Neuroleptanalgesia!" Sheri fanned herself. "You'll get me all hot if you keep talking like that!"

"What Sheri means," Dale told the dog solemnly, "is that I should learn to say *drugged* instead."

Sheri gave an approving nod, and the exchange put a Band-Aid over their horrified responses, and Dale took the dog into triage.

DALE, BACK FROM the sick animal rooms…dale, unhappy? wait, he's sitting on the floor! right beside me! sad face. here, dale, feel how I fit right into your lap? how sturdy i am? and strong! i can fix it, dale. whatever made the unhappy, i can fix it. let me sleep on you. that will fix anything.

THERE WAS SOMETHING to be said for a warm beagle in one's lap. Initially Dale had thought Sully would grow into the fifteen-inch variety of beagle, but he'd never gotten over thirteen inches at the withers. Over the course of the move, the advantages of having such a boundless supply of energy, hunger, and sleep bundled together in a smaller package became obvious. Moments like this, when Dale could sit on the floor and lean his head back against the wall, entirely comfortable with Sully snoozing—snoring slightly, actually—in the nest of his crossed legs…important moments indeed.

It didn't keep the images out of his head. The extent of the wound under the rescued dog's neck…the unnatural growth of skin around chain, and the strange feel of it under the scalpel. Isaac, hovering here and there, taking pictures, his habitually mournful expression tightening into something closer to anger.

The dog would be fine. Stitches, antibiotics, a few weeks to heal…and then re-grown hair would cover his new Frankendog characteristics.

"I don't get it," he said into the quiet office.

sleeping.

"I don't get Ledbetter, either. People bring in hurt animals, they stick around. They wring their hands, they worry, they want to know everything will be all right. This is the second time he's done a drop and run."

Sully shifted, sighing loudly. *SLEEPING.*

Pine Country Clinic. That's where Ledbetter took his own animals. The other end of town.

Laura Nakai's clinic.

Maybe she could shed some light on this guy. It seemed a safe line of inquiry, something to get his mind off murders and phone calls.

It certainly didn't have anything to do with the interesting afterglow when he considered how she'd given him her tea, stopping outside Foothills long enough to make sure he and his altitude sickness had something to drink even though she'd clearly been upset about something.

"Purely professional," he told Sully, assertively enough to rouse the beagle. "And much, *much* better to think about than what just went on in that triage room."

Sully crawled out of his lap, dragging each leg as though he barely had the strength to move and collapsing on his bed as soon as he reached it.

Enough about Ledbetter. Enough about the incomprehensible negligence that led to a fully embedded collar. First thing tomorrow, Dale would head for the Pine Country Clinic, taking shameless advantage of his still-flexible schedule to nab some time with Laura Nakai.

Now that was worth thinking about.

SULLY STAYED in the car. Now that the move was over and the SUV cleaned out, the vehicle had quickly reacquired its normal collection of interior detritus: Sully's larger wire crate, exchanged for the smaller soft-sided crate from which he could escape with glee. A tote with cleanup spray and towels, collapsible water bowl, tire gauge, and, for some reason, old windshield wiper pieces he never seemed to get rid of. Work gloves. A pair of old sneakers he'd ruined with creek crawling. A first aid kit, of course, along with a rudimentary vet kit.

There were also some things under the passenger-side seat that needed rooting out, but Dale thought he'd pretend not to know about that for a while longer.

There's only so long a man can linger near his car, he told himself, checking that his jeans hadn't ridden up his calves as he disembarked the Forester. He'd already given Laura Nakai enough reason to consider him Dr. Dork.

I just happened to be in the neighborhood...

Yeah, that would help.

But better, perhaps, than coming right out and asking for gossip on a client.

From inside the car, behind the half-rolled window, Sully gave a muffled, questioning sort of bark. *me?*

"Hang on, son, I'll be back soon." He looked at the clinic, this time actually seeing it. The Pine Country clinic nestled between a carpet store and a newly constructed low-end hotel, and though the parking up front was tight, the back of the building stretched into kennel runs and a long fenced open area.

Drought-dry could never look the part of the lush well-tended lawns from Dale's years in the Northeast and Midwest—*all in the past, where it belongs*—but neat little native plants lined the front of the building in planter boxes and the scant volunteer desert plants were neatly trimmed. A bright red plastic fire hydrant, securely anchored to the ground by someone possessing longstanding familiarity with Flagstaff's seasonal winds, gave Dale the first smile of the day. If Laura had put it there...or even allowed it to be there...she was someone with whom he could enjoy working.

He pushed through a double-door entry and into a welcome

area with a receptionist's counter off to the left, much like the Foothill clinic's arrangement.

This particular counter looked unmanned at the moment, with the muffled sounds of an unhappy dog coming from somewhere down the hallway straight ahead and a slight, well-groomed woman sitting quietly in the waiting room beside a little black Lab mix. The corner of the room held a dog and cat food display rack, on which the Lab mix—typically—cast an ever hopeful eye between her bouts of hand-licking. Dale gave the woman the kind of smile people give each other in the vet's office when they're acknowledging the wonderfulness of each other's pets.

Since Sully napped in Dale's little SUV it was a one-sided kind of acknowledgment, but Dale knew the ritual.

The little black Lab mix gave him a few tail wags of greeting, and it crossed Dale's mind that its eye was somehow too bright, its tremble not merely that of a slightly nervous dog, and its panting less panting than an unusually speedy respiration. And because his guard was down, he said the words that popped into his head. "Ate something you shouldn't have, did you?"

The woman gave him a look of astonishment. "However did you—"

The receptionist's head popped up above the counter, revealing a young woman with dishwater blonde hair secured in two wispy braids, an astonishing amount of freckles, and an equally astonished look on her face. "I thought you were here to do Chica's weight check, I didn't know you were waiting to see one of the doctors—" And then came the pause, the slight look of suspicion as she turned her washed-out blue gaze on Dale. "How *did* you—"

"Chocolate," said the owner, as the dog gave a tremor so hard it came in just shy of being a seizure. "Half a pound of bittersweet baking chocolate. Is that bad?"

The receptionist flipped a page in the schedule book, idly tapping her pencil on the counter. "Lots of dogs seem to get into chocolate," she said. "I think Dr. Nakai will be through in twenty minutes or so…"

Dale gave a sharp shake of his head, drawing their startled attention to him; his own was on the dog, and warily so. "Half a pound of bittersweet?" he repeated. "Too much theobromine. You need to get her into treatment *now*."

"But Dr. Nakai is in surgery. She's the only one here—"

"Then see if she'll let me handle this." He stuck out his hand, a belated introduction. Dazed, she took it more or less automatically, a small pale grip within his own. "Dale Kinsall, DMV—I'm new over at Foothills Clinic. I need apomorphine, charcoal slurry kit, a blood draw, and someone who can monitor her vitals while I work."

"But—you can't—"

The dog trembled again, releasing a generous rope of drool. *So much for making friends with Dr. Nakai.* Dale scooped the dog up, wrapping his arms around her chest and rump, and looked down to catch the owner's eye. The woman returned his gaze with a stricken expression. He said, "It's up to you."

"Save her," the woman said, already almost beyond speech. "I'll sign any release you want, but you have to *try*."

"She's going to kill me," the receptionist said. "I don't have a release for *this*—"

"Write one up," Dale told her. "And go tell Dr. Nakai what's happening. She's still got time to kick me out. Meanwhile, I need someone to help—"

"In there." The receptionist pointed to the first door on the left down the hallway as she hurried past on her way to the surgery room. "Trina's cleaning up. She can help. But don't get comfortable."

"I'll write something up." The owner, still standing helplessly in the waiting room, scrabbled for something to write on and ended up grabbing a West Nile virus handout, flipping it over to scribble on the back. From the looks of it, it wouldn't matter exactly what she wrote; no one would be able to read it.

And so Dale invited himself into the treatment room, carrying the trembling little Lab mix and already scanning the counters, cabinets, and shelves for their drug storage. Trina the tech gave him a wary eye, but she must have overheard the conversation; she held up a syringe. "I didn't know the dose—"

Dale stuck his head back out the door to the waiting room, not failing to notice it had gathered another client with a small pet carrier, a woman in formal wear and makeup, sparkly high heels, and a perpetual expression of plastic surgery surprise mightily enhanced by Dale's appearance. He said sharply, "Weight?"

"One thirty-five," the highly dressed woman said, blinking in surprise.

"Forty-five pounds," said the dog's owner.

Dose, .6 mg of Apomorphine. *And we're off.*

Five minutes later, when Laura Nakai pushed through the treatment room door, her expression tense and her body language radiating stiff anger, Dale had an arm around the thoroughly miserable dog while Trina held a lined wastebasket at the end of the exam table. Laura crossed her arms at her stomach, tightening her surgical scrubs over her shapely chest quite nicely. "You." The way she said it surprised him...as if it were confirmation of a previous conversation.

"Hi," he offered.

"HORK!" said the dog.

"Gawd," said Trina, looking away from the wastebasket. "I'm never eating chocolate again."

Laura's lips twitched slightly. Surely it wasn't anything

related to a smile, especially given the way her tension quickly
returned. "I think I can take it from here, much as we all appreciate your help."

"Hor-hor-HORK!" said the dog.

Dale cast Trina a sympathetic look. "They never do it just
once."

Laura gestured to the door, clearly meaning for Dale to use
it. "She's had apo, she needs the slurry, am I correct?"

"That's where we're at." Dale eased away from the dog,
giving Trina the chance to set down the wastebasket and supply
a restraining hand. "I'd be glad to—"

"I think you've done enough," Laura snapped, and for sure
there was anger in her voice that time. Anger and resentment,
and Dale blinked at the strength of it.

"I'm sorry," he said. "I'll wait outside."

Reeling a little from the edge of her censure—not unexpected, at that—he returned to the waiting room, where the receptionist was on the phone, hunched over the receiver with one
hand making a futile effort to muffle her conversation.

"Yes, he's *here*. And you were right, he's—" She glanced
over, saw him, and straightened. "Yes, well, I have to go. Talk
to you later." She hung up, and looked straight at Dale as if she
hadn't just been talking about him. "I told you she'd be mad."

"I don't think there was ever any question about that." He
scrubbed a hand through his hair even though he knew it would
leave him more or less irreparably mussed for the day. The receptionist gave an inexplicable sigh, sagging a little in her
chair. He frowned, glancing into the waiting room. The
formally dressed woman, attentive as she was, quickly looked
away.

Dale took the chair between them and stretched his legs out
into the room. Waiting. In the waiting room. Probably just to
get turned out of the office altogether.

The dog's owner remained oblivious to the byplay of undercurrents. "What about Bennie? Will she be all right?"

"She got rid of…" he tried not to envision the moment, couldn't help it, "…a lot." That didn't mean it was enough. "She's getting charcoal now, which will help soak up anything remaining in her stomach. The question is whether she absorbed enough to do her permanent harm, and it's going to take a day or two before we—I mean, before Dr. Nakai—knows for sure."

The woman hesitated, red-eyed and anxious and not wanting the answer to be *I don't have an answer*. But she subsided, sitting back in her seat slightly, crossing her legs to endlessly bob her ankle, her arms crossed and a red leash clutched in her hand.

The formally dressed woman regarded Dale from behind thick false eyelashes that could have done double-duty on Tammy Faye. He wasn't sure what that look meant—it could have been curiosity, and it could have been accusation. She, too, wanted an answer.

Fortunately, another vet poked his head into the waiting area—*must be a back way in*—and picked up the folder for whatever pet the woman had in her little carrier; he gave Dale a somewhat puzzled look and then nodded at the woman, who picked up the carrier and clopped after the vet, her high heels striking the linoleum in a no-nonsense step.

The freckled receptionist saw Dale looking after her and said in a stage whisper, "She's in the symphony. She told me they had an early performance at the university today."

So. Flagstaff had a symphony. Good to know.

Right, Kinsall. Think about everything but what you're going to say to Laura Nakai when she walks into this room.

I came to pry about a client and I took over your treatment room instead.

Surely he could do better than that.

I wanted to return your tea bottle.

That would have been good, if he'd brought it with him.

I—

It would help if he didn't keep interrupting his thoughts with the very distinct image of Laura Nakai entering the treatment room, her toasty complexion flushed, her lips thinned, her face set. He had the feeling that this was actually quite an unusual display of anger

"Here." Bennie's owner held out a piece of paper. "It's the best I could come up with. And thank you. I hope this doesn't get you into too much trouble."

The receptionist glanced down the hall as a door opened, and nodded at the woman. "You can go on back."

The woman jumped to her feet, and Dale hastily took the paper before she dashed off with it, stumbling in her eagerness. *I hope this doesn't get me into too much trouble, too.* He'd already found a body in this area with single-digit yearly murder counts…he thought that should be enough notoriety for his first weeks of residence.

It was then he found the receptionist looking at him, apparently feeling free to speak now that they were alone. "Define trouble," she said, not unkindly…but not encouragingly, either.

It sent his thoughts scrambling back to his apology and introduction. *I came to pry about a client and I took over your treatment room as well—plus I still intend to pry.*

Because surprisingly enough, he did.

Humble. Start with humble. *I'm sorry, I was inexcusably rude, I—*

The door opened again, closing quietly; it allowed the escape of the dog owner's tearful reassurance to her dog and the tech's barely audible reassurances in the background, and then Laura came down the hall and hesitated at the énd of it.

Dale rose quickly to his feet. "Ledbetter," he said, his mouth apparently overcome by alien forces with no social graces whatsoever. "He keeps bringing me rescue cases—" at which point he wrestled himself to a stop.

Laura, showing only the slightest surprise, beckoned him to follow. He saw with relief that she was no longer so flushed, and she moved gracefully rather than stiffly. He hastened to follow, and then matched his strides to hers, staying half a step behind.

The door at the end of the hallway led to a shared office with two desks facing one another, a shared phone, a lush and exotic-looking plant in perfect health, and various certificates and photos, inexpertly framed, adorning the walls. Laura closed the door to reveal a huge plastic three-month calendar hanging from the back of it with schedule notes in two different colors. *Birthday!! 32!* exclaimed green marker on May 19 and he wondered if it was Laura's, if behind the restraint she once again showed him was a person who could use all those exclamation points in green marker.

He opened his mouth, and this time better words came out. "I'm sorry," he said. "I was here to talk to you, and I just couldn't…" *Figure out what to say, that was it.*

Laura sat on the edge of her desk. She didn't offer Dale the single guest chair in the room, a battered and utilitarian thing. She said, "Bennie's owner is impressed by you," but she didn't say it like she believed it herself.

"That's…" Dale cleared his throat, still working through the final gruff vestiges of the asthma episode and buying time to boot. He couldn't read her quiet expression, couldn't read it at all. Finally he ventured, "That's good, right?"

It earned him the briefest tug of a smile. No lipstick on those lips, just good natural color. Nice.

Don't stare at her mouth. He jerked his gaze back up to hers.

"It certainly makes things easier, should the incident result in permanent damage to the dog's liver. I myself don't honestly know the ramifications of a situation like this. I've never even *heard* of a situation like this." She regarded him a moment, making no attempt to hide the assessment. "She says you picked up on the situation the moment you set eyes on the dog."

"It seemed pretty clear," Dale said, though at the moment he couldn't have said just why.

She didn't respond, and though at first he thought she was not saying something on the tip of her tongue, after a moment he realized she was simply comfortable with not responding.

"I *am* sorry," he said, not quite as comfortable with the silence. He made an effort to keep from bouncing slightly on his toes. "I actually came to thank you for the other day. The tea. And because I wanted to talk to you about an awkward thing with one of your clients, but that's pretty much even more awkward at this point."

"So it is," she allowed. She pushed at a strand of black hair, tucking it back into her short, business-like French braid. It had the look of a perpetual escapee, and Dale expected to see it back, arching over her forehead to brush against the refined line of her cheek. "But you're here. I won't promise any answers, but you may as well ask."

Yep. There it was. Hanging just to her jaw line.

Don't stare at—

Just don't stare.

"I'm in a situation with one of your regulars," he said, focusing with effort. Maybe this was what happened when you left family behind, changed jobs and climates, and then found a dead body. Early senility. "A man named Ledbetter—I don't have a first name. I'm trying to get a bead on how to handle things."

"Alfred Ledbetter," she said, finally gesturing at the chair.

He sat. And after a moment, when it became clear that it was his turn, he said, "In the last week he's brought in two rescued dogs. They were in pretty bad shape—they needed rescuing. But…I think he's lying to us about the circumstances, and I'm getting a…" *Oh, just go ahead and say it—* "bad feeling from him."

She didn't immediately respond; he was coming to expect this from her. This time she remained silent long enough that he wondered if it was still his turn or if she was actually biting her tongue—in annoyance or amusement, he wouldn't care to guess. He stopped himself from wiggling his foot. Barely.

She drew a breath, tapped her fingers against her thigh in a gesture that seemed momentous after all that silence, and said, "You have a knack for presenting me with difficult situations."

Dale winced, right out loud. Or at least with an expression that must have been loud to someone as self-contained as Laura Nakai.

She put her fingers over her mouth; it looked thoughtful.

It looked like she might be trying not to smile.

She cleared her throat slightly. "If this were a matter where we were concerned about an animal's welfare, I wouldn't hesitate to discuss details with you. As it is, I think we both agree Mr. Ledbetter is…assertively passionate about his causes. Enough so that…" she hesitated, clearly hunting words "…a period of adjustment to his ways might be necessary. That being said, he's…pretty independent. For the most part he's confined his rescue efforts to working with one of the local groups."

Dale looked up from the sneaker laces that had somehow caught his attention. Nothing to do with how awkward he felt. "Paws for Cause."

She nodded. "Sorting out the players already, I see. It's a wonderful organization. They gladly handle urgent rescues."

Unspoken was her puzzlement about why Ledbetter hadn't gone through the rescue group in the first place, but he had enough sense of her now to know it would remain unspoken.

He said, "They were in pretty bad shape—one of them barely made it. He may have felt an urgency in the situation—"

But not so urgent that someone hadn't taken time to brush out the second dog.

Laura stepped into his silence. "I'm sorry I couldn't be of more help."

Dale looked away from the thoughts he'd trailed off after, startled. "You've helped a lot, actually. I still can't say as I understand the guy, but when it comes right down to it, I guess I don't have to understand him. It's just…in my nature to try, I guess."

Not to mention it had been a good reason to stop by Pine Country Clinic.

She took pity on him. "How are you settling in? Aside from finding the second bizarre murder of the month?"

"And I'm not hearing much about *that*," Dale grumbled without thinking.

She gave a slight shake of her head; it barely displaced her short braid. "Feelings are running high enough with this drought—" She stopped herself, giving him a more attentive look. "Then again, you know all about that, don't you?"

"Yes and no." With a real conversation in gear, his sneaker laces held no appeal; he looked at Laura. "I learned I was odd right off the bat, but plenty of folks from home would have said the same. I think maybe I need to live here longer before I understand drought issues on more than a superficial level, though."

"Good for you." She looked at him again—a second assessment, he would have said. "Most people think they can move up here and apply their old climate's standards to this one."

"No problem here," Dale said. "I know I know nothing. Tell me I didn't just say that."

To his surprise, she didn't miss a beat. "You didn't just say that." And to his further surprise, she added, "If you're interested in learning more about the community, maybe you'd like to participate in the Environmental Fair. Paws for Cause sponsors a free rabies shot booth. It's usually quite an assembly line…we could use more help."

He sat straighter in his chair, unaccountably flattered even though the little voice in his head whispered *sucker!* at him. "Seems like an excellent way to learn more about the climate," he said. "It being so closely related to the environment and all."

Okay, that was definitely a smile.

She said, "I'll get some information for you and have it sent to Foothills."

Okay, that was definitely a closing line.

Especially with the little glance at her watch. She no doubt had patients to see, and he had work to do as well. He unfolded himself from the chair, surprised to find himself so much taller than she. Sitting there on the edge of the desk, projecting her quiet authority, she'd seemed to fill the room. "I hope you'll be at the reception tonight," he said. "The RoundUp is putting out a sandwich board—" But he cut himself short because her expression had changed entirely, and he didn't have the faintest idea what he'd said that made her go back inside herself, right back to the beginning of the conversation.

She stood from the desk. It didn't make her a whole lot taller. "Thank you," she said, rather formally. "I appreciate the invitation."

Dale thought a *clueless* sticker for his forehead might just be appropriate. Maybe they came in bulk packs. Cheaper that way. He faked it as best he could, thanking her for her insight as she opened the door for both of them and then followed him out.

The receptionist had propped open the inner door of the entry airlock, and through the outer door filtered a familiar sound. A familiar *howl*.

The receptionist gave Laura an exasperated look. "Do we

have a beagle on the schedule somewhere that I don't know about? Because someone's left one out in the parking lot—"

Never. Sully *never* howled in the car. He slept. He slept with glee and snorts and snoring. He slept with purpose.

"—and it's getting warm today. I've half a mind to go get the dog and—"

"Never mind," Laura said. "I think we've had enough excitement for the morning. And I doubt it'll be a problem much longer." At this she somehow refrained from looking at Dale, who somehow refrained from looking at *any*one. He muttered something about looking forward to the Environmental Fair and made his painfully casual way out the door.

As soon as he emerged from the clinic, Sully's howling stopped. Not at the end of a good long note or fading as Dale's presence finally cut through the concentration of the howling, but stopped short. Sully's tail waved with gentle contentment. *dale*.

Dale went to the half-open back window by the crate. "What were you thinking?" he asked, incredulous. "You don't howl in the car—and you'd better not *start* howling in the car, or you're going to spend a lot less time in it."

wagging.

Dale narrowed his eyes, an expression change that only increased the rhythm of the wag. "You did it on purpose, didn't you? The one place where I wanted to make a good impression…"

bored. singing!

Dale drew his hands down over his face, letting his fingers pull at his eyes and lips. Sully pawed lightly at the crate. "I'm losing it," Dale groaned. "You don't do anything on purpose. You just do what strikes your fancy at the moment. This is all your fault, you know. Lead me to one little dead body and my capacity for thought splinters into tiny little pieces."

Sully offered an exploratory *woo-oo*, a thoughtful pre-howl.

Oh, no. Not here. Dale thumbed the automatic lock control on his key ring and hastily slid behind the wheel…but could not help a long glance back at the clinic as he aimed the SUV toward the road.

SIX

LAURA DID NOT APPEAR at the reception. Everyone and anyone else packed the unprepared interior of the RoundUp Café. The five little round tables had been shoved up beneath the giant front windows and their astounding view of the Peaks. Elden rose up on the left, majestic in spite of the giant bare scar left from the 1977 Radio Fire; Agassiz and Humphreys rose even higher on the right, still capped with snow. The sun, recently set in the notch between the Peaks, backlit the sky a crystal-clear cerulean.

Directly in front of the diner, Route 89 hummed with the tail end of what passed for rush hour, and cars filled the parking lot—shared by the clinic and the café—to spill out along the generous road shoulder.

And inside, people filled the family-owned little café and spilled out into the parking lot. Like the diner, Dale, too, found himself unprepared. He'd thought he'd see a few long-time clients from the clinic, the staff and some staff family, a few local vets, and the Yazzie family who owned the diner. But the unfamiliar faces outnumbered those he recognized, and Terry Yazzie looked a little stunned at the number of people inhabiting the diner—no doubt far over any safe occupancy number. Behind the sandwich counter, he, his wife, and his teenaged children worked frantically to fill orders for coffee, soda, and sandwiches. The courtesy cheese and cracker plates on the tables had already been nibbled down to crumbs. The kitschy cowboy trappings of the diner, normally all-too-noticeable, were entirely overwhelmed by the occupants.

Dale had yet to figure out who most of them were, except that they seemed drawn by his exploits rather than his mere arrival in Flagstaff. He and Sheri had quickly worked out a nose-for-trouble system; he merely lifted his hand and she made another mark on the napkin she carried for that purpose. He thought she might be on the second napkin; certainly the count was far beyond what anyone had guessed. They'd have to start a new pool in the morning.

This evening he found a certain comfort in being the tallest one here. Unlike most people, he could grab a reassuring glance at the propped-open exit any time he felt the urge. And he could see who was coming his way, gauge the expression of intent they wore, and take evasive action if necessary.

Rarely successful.

He spotted Deputy Rena Wells as she entered the café, still in uniform. Unlike most of those people who had approached to ask him about the bizarre murder and speculate about the killer, she met his gaze across the room, gave a slight acknowledging nod, and parted the crowd to approach him directly. It was a relief in more than one way, for in the genial build-up of chatter noise, Dale had been forced to employ the old tilt-and-bend method of communication anytime he came upon someone of shorter than average height. Tilt of head, a slight twist at the hips to ameliorate the angle of bend, and then the bend itself—a little sideways, a little forward. Hardly noticeable—unless you'd been doing it all evening.

Dale's back knew.

Rena Wells waited until she got up close and tipped her open plastic water bottle at him. "You look better than last time I saw you."

"Checking up on me?" he asked, not meaning it at all.

"Sure." She kept a deadpan expression in cornflower blue eyes; even her too-much-sun freckles were deadpan. "You're a witness, after all. First one on the scene. Someone could decide you're a problem and try to off you." She gestured at the happily conversing crowd.

Dale glanced over said crowd—ten percent kids, ten percent elderly, a hundred percent socializing happily—and then back at Rena, complete with skeptical expression. Highly skeptical.

She shrugged, still deadpan. "You never know."

Dale snorted. Not a response Miss Manners would condone.

Wells grinned. "Or maybe I just came over to exchange a few words with you when you don't look quite so pale. I admit I won't pass by the opportunity to ask you if you've thought of anything you didn't tell the sergeant, but mostly it's just nice to see you actually breathing."

"Breathing is good," he admitted. "That was my own fault. It doesn't happen very often. I'm sorry, but I haven't thought of anything new. Really, everything I saw was just the same as when you saw it. Has the department made any progress on solving the murder?"

She cocked her head, absently sticking out an elbow to ward off the hefty fellow who was migrating toward her, backwards, as he chatted loudly to his companion. "They're going to up the ante on those water restrictions any time now, just you wait and see!" he proclaimed.

But Wells didn't let it distract her. She said starchily, "Why, you have some particular interest?"

"Aside from having found the guy dead?" Dale shook his head. "Nope."

Except suddenly it wasn't true. It wasn't true at *all*. He got the odd feeling at the back of his throat, a familiar feeling when he thought of the turning points of his life—a six-year-old combing through the skeleton of his arson burned-out house with no one the wiser, utterly convinced that if he could find his dog, the animal would leap from the ashes rescued and fine. That if he could find the fish tank, his favorite books, the new suit he was supposed to wear on Easter…then his life would go back to the way it had been *before.* That if he could find his parents, buried under the one crucial piece of protective rubble that everyone else had somehow missed, they would return to him. *Alive.*

Or at the least, that he might understand why all this had happened to him—instead of merely chronically irritating smoke-damaged lungs into bona-fide asthma. No answers, only scars.

Not to mention a whole lot of yelling when Aunt Cily learned what he'd been up to.

The Ohio clinic fire raked those scars open with vengeance. A desperate attempt at rescues, and most of the animals dead regardless. Arson. And no answers, only questions. Questions, asthma déjà vu, and too many ghosts for Dale to stick around.

Wells gave him a polite little nudge, a knuckle to his upper arm. "Still in there?"

Dale shook it all off. He gave a sheepish grin and glanced down at his plastic soda cup. "Too much sugar for one evening."

"You could join them." Wells nodded at a trio of young kids in the corner, dancing like poorly coordinated puppets to non-existent music and laughing at each other's antics. "That's too much sugar if I've ever seen it."

"You have kids?" Dale asked, a little startled. Lean, lanky hard-edged deputy…he hadn't thought of her that way.

She just smiled. "Two. Just about that age. They're with my sister. That put you off?"

Blink. Put him off? Put him off *what?* Since it didn't actually put him off anything at all, he just shook his head. "Of course not."

The smile changed, though he couldn't have said just how. Just that suddenly…it began to feel crowded in this crowd.

Wells suddenly turned her head slightly, rolling her eyes and clearly hiding the gesture from someone. Dale hunted, saw nothing but another woman headed their way, a perfectly pleasant expression on her face. She approached them with her hand held out, ready to shake in a limpid fashion.

Dale shook its limpidness. He had to do the tilt and bend to hear her introduce herself as Marcia Roth, and in the middle of that, Wells made a minor face behind Marcia Roth's back and gestured a *later* at him.

"Please call me Marcia," she said, allowing her hand to stay in his a moment after he released it.

Definitely getting crowded in here. And warm.

"I wanted to thank you," she said, and regarded him in a thoughtful manner. The assessing manner. Except that unlike Laura's thoughtful look, this one made him feel like checking for bulls-eyes that had somehow been affixed to his body. She said, "Why, they're green!"

Getting scary…

"Thank me for what?" Dale asked faintly.

She apparently didn't hear. Maybe it was the extensive dangle of jingling earring, making enough noise to obscure his words. They certainly suited her over-worked hair, with the kind of stand-up bangs that had (mercifully) gone out in the early nineties, and the dramatic eye make-up to match. Add in the long, manicured nails that had pressed into his palm only moments earlier, the tightly fitted bodice of her bright western shirt, and jeans tight enough to double as a hernia girdle, and she—and her intense waft of sharp knock-off perfume—was the most noticeable things in the room.

And she definitely hadn't heard, for she went on as if he'd said nothing. "From back there they looked brown, but now that

I'm up close—" and she moved even closer, leaning into him a little "—they're quite clearly dark green."

Suddenly he understood. "My eyes. You're talking about my eyes." *Whoa!*

"What else?" she asked, making the slightest pout of her lower lip. "Anyway, thank you."

He tried again. "For what, exactly?"

She looked surprised, as if it needed no definition, and put a languid hand on his upper arm. He could have sworn he felt the fingers tighten slightly, taking assay of his biceps. "For taking in those poor dogs, of course."

New strategy: get cool with never having the faintest idea what's going on.

"The rescues?" he ventured. *Rescue. Not a bad idea.* Now where was Sheri? "How'd you find out about those?"

She gave a wave of her hand; the nails flashed like bright pink weapons. "Word gets around, you know. And I hear the circumstances were…unusual." She looked at him from beneath lowered lids, inviting him to say more.

As if. "Nothing worth mentioning." He gave her his best blank expression.

"Of course, maybe you're used to *unusual,* after that body you found. I can hardly believe it—I walk in that neighborhood myself sometimes! At least, since the drought restrictions."

"Dr. Dale!"

There was Sheri. Equally as colorful as Marcia Roth, but in an entirely natural and oblivious way. Also a not-matching way. Orange and green? Ouch.

But Dale could have kissed her anyway. "Hi, Sheri. How's the count?"

She waved the bedraggled napkin at him. "Not sure. I'm going to have to give it a good look later on. There are some spots I'm not sure if they're barbecue sauce or actual counting marks.

At least forty-three, though—and that's just from tonight." She took his arm. She didn't try to test his muscle. "There's a reporter from the *Post* over here, wants to talk to you."

Marcia hovered between pout and minor huff, rightly figuring Dale was about to be stolen from her, and not about to be a good sport about it. Dale, rescued, could afford to give her a smile and mutter pleasantries about meeting her as Sheri dragged him away. As soon as they were out of earshot, Sheri gave him a little jab in the arm. "You owe me."

"I owe you," he agreed as they threaded through the crowd. Marcia's perfume faded behind them, leaving Dale relieved all over again. "Is there really a reporter?"

"There really is. But about this owing me—"

"Pizza Hut take-out," he said.

She made a discreet arm-pumping motion. "Yes!" They passed beside Brad Stanfill, who chatted amiably—and at length, to judge from the faint desperation on the man's face— with another of the local vets. Dale had met him earlier and now nodded at him, feeling a touch of survivor's guilt as Marcia's perfume faded altogether. Sheri gave a less restrained, "Hey, doc!" and dragged Dale on by.

"I thought I'd see Laura here," Dale said, mostly without thinking.

"Laura who?" Sheri kept them moving.

"Laura Nakai. From Pine Country—"

Sheri stopped so short that Dale bumped into her and re-bounded, although she appeared not to notice. "Why on earth would you think she'd be here?" She also didn't appear to notice just how loudly she'd spoken.

Dale waited for everyone else to get back to their own conversations and said mildly, "Because I invited her."

"You—" This time she realized it when heads swiveled back to look at her, and stepped in closer to Dale. He did the twist and bend. "Laura Nakai," she said, forming the words more distinctly than her usual wont, "wanted your job. And she thinks she should have gotten it, too."

Dale looked at her, feeling his brain spin. After a moment he managed to close his mouth.

Sheri took it as a sign that he was ready for more and gave a firm nod, moving another inch closer. "She even came over and gave Dr. Hogue a piece of her mind. Not that I was listening on purpose, of course, but I just accidentally overheard her say how Doc Hogue had a small mind, and that if it were even a little larger he might have been able to bring himself to hire a woman." She frowned. "Or something like that. It made sense when she said it, anyway."

"Not that you were listening." His mouth said it; his brain still whirled on a course all its own. One that suddenly made sense of how upset Laura had been when they'd bumped into each other in front of Foothills. Or how surprised and tense she'd been that morning at her own clinic. Thinking about how he'd walked in and taken over, he couldn't help but hide his face in his hands.

"Oh, it's not that bad." Sheri elbowed him. "I mean, for all I know she's right, but we got you out of it, didn't we?"

Dale dragged his hands down his face just enough so he could look over his fingers. "It would have helped if I'd known."

"What? You think someone's just going to offer that information up like a side of fries? No one around here's that kind of busybody." For a moment she looked offended, but then grew thoughtful. "*Any* size of pizza?"

"Any size." Dale let his hands drop and looked out over the crowd. Chatting, laughing, maybe a little wheeling-dealing going on back near the sandwich counter. And here he stood, suddenly not feeling like part of them at all.

Maybe she *should* have gotten the job.

He tried to decide if he'd have been as restrained, had he been in Laura's shoes. And then he'd gone and invited her to this reception…

He groaned.

"You're taking this awful hard for the person who *got* the job," Sheri observed. She eyed him a moment, then nodded her head toward the front corner of the room. Through the windows before them, the skyline had gone completely dark, waiting for an opportunity to show off its stars. "Reporter's over here."

It could have been a nightmare—questions about the clinic fire in Ohio, questions about the body he'd found. Dale went in wary, his professional persona face in place. He hoped it went with the nubby seed-stitch polo shirt he wore, and hoped harder that the reporter wouldn't look down to the cuffs of his dress jeans and discover he'd grabbed a pair of sport sandals from the car when his favorite loafers ended up fouled at work. Not to mention his socks. Not a good moment.

But the reporter asked him all the easy questions—how Flagstaff differed from the heart of Ohio, what he was looking forward to in his new home, what he hoped for the practice—*tread carefully there, and avoid any comment that might be construed as a criticism of how the clinic was now*—and eased back on an explorative probe about the discovery of George Corcoran's body when Dale simply said he'd been advised not to discuss it.

He hadn't been, but as an evasive ploy, it served him well.

He'd actually started to relax a little when the first whiff of trouble hit him. Literally. Hit the reporter at the same time, to judge from the expression on her face. Cigar smoke. Acrid, pervasive, and the last thing Dale could deal with when he was still calming his lungs from their last little adventure. "I thought there were laws here—"

"Oh, there are." The reporter looked more closely at him, tucking her stylus away beside the PDA on which she'd been taking notes. She had a tape recorder as well, but she didn't seem to have much confidence in its ability to record his voice clearly above the crowd noise and he didn't blame her. "I'm sure Deputy Wells will take care of it in a moment, off-duty or not. You don't look well—"

"Cigar!" Dale said, and beat feet for the open exit. End of the interview, and a graceful conclusion it was. Outside, he stood in the parking lot and tipped his head back to take in the desert-clean air. Just as well. A few hours of that much humanity and he was ready for a break.

The night air had already reached crisp territory; the wind gusted briefly, doubling itself. He headed for his SUV in the Foothills side of the parking lot and the noise from the café faded away, leaving him as grateful for the silence as for the clean air. He snagged his linen sport coat from the vehicle and shrugged it on, then went to lean against the tailgate and consider the stars. Not as brilliant as the view from his backyard; too much ambient light.

A moment of solitude and he thought of Sully, ensconced in Dale's office with a bone, his Sullybed, and water. It looked like the reception might go on for another hour or more, even if Dale wouldn't be able to return until the cigar smoke cleared out. It was a good time to grab Sully for walkies.

Sully greeted him with a demand that Dale account for his time and an inspection of every food molecule on Dale's fingers. He gladly stretched his head out for the leash and collar, and trotted at Dale's heels, tail flagged, as they headed out to the parking lot.

mine.

"It's everyone's parking lot," Dale told him. "But feel free to write all over it anyway."

He almost missed the hesitant figure walking down from the road; between the darkness and her soft way of moving, she might have been upon him before he saw her if Sully hadn't lifted his head from the gravel he'd been so assiduously examining and given a brief, business-like wag of his tail. *i know you. but…busy.*

"Dr. Kinsall?"

Familiar voice. Familiar manner, even in the dark. Just the last person Dale expected to find out here after what he'd heard from Sheri. "Dale," he told Laura Nakai. "Just call me Dale."

She came close enough so he could see as she glanced at the reception, her expression uncertain.

"I'm glad you came." He stuck a fidgety hand in his pocket, and knew it had been a mistake when Sully immediately alerted. Pockets meant cookies, no two ways about that. "And…I'm sorry. I only learned a few moments ago that I put you in an awkward position by asking."

After a moment in which she turned her head into shadow and he couldn't see her expression at all, she said, "To tell you the truth, I'm not even sure why I'm here. I guess I decided it wasn't fair to take the situation out on you." Amusement entered her voice. "It seemed pretty plain you had no idea I'd been the least bit interested in the Foothills opening."

"I'd have appreciated a heads-up from someone around here, I can tell you that much." Dale eased toward the barely sprouting wildflower greens by the side of the road—or rather, allowed Sully to lead him that way, up the short, steep hill and away from the clinic.

"Oh, I don't know," Laura said, easing toward the road beside him. "You'd never have asked if you'd known, would you? And then I wouldn't be here. Though I didn't think to find the guest of honor avoiding the festivities."

"That obvious? I just needed some fresh air."

"You're wheezing," she observed.

"I—" He stopped short on the glibly dismissive words ready at his lips, unwilling to brush her off. "I have asthma. For now. That is, I had it from the first fire and pretty much outgrew it, but then the clinic—"

There was declining to give a pretty woman a glib brush-off, and then there was babbling. Dale managed to shut his mouth.

"Ah," she said. In tacit accord, they walked the shoulder of the road, facing the headlights of the rare vehicle. Sully was delighted. "The heroics I keep hearing mutters about. To be honest, I'd assumed it was merely rumor gone amok."

Sully alerted to something just off the shoulder, leaning against the leash with a quiver Dale felt through the leather. *Not another body, please!* But no; as they closed on the spot, the light streaming out of the café windows reached just far enough to reveal a man sitting cross-legged in the dusty gravel, hunched over his lap and making a slurping noise. He glanced up at them, hesitated, then asked with some reluctance, "You want some?"

No need to think about that one. "It's all yours," Dale said, trying to sound much more offhand than he felt. He could have sworn he heard Laura smile. Then the vehicle bearing down on them swept past to offer a headlight flash of a bearded and grizzly older man with a soda in one hand and one of the cheese and cracker plates from the reception in his lap. As soon as he was certain they'd pass him on by, he fell back to his noisy consumption of same. Sully dragged behind, disbelieving that they could just walk away from such bounty, and abruptly gave up to trot out ahead again.

After a moment, Laura said quietly, "It wasn't, was it?"

He could pretend he didn't know what she meant. *Wasn't rumor gone amok.* He didn't. "No. There was a fire. Unsolved arson. I lived in an old farmhouse behind the clinic—it was just a big old converted house itself, with kennels off the back. Tinderbox, really. Sully was just a pup, but he woke me and I—" He stopped, overwhelmed for the moment with the surround-sound memories of that night, the incredible roar of the flame and the smoke searing his nose and lungs, the screams of the animals he couldn't reach. Two cats, perfectly healthy guests while their owner traveled. A dog recovering from spay, and another with a faltering heart, under observation until Dale could stabilize him. A ferret that'd just had a cancerous sore excised. And the animals he'd reached…smoke inhalation quickly claimed them on the lawn, wet by then with windblown spray, the roar of the flames replaced by the rumble of fire trucks and the static-laced interruption of the captain's hand radio. Until suddenly Dale, too, realized he couldn't breathe. Passing out had been a mercy, he supposed.

A hand touched his arm. A brief touch, but one that held startling understanding before it went away. And suddenly there they were, standing by the side of the Flagstaff road with the sound of socializing coming up from the café; someone burst into a rendition of the old Statler Brothers' hit "Elvira" and a lot of other people joined in, but they only seemed to know the beginning of the chorus, resulting in a lot of muddled *nah-nah-nahing*. Sully stood against Dale's leg to nudge his hand. Somewhat befuddled, Dale asked, "Did I say any of that out loud?"

"You said some things."

"Aurgh." Dale voiced the word distinctly. Then he gathered himself and added, "Anyway, someone lit a cigar in the café."

"So I found you in the parking lot."

Somehow it didn't occur to him to ask her to keep his babbling in confidence; some part of him simply knew she would. He gave a nod in the darkness. "I'll go back in after a while, if it clears out. But cigars…they always get me." And then, almost fiercely, he said, "It'll get better. Now that I'm here. It got better before."

"And in the meantime you'd just prefer not to be a hero."

"That's just exactly it." He took advantage of another passing car to look her fully in the face, making sure he saw the understanding there. "*Hero* is just a word. I'm not, for one thing. And it takes an event…an experience…and turns it into that one meaningless word. I don't think it's respectful of what really happened that night. Of how it affected other people."

The approaching semi rumbled up upon them; Dale ducked his head against the headlights, realizing they'd come further than he intended. Realizing, too, that his breathing had eased; he wouldn't even need Big Blue.

The semi's road noise trailed out behind it, finally leaving them in silence again. Laura must have had the same thought as he; she turned to reverse course even as he did, ably shifting Sully between them when he got confused and tried to walk on her left instead of Dale's. "You're not what I was expecting."

"Everyone always thinks I'll be shorter," he said.

"There is that." She didn't do the obvious, what everyone did at that point, even those people who weren't of her diminutive stature—to look up at him and make a big deal of it. She kept to her own thoughts. "I was thinking, someone who would be easy to dislike. To resent."

He winced. "I'm not sure I'd blame you."

"I'd blame me." Then her voice turned lighter. "Besides, it looks like you've got enough to contend with for your first week here. Ledbetter, adventures with the police…" She stopped suddenly—the walking and the talking both. "A strange thing happened today."

Dale thought at this point, a strange thing would be if there were no more strange things, but somehow managed to refrain from saying so as they resumed walking. They passed the homeless man, who greeted them with a loudly satisfied belch and no apparent recognition.

Sully growled at the belch.

"Glory Heissman," Laura said. "She came to see me today."

"Glory…?"

"Creative Breeder."

He gave her a sharp look in the darkness. "I saw her at Foothills last week. The dogs seem a little…frenetic."

"The dogs excel in frenetic. It's why she's been in so many disputes over them. But the one she brought in today had been hurt—a very deep, clean cut on its pad. And not a fresh one, either." They turned back into the parking lot, taking the short, steep grade from the road to the parking lot itself.

Dale probably should have said something, taking his turn in the conversation. But his mind filled with images, distracting him. Images of countless little paw prints around George Corcoran's body. Paw prints and broken glass.

"The thing is," Laura added, "she's a Foothills client. Ever since she moved out behind Elden Trail Road."

Dale jerked away from his mental images of the murder scene. "But that's—"

Laura nodded. "About half a mile from the dead man you found."

SEVEN

GLORY HEISSMAN.

The day after the reception, Dale considered her. How she'd mixed up her appointment for her diminutive dogs, and how in spite of her cute country-themed lifestyle, she'd made it clear in an entirely uncute way that the world owed her an appointment whenever she managed to make it to the clinic.

How it's not my problem.

Back at home in the late afternoon after taking the morning clinic appointments and then some, Dale booted Sully out into a yard of tufty natural grasses, mostly tiny hummocks of dryness between the fine, silty soil of the area. He contemplated the narrow storage outdoor-access closet between the back patio and the master bedroom and once again determined to put a dog door in the bedroom and turn the storage into storage/dog shelter.

No doubt the realtor would be appalled.

Other aspects of the house were falling into place. He could almost see across the living room-dining room combination, if you weren't fussy about the boxes piled up on the counter that divided the dining room and kitchen. He'd assigned himself the remaining kitchen boxes for this afternoon, with the goal of cooking an actual dinner meal his own actual self. Okay, pasta, no biggie with chili from a can and grated cheese from a bag coming together for Cincinnati chili.

So here he stood in the third bedroom—already nicknamed

the puzzle room—with its huge windows overlooking the patio where Sully sunned himself, covered with a thin film of dust from an enthusiastic roll. The sturdy puzzle table stood before him, an old Escher favorite spread on top. Not a hard one, not at this point. And not a big one. Just right for letting his hand wander over the pieces and his mind wander over the past days.

Ditto the music. Rather than hard country Montgomery Gentry or an old Jim Steinmann CD, he'd stuck Kay Thompson into the well-used boom box that currently served as his only assembled music system. Not because it was his favorite— swing music wasn't. But because after so many years of listening to it, cementing the only clear memories of his parents, it had come to evoke feelings of home and contentment.

Dale badly needed to feel content.

New job, new town, new life…plenty of things to be planning. Planning with glee. He hadn't yet been to the Lowell Observatory, or the arboretum. He hadn't been to the nursery, the one that specialized in hardy native plantings. He needed to stop by the local national forest office and check on hiking options for when the trails opened again.

But Dale wasn't planning with glee. Dale couldn't get his mind off that moment he saw the water rising in the mouth of a dead man. He couldn't get his mind off Alfred Ledbetter and now Glory Heissman. Ledbetter, an unsettling man with unsettling ways who'd shown up with the Dane who lived near the first murder site. And Glory Heissman, an abrasive woman with a cotton-candy coating who lived near George Corcoran and whose dog, of just the right size to have left paw prints near broken glass, showed up with a cut pad a couple of days after the murder.

He wanted to know more about both of them. He'd been uneasy for days, chalking it up to the annoyance and disappointment of dealing with such a difficult asthma episode so soon after his arrival. But maybe it wasn't the asthma at all. Maybe this time he had the opportunity to find answers, and he wanted to take it. It's not like he had any intention of going to Rena Wells to say he had a client who acted oddly and could that be important? Especially not when for Alfred Ledbetter acting oddly seemed to be par for the course. He'd only get the man in trouble for rescuing two desperate dogs.

Earth to Dale. It's still not my problem.

Well…maybe the asthma had just a little bit to do with his uneasiness, too. But he was halfway through the course of oral steroids and knew they were doing their job. He'd reacted to the cigar the evening before, but it hadn't turned into a big deal. No dying fish gasp and wheeze before Laura…only someone of unusual perception would have noticed at all.

Then again, Laura struck him as unusual in all respects.

A glance out the window showed him Sully on the trail of something, nose to the ground and following a track that wandered in squigglies and loopedy-loops. Horny toad, no doubt. Soon to be deceased, if it hadn't gotten its spiky little butt out of the yard—and maybe even then. Dale had yet to beagle-proof the yard with chicken wire along the bottom of the fence, which meant Sully only had extended freedom when Dale could watch. As new as he was to the area, if Sully got out he'd probably end up as Ledbetter's next rescue.

Ledbetter.

Dale put down the puzzle piece he'd been turning over and over in his hand as the impulse to gather *answers* became too strong to ignore. He gave a last glance at Sully—very busy indeed—and went to the living room to rummage for the phone book that had landed by his mailbox a few days earlier. He wasn't at all certain Paws for Cause would have a phone number, but when he pulled the phone book out from under the curtains he should have hung three days earlier, he looked them up anyway.

Be lucky if anyone's actually there.

He grabbed the portable phone—also under the curtains—and dialed as he headed back to the office, punching the last number as he spotted Sully with his nose under the fence, sniffing mightily as if he might simply vacuum his errant quarry right up to his nose. And while the phone on the other end of the line rang, Dale waited to see if those white front paws would set against the earth in finest "Escape Beagle" style…

"Hello?"

But no, Sully gave it up with a sigh visible even from Dale's perspective, and ambled back toward the porch with napping in mind.

"Hello?"

Dale gave himself a mental kick. "Hello!" he said, apparently just in time to judge by the various rustlings, hesitation, and reverse rustlings. "Is this Paws for Cause?"

"Yes." The voice was wary and he didn't blame the woman; he had the impression this was her home phone and so far he'd sounded more like a crank call than a legitimate one. "This is Anita speaking. Can I help you?"

He hadn't thought about it ahead of time, of course. How to inquire about someone who worked with them without getting a big loud hang-up click in his ear. So he went with his work voice, which somehow sounded quite a bit smarter than his usual voice. He introduced himself, mentioned that Alfred Ledbetter had dropped off two dogs in recent days and that as a new vet in the area, he needed to check on their rescue procedures—and to double-check that Ledbetter was, as he said, someone who worked with them and whose rescues would be financially supported if necessary.

The woman became cheery. She'd heard of him. *My, didn't*

his own little dog have a nose for trouble (number fifty-three)! She discussed their procedures in much depth, letting him know they tried to find sponsors for animals in as much need as the two currently at Foothills, and that if she could send someone down to get pictures, that would be great. If he wanted them to help pursue any prosecutions for the abuses, they'd be glad to do that, too. He had to admit the animals had been brought in as strays, owners unknown. He didn't mention the all-but-certain fact that the dogs had been liberated.

But he did wonder out loud, "Mr. Ledbetter seems pretty dedicated."

She gave a little laugh. Closer to a giggle, it was. "He's always helped us out—he's always been involved in several of our local groups—some of the environmental groups, the Dark Skies people, and of course our own efforts. He's always such a loner, but he does find ways to help, especially lately. I don't know where he finds the energy! I think it's the drought."

"Where he finds the energy?" Dale thought to look outside; no Sully in sight. He wandered over to drum his fingers on the window. Sully popped up directly below him, propping his front legs against the house to just barely peer into the house, only the top of his head and his eyes showing. Dale waggled his fingers in a wave, an affection gesture to which Sully was well accustomed. He wagged his tail in a *hi, dale* and dropped back out of sight.

"No, not the energy," the woman said, then paused. "Well, not precisely. The drought has upset him, as it has many of us. Not the drought so much as the way people are responding to it. Or *not* responding to it, you could say. My friend Celeste commented on it just the other day."

"People and the drought," he said, pretty sure he had it right this time.

"No, Alfred's intensity about it all. You know, if we were

all as dedicated as he is, this area would be in much better shape. He's so dedicated, working on his own to do what he can."

"No computer cases littering Lake Mary," he said, remembering the newspaper photo from his first day at Foothills.

"Exactly." She beamed; even over the phone he could tell. He thought it was time to thank her, to tell her it would be a privilege to work with their group and how their accomplishments impressed him—all quite true, but more to the point it turned the phone call official again and gave him the chance to end it before his uncertainties about Ledbetter leaked through.

Nothing she'd said reinforced the impression he'd gotten of Ledbetter—the unsettling intensity of his eyes, the underlying belligerence in his manner. Maybe he'd just caught the man on an off day. Or two off days.

Or maybe not.

KAY THOMPSON finished crooning "Moonglow," and Dale left the puzzle to switch the boom box over to the radio—93 KAFF Country Radio—the only station he'd been able to tune in clearly so far. He turned it up loudly enough to filter through to the entire house and went out into the living room to open the patio door for Sully. Outside, a casually stupendous sunset of orange and crimson cloud underbellies topped by deep bruise-purple columns made him linger until Sully discreetly pinged off his knee with two front feet.

dinner. Sully pinged his knee again.

"Maybe we'll eat tonight, maybe not," Dale told him. But the tone of his voice didn't worry Sully, who trotted busily between the door and the kitchen until Dale went to the kitchen and shoved enough boxes around to rediscover his microwave. He'd put cooking off too late, and suddenly starved, only wanted to zap something instant and chow down.

dinner!

"Yeah, yeah," Dale muttered, pulling a big microwavable breakfast offering from the freezer.

A barely-there whine accompanied Sully's pleading gaze. *i could dieeee.*

"Pathetic," Dale told him. "And so convincing." But somehow he found himself in the corner of the dining room with Sully's placemat and bowl and food bin, scooping out dog kibble. Some kind of canine mind control, no doubt.

As Sully inhaled dinner and Dale frowned thoughtfully at the heating directions for the frozen meal, the phone rang. He punched a couple of quick commands into the microwave keypad, stabbed the meal's cellophane covering with a random violence that would make any pet owner wince to see those surgeon's hands so engaged, and loped for the puzzle room where he'd left the phone.

"Dr. Dale?"

"Sheri? What're you still doing at the clinic? It's—" He'd taken off his watch. Past sunset, he knew that much. Past clinic hours.

"I'm not," she said. "See?" And she held the phone out to take the full impact of an enthusiastic child playing some sort of computer game, complete with sound effects from both child and game.

"Thank you," he said when the noise faded and it seemed the phone was back at her ear. "Things are so much clearer now."

She ignored his dry tone. "Did anyone call you about the faucet today? I'm thinking not, which is why I wanted to make sure."

"The faucet?" he repeated, and would have said more but decided that would pretty much answer her question.

"The outdoor faucet. At the end of the building."

"I know the one. What about it?" Distracted, Dale moved

the phone away from his mouth to sniff the suddenly pungent air. Was the meal supposed to smell like that as it heated?

"It's our water day, so right before we closed up Dru went out to water what passes for flowers in our planters. 'Cept the faucet was welded closed."

Now she had his complete attention, even if Sully was suddenly barking at the microwave. He stuck his finger in his other ear and said, "Welded? Did you say—"

"Welded. Wrecked. Busted."

"Vandalized?" *Damn it.* Not *the clinic.*

"I know you're more familiar with animal plumbing than plumber plumbing," Sheri said, the clatter of dishes and rush of running water suddenly taking over her own background noise, "but trust me on this one, Dr. Dale. These things don't just weld themselves."

He would have met her sarcasm in kind, but he heard the tension beneath her words, so instead he took a deep breath and managed to say mildly, "Did anyone see anything?" He couldn't help but think of the sullen kennel help he'd annoyed—the teen who'd registered on his trouble meter. It'd almost be a relief to learn the damage had been Jorge's work.

"Nope. Coulda been done last night for all we know, unless you were using it earlier today."

Dale shook his head, realized she couldn't hear it, and said, "No, I wasn't even out there. Has anyone called to have it repaired?"

"Naw, it was after five. I'll call tomorrow. But since you're coming in early again tomorrow, I wanted to let you know." She let out a big noisy breath, splashing softly in the background. "Tell you what, Dr. Dale, things sure have gotten exciting since you got here. We never had anything like *this* happen before."

And I'll bet no one on staff ever found a body before, either. Not to mention the Ledbetter dogs…

"That reminds me," he told her, rapping his knuckles on the room's door to make a satisfyingly loud noise that would hush Sully. The dog barked another time or two just to show he could and then grumbled around the living room. A moment later came the loud grind of teeth against Nylabone. "Add another one to the nose list."

"I wonder can we get some sort of world record?" In the background, a child suddenly burst into loud, offended wails; Dale held the phone away from his ear slightly. Not surprisingly, Sheri said in a rush, "Gotta go. Just keep an eye out when you get into the clinic tomorrow. Who knows what else that damn vandal might have been up to! No, now, Tremayne, you didn't hear momma say that bad word. And what is this all over your face?"

After a moment Dale realized that Sheri wasn't necessarily going to say an actual good-bye, and hung up the phone.

Vandals at the vet clinic. Wonderful. The faucet could be fixed, of course…but *why?* Why weld it in the first place?

He got the feeling it was personal. How could it not be? Welding…that took time and effort. It wasn't just a random egging or kids with spray paint making their way down the street. Then again, it was hardly fair to immediately blame Jorge. All teens had an attitude about loud music. Dale had been no exception.

And he really hoped his now-cooling dinner was supposed to come with that particular aroma. Maybe the sausage—?

He was on his way out of the room when the phone, still in his hand, rang again. Startled, he dropped it, but quickly swooped to snatch it up again, suddenly certain Sheri hadn't meant to hang up at all and that he'd effectively hung up *on* her. "Sheri?"

"Guess again." Not Sheri's upbeat voice. Not even a friendly voice.

A distinctly *unfriendly* voice. Familiar, and with a sneer

around the edges. Dale's eyebrows went up with the *huh!* of it. "Sorry, my dinner's ready. You'll have to find someone else to play games with." And his thumb hunted for the button to cut the connection.

"Dale Kinsall," said the voice—almost a shout, really, a shocking revelation that someone had cared enough to locate his brand-new phone number. "This is no game. You have no idea who you're dealing with."

"No," Dale said, most equitably. "As far as I can tell, that seems to be the point."

"The point," snarled his entirely unwelcome caller, "is that you need to pay attention before someone gets hurt. Do you care about your new friends? About your dog?"

Oh God. "I—"

But he spoke to dead air. Just as well, really. He had no idea what he'd intended to say. He took the phone from his ear and gave it a horrified stare, and then on a quick impulse he hit star-six-nine, only to be informed the number was unlisted.

KAFF Country Radio jarred its way past his frowning contemplation of the phone. The normally jaunty evening DJ came on with his Serious Voice, announcing breaking news. "Another murder in Flagstaff," he said, and then Dale seemed to catch only the few really important words. Words like *Old Cave Trail and Cinder Hills area—his* Cinder Hills—and *bizarre circumstances.*

Vandalism at the clinic. A threatening phone call. And another murder in Flagstaff.

A murder in Dale's own backyard.

EIGHT

DALE WRESTLED WITH dreams that smelled like smoke and roared like flame, drought-dry West Winona going up in flames around him. But when he ran to save the clinic he couldn't turn the water on, and somewhere Laura screamed. He'd never heard her scream, but he recognized her without a doubt. And even though his innately sensible self immediately got suspicious and kept waving a hand like a frantic kid at school—*Ooh! I know, I know—I bet it's a dream!*—Dale ran from place to place, hunting a phone to call for help and tripping over an inconvenience of dead bodies along the way until his lungs were as fiery as the flames around him and he tripped and fell, his face only inches from the dead, dull gaze of George Corcoran. Water poured from Corcoran's mouth, and Dale sputtered himself awake—

And sputtered for real at the tongue washing his face, quick sloppy licks of worry. *dale, dale!*

Dale flung the covers back and let the cool early morning air wash over his body, bare but for running shorts. Sully immediately put a foot on his chest, flexing it just enough so Dale knew he was about to be pawed as well as licked awake. "Ohh, no you don't—" He grabbed the beagle and rolled him over, snugging him up on his back with legs flopping loosely, tongue never ceasing its effort to reach Dale's now out-of-range face. Sully got a lick of dream-sweaty neck and finally gave up, lying at ease to contemplate the lazy movement of the ceiling fan along with Dale.

whirlywhirlywhirleee… Sully swallowed convulsively.

"Don't look." Dale covered Sully's eyes, closed his own. Don't look at what? At what had suddenly become of his new life here? Murders and threatening phone calls…

Not that he knew if the one had anything to do with the other. Or how to figure it out if they did.

Well, he pretty much had to start with getting out of this bed. No matter that it was an hour early; he wouldn't go back to sleep. Not after…

He still thought he could smell the smoke.

"Hey," he said to Sully. "You ready for an early breakfast?"

Amazing how fast that dog could flip himself over and race out the door.

DALE'S FORESTER took up a lonely vigil in the early morning parking lot, the windows cracked in anticipation of midday heat, the doors as unlocked as any car in this end of town. Jorge hadn't parked his bike up against the side of the clinic yet, Sheri wasn't here, and Dale had even preceded the inevitable early customer.

But someone had been here before him. Been and gone, and left behind a special treat.

It eyed him from the porch, ears back in suspicious warning, legs slightly spraddled, stumpy tail sticking straight out behind, and a sparse fringe of sandy terrier hair sticking out everywhere else.

Uglee. When Dale opened his car door, the whiskered lips lifted in a warning snarl, revealing a crooked bite and equally nasty teeth. *UgLEE!*

"I hope you're tied here so we can stop you from contributing to the gene pool," Dale told it. Still fastened in his doggy seat belt, Sully crowded Dale—perfectly capable of smelling the new door guard even if he couldn't yet see him.

"Never mind," Dale said. "You won't be making any play dates with that one." A note taped to the porch post fluttered in the wind, and Dale tried to estimate his chances of getting past the dog before the paper blew away. The terrier mutt settled into a prim sit beside the post and stared back at him with beady, warning eyes.

Coffee.

Ignoring the fierce snarling warn-off of the tied dog, Dale extricated Sully from his safety harness, sliding out of the Forester to head toward the RoundUp diner. *Please let there be coffee.* He'd never been here this early before, and rarely felt the need to scald his tongue so early in the day anyway. But Terry Yazzie greeted him as though he'd been here every morning since the welcome reception, and smiled at Sully, too. He was a big-bodied man with a square face and square shoulders and an understated manner, and Dale responded to the welcome with relief—and a nod toward the clinic. "I don't suppose you saw who left that dog off?"

Terry shook his head, carefully capping Dale's coffee cup—black, too much sugar—and pushing it across the counter. "You mean that pig-shaped thing with the bad case of static-head? Nah. It was here when I came out front." The door to the back led to more than just the kitchen; it led to the small add-on at the back where the Yazzies lived, a comfortably crowded family. "Sorry about that."

Dale lifted a shoulder in a *what're-you-gonna-do* gesture. "Too bad it's got teeth."

"Yeah," Terry said. "I noticed that when I went to pick up the paper—the kid always throws it way over there, lousy aim. You hear about the killing? Amos Weatherby?" Dale barely nodded before the man lifted his square chin in realization and added, "Sure, you'd hear about it. You found the second one, after all. You and your dog, there. He must have a nose for trouble, eh?"

Number sixty-five. "So they're sure this one is related?"

"Nah, but everyone else pretty much is. It's too bizarre, what with the guy being hit on the head and strangled—as if being killed once wasn't enough—and then all those cigarettes up his nose. Even the surgeon general never figured on cigarettes killing anyone like that."

Cigarettes. Up the dead man's nose.

Coffee. Dale reached for the cup, poking out the little drinking hole at the edge of the lid. Caffeine would help. It would have to. He took too much of a sip, scalded his tongue in fine style, and felt the liquid burn all the way down. He'd hear about the dead man soon enough. Unless he was exceptionally lucky, he'd probably find Sheri's little rag doll with toothpicks sticking out its nose and a string tied around its neck and another new toe tag. *Amos.* "How about yesterday morning—you notice anyone messing around the clinic, the side you can see from here?"

"Heard about that." Terry took Dale's money, handed back the change. "Wish I'd seen something, but…they were pretty quiet. I heard a truck right about the time I was getting up. Dodge, probably—you know how noisy they are. But that's all I can tell you. They made a mess, Sheri said."

"It astonishes me that Sheri would think to mention it," Dale said dryly.

"Ah." Terry pulled a couple boxes of doughnuts from behind the counter and put them on top of the glass-covered deli case, flipping the lids open so the customers could choose. "I see you understand the way of things around here already. Do you want a doughnut? Fresh from the bakery." He waited for Dale's doubtful reaction and added with a grin, "Just not *our* bakery."

Dale looked at the doughnuts a moment. He especially looked at the chocolate glazed doughnuts with sprinkles. "Fresh is fresh," he decided, and put his change back on the counter. Sully did a little front-foot dance beside him, daring to hope. Dale told him, "I'm not looking at you."

foodfoodfood—

Dale nodded to Terry and headed for the door in his best beagle-ignoring manner. By the time he reached the vandalized spigot, he had doughnut sticky fingers to offer Sully as he crouched to examine the damage.

No, this hadn't been an accident. Someone had had solder to spare…and hadn't stinted in using it. Solder around the faucet, solder built up inside the opening, solder dribbled all around the cinders that bordered the clinic…

It smacked of anger and warning…just as the phone call the night before. "Someone doesn't like me," Dale murmured. "Because…why? Because I found a body? Because *you* found a body? Or just because we're here?" He thought of the last time he'd used the faucet, shook his head. "Surely not because of the odd/even days thing…"

Or maybe it was just that simple. A message in response to his perceived carelessness. Waste Not-Water Not on the prowl.

Sully wiggled briefly and went back to sniffing the grass. "Message received," Dale grumbled, but felt a certain relief nonetheless. He'd fix the faucet and watch his step, and that would be the end of it. He squelched the remembered alarm from the previous evening, the clarity of threat in the voice on his phone. Sully looked up at him, and Dale cleared his throat, changing the subject of his internal conversation. "At least the dog people left a note," he told Sully. Not that anyone could read it just at the moment, but he had no doubt that Dru would concoct a way to get her hands on both the dog and the note. Otherwise, how would she know more about it than anyone else—and more importantly, how would she know more than Sheri?

"C'mon, Sullydog." Dale stood, wiped his hands on his

jeans, and instantly regretted it. Well, his lab coat would cover that far down…he was safe.

But he wasn't so sure about the clinic.

SMELLS WEIRD. sharp stinging metal smell, mad person smell. and people, lots of them. people smells i know. and food smells on dale. lovely smells! i want to follow them. dale! dale, come with me and play the smells game!

leash says no. time to go inside. dale! there goes the dog thing! smells like a dog, looks funny. smells like people I know, too. there it goes! let's go, too!

leash says no.

poop.

and i didn't get enough to eat.

AS DALE STOOD, he got a good look at Jorge's arrival—and at the expression on Jorge's face as he dismounted his bike and wheeled it up to the side of the building. Wary. Defensive.

Defensive enough to look back at Dale and say, *"What?"*

"Tell me you'd speak to Dru that way." Dale didn't look down, but he knew well enough that Sully had casually moved to an inconspicuous spot behind Dale's legs. Not exactly Sully-like.

Jorge aimed a sullen glare at the ground and became very busy with the usually simple procedure of parking his bike.

"Fine. You don't get to talk that way to me, either." Dale gestured at the faucet. "You know anything about this?"

"Why should I?" Jorge briefly aimed the sullen glare in Dale's direction. "Just because I'm a kid? Because I like loud music? Because I don't like it that you've come in here and changed things? Because—"

"Because," Dale interrupted, and loudly, too, just to get Jorge's attention, "you're often the first one here in the

morning. I thought you might have seen it." But he had to admit…the kid's behavior painted him in neon guilt.

Jorge looked like he'd been punched in the stomach. "I didn't mean—"

"Yes, you did."

This drew a prolonged scowl. Jorge scrubbed a hand over his tightly cropped curls and then dropped it to stand in awkward silence. Finally, he took a deep breath and blew all his words out in an angry blurt. "I didn't see anything. No way I can hear anything when I'm working in the kennel. Believe what you want, that's how it is."

Dale hadn't phrased the question with Angry Young Man syndrome in mind; he took a deep breath, realizing he'd set Jorge up for his belligerent response. So he said simply, "Okay."

"Okay…?" Jorge's eyes narrowed in suspicion.

Okay for now. "Okay, get to work. If you remember anything, let me know."

The suspicion never faded, but Jorge moved toward the back entrance of the kennel area—slowly at first, as if Dale might change his mind at any moment, and then at a jog. Sully woofed softly, a puzzled sound.

"That makes two of us." Dale sighed, scrubbed his hands through his hair and over his face, and said, "Good morning, us! Let's see about calling a plumber. If we can get past that dog. And let's see about that dog." He scooped Sully into his arms; the dog went into rag doll mode and let his limbs dangle in total pathetic surrender to his undignified circumstances. Dale carted him around the corner and stopped short at the sight of the porch post, free and clear of its doggy encumbrance. The stout nylon leash tied around the post now dangled in a short ragged tail, and a quick glance showed no sign of the porky little mutt. The note caught Dale's eye.

PLEASE CARE FOR ORPHANED DOG.

That hadn't turned out so well, had it?

Sully shifted in Dale's grip, his tail beating against the side of Dale's leg. It was the only warning Dale got—that and the flash of sandy movement out of the corner of his eye. The terrier mix sprinted around the corner of the building, growling with every bounding leap, heading straight for Dale. *Don't run...don't look it in the eye*... That pretty much left standing there stupidly as the dog strafed by, snagging pant cuff and racing away.

Something ripped.

The little dog whirled to a stop at the other end of the building, gave three sharp barks, and dashed around the side.

fun! Sully's tail beat against Dale's leg with even more enthusiasm.

"Not everyone's a big friendly goof," Dale muttered at him. He unlocked the clinic door with unseemly haste, locking it behind him with particular care on this day when he had a plumber to call and a wretched phone threat ringing in his head. He put Sully down on the linoleum and unsnapped his leash. "Go find the Sullybed."

Sully trotted off and Dale stuck the leash in his back pocket to lean over the counter at Sheri's station and cycle through the messages on their machine. Maybe someone had called about the dog.

Or not. There was a message from a pharmaceutical company on the East Coast, someone who hadn't bothered to remember the time difference. Two cancelled appointments— no big deal this time of year, when spring shots and heartworm tests had the calendar overflowing. A hasty, hard-to-understand cell phone call that he finally deciphered to be a heads-up on a rattlesnake bite coming in. Two calls where the caller stayed on the line long enough to start the machine and then didn't say anything before hanging up.

Dale erased the hang-ups. They might be nothing—wrong

number, someone deciding not to leave a message after all. Given the vandalized faucet, he didn't want Sheri spreading the word they were under siege of some sort.

Even if he was afraid it might be true.

No one had called about the dog.

On the other hand, having that dog around might turn the conversation in directions other than the most recent murder.

Dale glanced down at Sheri's lower desk as he pushed the answering machine back in its spot. Yep, there was the rag doll. Pathetic little thing, staked and drowned and strangled and bashed and—yes, broken toothpicks stuck into its face where the nose had been before the drowning smeared the penned features. He had the sudden impulse to steal the thing away, give it a decent and merciful burial…

But there was no telling what Sheri would come up with to replace it. Some things were best left alone. Dale put another mark on the NOSE FOR TROUBLE board and went to prep the treatment room for the incoming snakebite; the expensive antivenin needed to be mixed gently into suspension. He set it out to warm for a few minutes and grabbed up one of the clinic's cheap woven loop-end leashes, stepping outside the double entry doors to breathe in the amazing chill of the high altitude morning air, check the rising breeze that would turn into ceaselessly blustery winds in early afternoon, and tip his head back to take in the always impressive Peaks, still snow-capped and squint-worthy in the bright morning sun.

Grff-grff-grff-GRFFF, and the terrier launched another strafing run. Dale waited until the last moment and stepped aside. Undaunted, the dog whirled to a stop, gave his three sharp barks, and retreated around the corner. Dale looked at the snare leash, looked at the corner around which the dog's butt had disappeared. Definitely out of his league. He made his own retreat, back to the treatment room to commence the slow process of rolling and swirling the antivenin, a tedious process relieved only by the challenge of balancing the phone on his shoulder as he left a message with the plumber. When Dru arrived he'd set her to work on the terrier.

Sheri made it in next, announcing her arrival with a shriek of surprise followed by the three triumphant sharp barks. She hustled through the inner door, slammed it shut behind her, and leaned against it as though keeping a large monster at bay. When she saw Dale at the treatment room door, swirling his several hundred-dollar bottles of antivenin, she glared. "What," she demanded, "was *that?*"

Deadpan, Dale said, "In my highly schooled opinion, it was a dog. But I think we'll need to get our hands on it to be absolutely sure."

Her glare notched into dangerous levels as she smoothed her top—big colorful pansies—down over a pair of stylish striped pants that might even have not been blinding in a different color and pattern combination. "That thing better not be out there when people start coming in." She looked pointedly at her watch. "Half an hour from now."

"Sooner." Dale lifted the antivenin. "We'll just have to have someone run interference when they get here."

Sheri plunked her substantial tote of a purse over the customer counter to the lower desk behind it, careful not to smoosh the doll. This made sense to Dale—no one had been murdered by smoosh. Yet. "When's Dru coming in?"

"Great minds think alike," he told her. "If Dru can't grab that little…"

"Bastard," Sheri filled in for him. "You can say it. Technically, it's true. Even in the new age parts of town they aren't marrying dogs yet." She frowned. "I don't think."

"Bastard," Dale said, more obediently than with intent. "If she can't grab him—or send him running—no one can."

"What's he doing there?"

"Didn't you see the note?"

"I *saw* it. I didn't stick around to *read* it."

"Please care for orphaned dog," Dale recited for her. "I don't know why they didn't take it to animal control."

Sheri lifted her chin, raising her eyebrows. It appeared that she'd underlined those brows with something sparkly. "Because," she said, wisely, "it's busier there. All sorts of official people going in and out. Someone would have seen whoever left that *creature* and made them explain that whole orphaned thing."

"And that's a big deal?" Dale took care not to unduly jostle the antivenin. Another ten minutes and it might actually be mixed and usable. All they needed was the patient. And in the background of his chaotic morning thoughts, there was something about that dog…

"Apparently so." Sheri stopped herself as she headed around to the door that would take her into the office area, a hand to her mouth and what looked suspiciously like a smile mostly hidden beneath that hand. "Mr. Dr. Dale, you have such personal style. Heaven forbid you should come to this office one day without dirt on your shirt or hand-prints on your jeans—on your *butt*, usually, if you wanna know. But if this don't beat all."

Dale looked down at himself. The doughnut smears on his thighs were barely discernable. "What?"

"Tsk!" She put her hands on her ample hips. "Didn't you ever see that movie, that one where that blonde chick uses something that *ain't* hair gel to—" But Dale's baffled look must have gotten to her, because she rolled her eyes and rolled forward like a tank, reaching for his head. With the greatest of courage, Dale stood his ground, antivenin in hand, as she pulled his head down and artfully rearranged his hair. "My Lord, Dr.

Dale, what have you got in here? You don't gotta tell me how you did it—I've seen the way you mess your hair. I've just never seen it stay that way."

Ah. "Might be some doughnut frosting," he admitted. And Sully spit, but he wasn't about to say so.

And still, there was something about that orphaned dog…

"Well, that there is just going to have to do." She flicked one last hair into place and released him. "Keep your hands off. I might not be able to fix it next time, least not until you get that frosting out of there." She rolled her eyes again, muttered something that included the word "hopeless," and marched off to the office entrance.

Grff-grff-grff-GRFFF, faint but distinct outside the office door. And a little shriek, more annoyed than fearful, and three sharp triumphant barks as Jade the tech bolted through the door, throwing herself against it just as Sheri had done. "What," she said, her frosted, spiky hair looking more frenetic than usual and her eyebrow rings enhancing her mighty scowl, "was—"

"Dog," Sheri said shortly, glancing at Dale. "We don't get it caught soon, you'll have to go out and decoy it while the snake-bit dog comes in."

"Where's Dru?" Jade demanded.

Grff-grff-grff-GRFFF, faint but distinct outside the office door. And a then great big wordless human *BAHHH!,* followed by a yip of startled retreat.

Sheri and Dale looked at one another and at Jade. "Dru," they said together, three identical tones of satisfaction.

And here she came, blasting through both front doors, a backpack slung over one shoulder, waving the porch post note in the air. "Damned stupid punk dog. Why hasn't anyone caught it yet?"

Dale cleared his throat. "We've been waiting for the one person who could do it."

That stopped her short. "Oh, nice," she said after a moment. "Flatter the old lady into doing the dirty work, why don't you? And what'd you do to your hair? I like it. More style than usual for you."

Dale felt a secret triumph that the whirlwind byplay no longer left him spinning like a top. "Thank you."

Sheri smirked.

But Dru took to waving the note again. "*Another* drop-off dog. At least this one's not hurt."

"It's gonna be, if it comes at me again," Sheri said meaningfully, but Dale wasn't quite paying attention, stuck on Dru's words as he was. *Another drop-off dog…*

Because here they'd come. All of them, within twenty-four hours of one of the murders. Three dogs, three murders.

That couldn't be good.

He didn't know what the hell it meant, but considering how quickly he could tie the Dane to the first murder…and quite suddenly he remembered that feeling of familiarity when he'd seen Ledbetter with the shepherd mix. No wonder he hadn't recognized it—when it had been in the backyard beside George Corcoran's house, no one had brushed out its thick, tufting undercoat. Now it looked half the size.

Three dogs, and two of them from murder scenes. Maybe the third, too.

No, that couldn't be good.

"You're staring." Blunt as ever, Dru stared back, narrowing her crinkle-edged eyes at him.

The conversation hesitated as a vehicle pulled up, right up front instead of to the side where the staff parked. Sheri peeked out the window. "Your snake-bit dog's here, looks like."

"Catch the punk dog later," Dale said, dropping into triage mode. He handed the vials to Jade. "We'll need Ringers ready to go—one for infusion, one ready for push fluids if necessary."

She nodded, ducking into the treatment room. "Dru, back outside. Keep that dog away from these people."

Dru, being Dru, didn't hesitate when it came to the crunch. Out she went, blocking the inner door ajar and opening the outer door on the terrier's wind-up. *Grff-grff-grff-GRYIPE!*

Silence. The fading sound of nails against the concrete porch.

"Yeah, you'd *better* run!" Dru called. And then she said, "Go on in, they're ready for you."

In came a woman staggering under the weight of a large Australian shepherd. Dale took the animal from her and straight into treatment. "Paperwork!" he said over his shoulder.

"Who do you think you're talking to?" Sheri waved the papers so broadly he couldn't fail to miss them in peripheral vision, and he smiled as he headed for the stainless steel table awaiting the sick Aussie. His clinic, his people. Strange as they all were, they knew how to get things done.

His clinic. His people.

The phone calls, the faucet, murders all around them...whoever had it in for this clinic would have to come through Dale first.

NINE

BRAD STANFILL ARRIVED IN unexpectedly short order—Dale sensed Sheri's hand in play—and ably filled in for the routine exams, spring shots, a litter of three-day puppies ready to have dewclaws clipped. By then the Aussie was stabilized and Dale had time to indulge in the unique puppy breath that came with puppy kisses before heading to the lobby to check on the status of the punk dog and, more importantly, the looks of his rear-ranged schedule.

At the sight of the empty waiting room, he stopped short. Sheri glanced up from the elaborate salad to which she was applying the finishing touches right there at her desk—a cherry tomato here, an artful fling of almond slices there, spilling over to the out-of-place stack of old newspapers beside the bowl. "You done for a while? Good. I'm taking this into the back."

"What about—"

"They went to lunch."

His gaze flicked to the door. "What about—"

"Dru went to lunch, too."

"And what about—"

"It's gonna take more than two people to get that thing we're calling a dog." Sheri stood, picking up the completed salad, and stuck the papers under her arm. "So it's still there. Being ugly."

A certain weariness descended upon Dale. In the grand

scheme of things, the dog barely rated a flicker of annoyance, and yet here he was, annoyed. "You," he said, more decisively than Sheri expected; she brought herself up short in that one casual step she'd taken to leave the office area. "You're the woman with all the power around here. Use it. Get that dog into a crate. Whatever it takes."

She hesitated on a protest, looking down at her masterpiece of a salad.

"*After* lunch."

"Oh, okay then. Sure. You shoulda said something earlier."

"I am not rolling my eyes," Dale said, a mutter of the besieged. "I am not rolling my—oh, damn. Couldn't stop myself."

"Ha. Ha."

Unaffected by Dale, Sheri nonetheless stopped short smartly enough at the sound of a vehicle in the parking lot. "Oh, man," she said, and put down the salad to rush to the window. "That's Hank's Jeep!"

Dale's brain stuttered to a stop at the imminent collision of forces, but not before it all started. The little terrier mix set his plump body in motion, growling at every quick bounding step. *Grff-grff-grff-GRFFF—*

"AW!"

Sheri peered avidly out the window, action too close to the side of the building to get a true bead on, hands clenched into fists in anticipation of the outcome. Eager anticipation or dread, Dale couldn't have said.

"Aww! C'mon!"

And silence.

And then, muffled by glass, "Hey…hey, you're kind of personality-ish." Whining noises from the dog. Pathetically eager whining noises. "Face like that, you gotta be, huh? Well, I'll bet you shouldn't be outside here like this. Come on inside."

Sheri looked at Dale; Dale looked at Sheri. Sheri said, "Wuh!"

And before either of them thought to prepare, Hank opened the doors to admit the dog. It preceded him like royalty, pausing only to eye his leg. For a moment, the entry area hovered inside a surreal moment into which Dale's imagination inserted the triumphal Star Wars procession theme from the first movie. Or maybe that was the fourth movie. Part four. Part four filmed first. And by the time he'd sorted out the details, the dog had stopped short, looked around, and come to a succinct conclusion about his new surrounds.

"Grff-grff-grff-GRFFF!" it said, and bounded away down the hall toward Dăle's office, nails skittering on concrete.

"Uh-oh," said Hank. "Say, you got that little beagle of yours here toda—"

Sully's astonished cry echoed back down the hall with the power of hound lungs behind it. *"Bawh!"* Terrier nails skidded, reversed course, and scampered briefly through the hall to fade to silence.

"Yeah," Hank said sadly. "I guess you do."

"Tsk," Sheri said. "I am not rolling my eyes. I am not rolling my—oh, damn. There they go!"

"Watch it," Dale said her, pointing a stern finger of warning in her direction.

Sully's indignant and totally baffled objection repeated itself to the now empty office. *"Bawh!"*

Dale said, "I will not hide my face in my hands, I will not—oh, damn."

THAT WASN'T RIGHT. this is my room! my sullybed! my dale! beagle grrr. smelly intruder…all people-made smoke. people smoking stick, crackly little fire smoke. people blood. familiar people smell. don't trust that smell. i feel grumpy.

maybe dale will feed me.

"You guys are really in the middle of it." Hank dropped a stack of rubber-banded envelopes on Sheri's desk and she snatched them up.

"Ooh, blue rubber band," she said, and fumbled the newspapers under her arm. They spilled across the floor; she didn't seem to notice.

"In the middle—?" Dale said, and stopped. Chaos, that's what they were in the middle of. With odd Alfred Ledbetter and his timely deposit of dogs at the clinic—two of them, at least. Damn, the man rubbed Dale the wrong way. Or maybe that was still irritation over the faucet, spilling over to Ledbetter via a stray dog the man probably hadn't even dropped off here...

"Wow," said Hank, hitching his pants up over his little potbelly. "That's a mighty frown, Dr. Kinsall."

"Dale." And Dale rubbed a hand over his face, scouring away the frown in question. "And I—"

Let it go, Dale.

"Never mind," he told Hank, who still waited, eyebrows politely raised in expectation.

"Wokay," Hank said, as if this sort of thing happened all the time. "Hope you get that little dog. He was kinda cute, come to think of it." He made an absent-minded exit, fingers twitching as if already pulling out the mail for the next stop.

The phone rang; Dale reached for it.

"Hey," Sheri said from where she crouched to pick up the scattered papers. "Let the machine get it. Lunch is lunch. You gonna eat any?"

"Leftover pizza." After a walk for Sully. Both after a big whiff of the daily inhaler, which he'd meant to do after his early arrival but somewhere between the soldered faucet, the snakebite, and the strafing terrier, he'd forgotten. Stupid. He'd never beat the asthma back into nothingness if he let things get out of hand again.

It was just so much nicer to pretend the problem didn't exist at all.

He imagined Dru's expression if she were there and could read his thoughts, and he made a face.

"Hey, if you don't want the old pizza, I can trade you this nice big salad," Sheri said, plopping the papers on the counter.

"You must be kidding. It's just now getting good."

She scowled at him—she'd clearly thought she'd had a chance—and shuffled the papers back into order with a mutter. "Gotta read these things as they come in."

They both looked at the phone when it rang, but when Dale reached for it, Sheri waved him off. "Lunch," she reminded him. "We'll never get them trained if we keep answering the phone. The machine'll pick up."

"Lunch," Dale told himself, pulling his hand back. Lunch, and a mournful woo-oo from his office. "Okay, give me a shout if it's important."

But even from halfway down the hall, he could hear the harsh blast of someone's breath into their phone mouthpiece…it sounded less like heavy breathing and more like exertion, but the click of the hang-up was undeniable.

"Grr," said the terrier from somewhere mysterious.

"Hey," said Sheri, giving up on lunch in the back room and speaking around a mouthful of salad. "Lookit this."

woo-oo.

The phone rang again, and Dale fled. First to the office, then out the side door, taking Sully for a brisk walk where the clinic property butted up against national forest. That worked up enough of a cough so he grabbed for the inhaler first thing upon return, then let Sully amble out with him to the waiting room.

Dale gnawed pizza; Sully carried a small corner of crust, trotting proudly.

Sheri looked up from her mostly consumed salad and said, "Chicken."

"Pepperoni," Dale corrected her, pretending to misunderstand. "Who was the second phone call?"

She shrugged. "Whoever it was the first time. He really needs to slow down, though. All that huffing and puffing…he's gonna have a heart attack."

He might have asked more, but he saw the line of worry on her high brow and took another bite of pizza instead.

She grabbed the opening and shoved a paper across the counter at him, stabbing a finger at one of the photos. "Lookit this."

Dale looked. A group of angry people, including a familiar face. "Our friend Mr. Ledbetter."

"Our *weird* friend Mr. Ledbetter," Sheri corrected him. "Scarecrow Man. And don't give me that look. I don't care if he brings in hurt dogs, the man is strange and you know it."

Dale thought it a good time for a socially incorrect portion of pizza and filled his mouth. Sheri didn't need any encouragement to continue. "Look at the date. And the caption. The city trail use forum, just like he said."

Like he'd said when he'd brought in the Dane, and a woman accused him of snooping around on the night of the first murder. And he'd said he hadn't…and here was the proof. Dale swallowed a funny gulp of something that didn't quite taste like pizza…more like unspoken words, as he realized he'd not only found Ledbetter strange, but he found the man strange enough that he'd half-believed the woman's accusation in the waiting room. *Ledbetter had been there at the murder.*

Except he hadn't been. He'd been spreading his charm at the water forum. Ledbetter might be strange…but apparently that's all he was.

An unbidden image of Glory Heissman came to mind—and Dale gave himself a mental slap on the wrist. *From one false trail to another.* Okay, she lived in the neighborhood. And she'd snarled with the dead man. And one of her little faux huskies had cut its foot right around the time of the murder. True, all of it. But the police were the police for a reason, and Dale...

Dale was a vet. A vet with a clinic under some unreasonable siege. If he had flights of fancy to spend on solving problems, he'd spend them on the clinic. On figuring out who had developed a grudge.

Given the clinic insurance deductible, he'd probably also be spending them on the plumber.

DEAR AUNT CILY...

And Dale stared at the screen of his laptop, plugged in to the clinic's cable connection and waiting in its patient computer way for Dale to finish and send the email. "You can wait," he told it. "I wait for you all the time. And don't even think about your blue screen of death."

But as the words came out of his mouth into the quiet office, they sounded flat and stupid. And they did nothing but remind him of the current circumstances. *The faucet is fixed,* he wrote Cily, determined to quit obsessing about the deaths that had welcomed him to this small town.

Sully gave one of his most dramatic sighs and rolled over on his back, legs dangling in the air. Rather like the "Dead Possum" display with which Dru had greeted Dale on that first day. *bored. dinnertime.*

Dale spared him a glance, bit his lip on a smile. "I give that one an 8.5."

On that first day. Not even so long ago. It seemed like too much had happened in the days since.

Sully groaned, stretching one leg in a fainting-diva pose.

"Soon," Dale told him. "This connection is a zillion times better than our dial-up at home. Amuse yourself a few more moments."

Catching the tone of his voice, Sully rolled to his feet, shook off, and put his nose up, air-scenting. The pizza box, probably. He didn't so much as flinch when the phone rang, even though Dale jumped and had to act fast to keep from deleting his email. What little there was of it. And though he half-expected a hang-up, what he got was a pleasant, vaguely familiar voice—one that sounded almost as startled as he did. "I'm sorry," she said, "I thought I'd get an answering machine."

"I can fake it," Dale told her, with no idea who she was. His little voice guessed *Laura?* but it was only wishful thinking. He knew it wasn't Laura. As pleasant as this woman was, she lacked the soft-spoken tones he already associated with Laura and with many from the Navajo Nation. "I don't have the beep down really well, though."

"Dr. Kinsall?"

"Yes," Dale admitted, a little abashed at his silliness. As with Sully, it always seemed to sneak out. The Sully in question had pinpointed the object of his desire, and, glancing back at Dale, considered raising up on his hind legs to acquire it—something in Jorge's stubborn pile of things not thrown out yet. Dale frowned at Sully and pointed at the Sullybed.

Sully didn't look at him. *i don't see you.*

The voice in his ear said, "This is Amelia Dresser."

"Is it?" Dale asked politely, racking his brains to figure out why the name should mean something to him.

She laughed. "From the *Post*. I spoke to you at the RoundUp reception?"

His brain made an internal clicking noise. *The reporter.* She'd done a decent job...and she hadn't poked any of the things Dale didn't want poked. "Hi," he said. "Sorry. Long day…I probably shouldn't have picked up the phone at all." And suddenly realizing how that had sounded, he quickly added, "I mean, not that I wouldn't want to talk to you. Just that…well, listen to me. Not even caffeine will make a difference now." And that was, he suddenly realized, truer than he'd known. He squelched the unexpected impulse to curl up on the Sullybed and close his eyes until morning.

Not a great idea. Sully was a real bed hog. He'd also correctly perceived himself to be unobserved, and now stood half-crouching on his haunches, a delicate balance as he reached oh-so-stealthily for a corner of…something. Dale pointed a sterner finger at him and Sully eased back and continued his tour of the room as though it had all been his own idea.

"—interview," the reporter was saying. "What do you think?"

Dale frowned and regarded the phone cradle, as if it could offer some magical wisdom. "You already interviewed me."

"Not about caring properly for pets and small livestock without over-using water in this time of drought," she said patiently, and Dale realized she was repeating herself. Oops.

"I'd be happy to talk to you," he said, but had to hesitate. The computer screensaver kicked in and he hit the space bar out of habit, bringing his barely composed letter back to the screen. "I'm not certain if I'm your best resource, though. Someone like—" *yeah, say it* "—Laura Nakai has a lot more experience with this area."

"But that's exactly it," Amelia said, enthusiasm creeping into her voice. "Yours are fresh new eyes. You'll see things differently…but at the same time you know how devastating fire can be—"

"What?" Dale couldn't hide his incredulous response, or the anger quickly rising behind it.

"Fire and drought," she said, undeterred. "They go together.

Your experience will give the article a personal touch; it'll reach people."

"I am not," Dale said distinctly, fighting a rush of resentment that had more to do with past reporters and not so much to do with Amelia herself, "going to talk about my *experience*. I am not even going to allude to it. I will not drop hints, and will not say 'or this could happen to you and your animals just like it happened to mine,' or make big solemn eyes for any pictures. If you bring it up anyway, I'll grab your notebook or your tape recorder or whatever you're using and I'll turn it inside out."

Sully whined. Dale crooked a finger at him and the little hound came over to tip his chin up and rest it against Dale's leg.

"Touchy," Amelia said, not sounding the least deterred. "Well, then, how about you see if Laura Nakai is interested in sharing the interview and we'll turn it into a newbie's view versus the voice of experience."

"Not versus," Dale said firmly. "Combined."

She gave the slightest of snorts. "Not so amiable as you once seemed. You know, I could just get Dr. Hogue's usual seasonal interview for this article."

"Okay."

Silence.

A sigh gusted into the earpiece from the other end of the line. "Well, this could be interesting, too. You check with Dr. Nakai. I'll be back in touch."

Dale hung up the phone and looked at Sully, who'd dropped his head to fasten a stare of immense woefulness on his person.

fooooood.

"Guess what," Dale said, ignoring the look with the ease of long practice and thinking instead that maybe finally he'd have a chance to make up for his vast social blunders upon arrival at the Foothills Clinic. "We have to call Laura. Bummer, huh?"

sighhhh.

DALE SOMEHOW MANAGED to make it home and dish out dog kibble before Sully expired from hunger. He amused his own stomach with a triple-decker peanut butter and honey sandwich, and he pulled out the phone number he'd scrounged from Sheri's Rolodex when the Flagstaff white pages hadn't been as useful. He eyed the number a moment, reaching for a well-deserved Dos Equis to wash down the last of the peanut butter. Sheri was right. She *did* have all the power.

Not that it would do him any good unless he dialed the phone.

He glanced at the clock—nearly eight—and reflected that he didn't have much time, but that didn't stop him from taking both the beer and the phone number into the puzzle room, misting the puzzle table to keep the dust down, and wasting ten minutes looking for a piece he'd chosen simply because it was so nondescript he had no chance of finding it any time soon.

Coward.

Sully trotted into the room with a Nylabone hanging from his mouth like an unlit cigarette, and Dale sat down to cross his legs, providing a lap. Sully made himself at home and Dale, somehow without thinking too much about it, dialed the phone.

She picked up the phone on the second ring. "Dale."

"How did you—"

Hold on, that hadn't been how he'd intended to start this conversation.

But she didn't need the end of that sentence to answer the question. "Caller ID."

"Ah," he said, embarrassed. That's what came of being a technological Neanderthal.

"You thought I just guessed?" She laughed, not as unkindly as she might have—just mild, honest amusement. "I'm afraid if I want woo-woo, I have to drive down to Sedona."

"You never just get a feeling?" Oh yeah, like the intense

feeling of astonishment washing over him that he'd actually said those words.

"Feelings of the sort you mean," Laura told him, "are just a collection of subliminal observations that add up."

"You're kidding." Dale tugged absently on Sully's ear. Sully pretended not to notice. "Have you been practicing that phrase?"

"You inspired me. Now, tell me how you got this number. It's unlisted."

"It—" Dale glanced down at the paper. Nothing more than a scrawled number written on the bottom corner torn from the papers left on Sheri's desk. He tried to remember if there had been any notations next to the number in the Rolodex; couldn't. "I stole it from Sheri's files," he admitted. "I don't know where—"

But he stopped short, not wanting to go there—because he suddenly had a collection of subliminal observations add right up to *oops*.

"My resume and application," Laura said, her voice suddenly tight with anger. "For the position I wasn't *man* enough to deserve."

Dale took a deep breath. "Or that Dr. Hogue wasn't man enough to give you?"

She hesitated long enough that Dale thought she might hang up on him. In his lap, Sully filled the silence by grinding away at the Nylabone, happy to prop it against Dale's convenient leg. Dale said, "Laura—"

"I'm surprised." Her loss for words came through in her tone. "I didn't think…"

"Hey," Dale said, speaking up over Sully's assiduous chewing. "I like the man well enough. It doesn't mean he did the right thing by you."

"*Ayóí ádíl'á*," she sighed, and then didn't make him ask. "It means, literally, *remarkable he makes himself*. As in, he's a little too big for his actual boot size."

Dale gave a soft snort. "I've seen some of that. I just don't know how to make it right, not now. Other than moving back to Ohio, and I really—"

"No," she said, and her usual quiet assurance had returned. "I don't think anyone would be happy about that."

"My Aunt Cily," Dale said without thinking.

"You have an aunt… Silly?"

"Cecelia." Dale relieved Sully of the bone and tossed it across the room, but Sully bounded after it and patiently returned to brace himself against Dale's leg, offering a reproachful look.

my spot.

Dale looked away, knowing that with his attention divided, Sully could easily guilt him out. "She raised me," he said. "Wanted me to come here, but wants me back there, too."

"Ah," Laura said, as if she understood a whole lot more than what he'd said. "She must really hope your health improves."

"She thinks," Dale said—stiffly, because he'd hoped for better from his lungs by now and hadn't gotten it, "that I'll find myself." Though Dale knew he wouldn't. If there was any part of himself missing, it could be found in the dead embers of not one but two fires. And it wasn't the sort of thing he'd expected himself to say to Laura Nakai, anyway. Maybe if he took a good quick chew on the Nylabone, he could get his mouth more closely connected to his brain.

But Laura said simply, "People do."

"What I'd like," Dale said, desperately trying to claw his way back to the reason he'd called, "is to find myself in an interview with you. The *Post* called me this evening, asking about it."

With brittle care to her words, Laura said, "They called you, looking for me?"

Dale climbed to his feet, leaving his disapproving dog

behind. "Hey, your number's unlisted, remember?" Not bad for a quick comeback. He glanced over the puzzle and tried a piece in the spot that had grabbed his attention before the call. It didn't fit and he put it off to the side. The table shuddered slightly as Sully leaned against the table leg in lieu of Dale's relocated leg.

"Right," she said, as dry as the desert air in drought. "And they'd never think to call me at the office. Where'd they call you?"

Time for out and out evasion. He tried another puzzle piece, discarded it. "I guess they do a piece on animals and summer care every year. This time they want an emphasis on the drought…so they decided to do it differently. It's the two of us, if you want it."

She waited long enough to worry him. "And if I don't?"

He cleared his throat. "I guess I'm not into a solo," he said, and meant it. No more news stories with too much focus on Dale Kinsall. And that meant no solos. "I'm sure Dr. Hogue will do it. I guess he usually does."

There. Take *that* bait, Laura Nakai. Take the chance to usurp a little attention from the man who wouldn't hire you.

"Damn it," she said, but resignation filled the word. "You really worked this out, didn't you?"

"My brain food today has been pizza and peanut butter. Better chalk it up to dumb luck." But Dale smiled to himself and bounced slightly on his toes.

She snorted. It was quiet, but it was a definite snort. "Summer animal care. Better study up on it. It won't be quite what you're used to."

"No problem," Dale said. "I'll just ask Dr. Hogue."

"Oh," she said. "You are a brat." And hung up.

Dale bounced on his toes again and set the phone aside. And then he picked up a puzzle piece that looked just right, and put it into the space he'd been trying to fill. "There, see?" he told Sully. "All the pieces are starting to come together."

HE REMEMBERED his nightly inhaler dose. He changed into an ancient stretched-out T-shirt and cutoffs to walk the yard perimeter with Sully, loudly admiring the height Sully managed when he hiked his leg. He saved another horny toad from beagle predation, and he walked back into the house still humming. Not out loud, but a happy body hum that made Sully frolic ahead of him.

Then the wind shifted, and Sully stopped short, his ears pulled forward as he stared through the dusk. Dale followed his gaze, expecting to find a neighbor's cat in the native plants lining the fence or the cluster of pines at the corner—still his property, but outside the fence line. Sully took a step or two and stopped, his nose in the air and his attention caught more by scent than by the potential of an intruder. A live-and-let-live beagle. But his interest in the corner didn't change and Dale's curiosity got the better of him. He angled back out into the yard. By then Sully had reached the fence, his nose stuck up against the narrow strip of an opening that Dale hadn't yet reached with his beagle-proofing work. He inhaled mightily, his tongue reaching—and then pulled back from the fence, expression content, jaws already working.

"I don't think so," Dale told him, and crouched down to fish around inside Sully's mouth, surprised to find something of significant size and—*ow!* "What the—" He rubbed his pricked finger on his shirt, still peering at the object. The failing light didn't do him any favors. Neither did Sully, who made his ears very long and pursed his mouth in extreme offense, aiming. "You really didn't want it," Dale explained to him, pretending to be unaffected by what was, after all, a very effective expression indeed. He stood up to rub the flat circle clean of spit, sacrificing his shirt hem without a second thought. Definitely a button of some sort. He held it up to what remained of the daylight and squinted as though that would help him make out

the logo stamped on the thing. Shortly after his move he'd
found a Smokey Bear button so old as to be an antique…but
he didn't think Sully would suddenly alert to something that
had been here all along. *Squint.*

Never mind. He'd have to take it inside, which is where he'd
been headed in the first place. He turned away from the fence.

Whap! Sudden impact against the corner of his eye staggered him, startling as much as painful. He jerked away and
then stood frozen, too stunned to do anything but the instant
assessment that okay now it hurt and *what*— Only subliminally
did he notice the rustle of sound from within the pines.

Sully forgot his sulk and rushed the fence, growling suspiciously. Just as quickly, he ran back to Dale, who stood with
his fingers pressed to the warm flow of blood down the side of
his face. *dale! dale!*

And Dale said, "What the hell," finally finding his voice but
still unable to make any sense of the situation. Berserker bird?
As if. Probably a rock. But how and who…

There'd be no easy answers to that one.

With darkness closing down fast around them, he stood
there only long enough to regain his equilibrium, searching the
yard perimeter in an effort that would have been futile even had
he not been stunned. Then he pulled the hem of his T-shirt up
to the corner of his eye, soaking up the blood that still flowed
fast enough to drip down his elbow, and headed for the patio.

By the time he reached it, Sully walking so close as to trip
him several times, the bleeding had already stopped. He pulled
the T-shirt off, used it to swipe down his arm and wipe the side
of his face, and tossed it in the general direction of the back
door.

Sully rose up to prop a light foot against Dale's thigh, licking
at his fingers. *blood. not right.*

Dale gave him a moment, and then wiped his hands on his

shorts, gingerly checking to see that the rising lump at the corner of his eye had indeed stopped bleeding. The eyelids were already swollen along the outside and though he thought it could probably use a stitch, he opted for a couple of ice cubes and a beer. Berserk bird? Stray stone from a distant slingshot? What were the chances?

But when he stepped inside, the phone rang. A raggedly disguised voice said, "I'm watching you. Be careful, or you'll be next."

Apparently, the chances weren't all that good after all.

TEN

"WATER, SHADE, HEAT STROKE…" Amelia Dresser checked her list of questions, her mini tape recorder held at the ready, the most obvious questions already asked and answered. In the periphery of the conversation, the photographer prowled the edges of the forest, looking for the most dramatic shot—the best place to arrange Dale's height and Laura's lack thereof. Amelia paid him no attention. "Evacuation necessities in case of fire…" She glanced up at Dale, her face dappled by lunchtime sunlight at the edge of the clinic property where they'd decided to set up for photos. "Tell me, Dr. Kinsall, do you keep an evacuation kit for your dog now?"

Now. Since the clinic fire, she meant. Dale tilted his head slightly and looked at her from beneath slanted brow. *Danger, danger—forbidden turf ahead!* The corner of his eye ached fiercely, although a butterfly bandage held the cut closed and the swelling no longer interfered with his eye. It was a cunning little bruise, deep and colorful, and the newspaper photographer had already muttered about being unable to keep it out of their pictures. Somehow he managed to keep his voice casual. "I expect I'm about average in that respect. I have some things ready and other things…aren't. But my car always has the basics."

Amelia ignored Dale's unmistakable warning. "So your previous experience hasn't really changed how you deal with the potential danger."

Dale reached for her recorder as promised and Amelia took

a quick nimble step backward. Probably used to it. "You know," she said quickly, "I guess we're pretty much done here. Unless Deputy Wells has released you from your vow of silence—?"

Dale growled. Sully, his butt plunked squarely on Dale's foot, looked up. *woo!*

"Maybe later," Amelia said, unabashed now that she was out of reach—pencil tucked behind her ear amongst a wiry explosion of curls, recorder tucked away in her canvas sling-tote.

"That doesn't seem likely."

"Oh, come now, Dr. Kinsall. Dale. Can I call you Dale?"

"No."

"Let's face facts here, Dale." She adjusted her pencil. "You're interesting news. You came from mysterious, heroic circumstances and you arrived to discover one of the strangest murders in Flagstaff history. You can't avoid questions forever."

Dale closed his mouth. Hard. He imagined that heroic muscles rippled across his jaw in his self-restraint.

Imagine the questions she'd have if she knew about his berserk bird. Or the phone calls.

"Not only that, one of your clients is on the short-list. Personally, I don't think she did it. I think George Corcoran met all her little dogs and drowned himself in horror. Of course, we still don't know who put the hose away. Do we?" She tipped her head, rubbing a finger across her lower lip in speculation.

"Sully," Dale said, "bite her."

Sully looked up at him with a vastly puzzled brow.

"I think we'll want the dog, too," Amelia said abruptly. "In the picture, I mean." She beckoned to her photographer, and they put their heads together a moment. Dale took the opportunity to notice that Jorge stood at the end of the short row of stalls with a gaggle of friends at his back. A separate group stood off to the side, some with dogs on leash, and Dale surmised they were clients, taking a look at the action. Or what passed for action on a warm May afternoon in West Winona on a day when the spring wind had lulled to a mere erratic breeze. Sully lifted his nose and grumbled, but settled back to a wary eye.

"Interesting interview," Laura observed, moving back up by his side and taking a moment to bend to Sully. Up until those last questions, she'd been an active participant in the interview. Wise woman, she was, to have stepped back at that point.

"Ah," Dale said. "She…at the reception, I thought she was different. I'm sorry—I wouldn't have invited you to join in if I'd known she was going to be like the rest of them."

"The ones back in Ohio."

He aimed a sharp look her way—or started to, until his gaze met only her serene brown eyes and quiet understanding. She wasn't baiting him. So he simply nodded. "I'll just count myself lucky she hasn't figured out about the dogs."

She raised an eyebrow at him, and he found himself explaining. "Right after each of the murders, we've been on the receiving end of rescue dogs." If you counted the terrier as being in need. A whole day passed, and the dog still lurked in the back rooms, stealing food and leaving the occasional calling card. The whole staff had come to dread its bounding growl, but it hadn't drawn any blood.

Dale got the impression it was laughing a lot, though.

And Laura, not lost in Dale's thoughts, had gone on to say, "It's hard to draw a connection there."

"Maybe not. One of the dogs came from near the first murder. But Alfred Ledbetter brought her in, and he's got a picture perfect alibi in our friendly paper, so…maybe. The second dog, not so obvious—but I remember seeing him there. The third…well, there's no direct connection that I know of. Just the timing."

Laura gave him a truly startled look. "You haven't read the paper today?"

"Avoidance," Dale admitted.

"Let's just say there's a dog missing. A terrier." She sounded almost reluctant to give him the news.

He didn't blame her. "Three for three, then, not that it makes any sense. And only if you admit that round little rat is a terrier." Dale rubbed the bridge of his nose. "I'll have to let the cops know. Though…it'd be less embarrassing if we could catch the damn dog first." Yes indeed, things just got stranger and stranger…

Sully woofed at the sound of a cracking branch; Laura and Dale both turned to the woods to discover the photographer and reporter in discussion there. Dale shook his head. "They've got to know that forest is off-limits. And they've got an audience, too."

"You're assuming they care," Laura reminded him.

He looked down, gave her a grin that felt like the first real grin in days just because he hadn't been expecting such a blunt response and he found himself oddly flattered. "Yeah," he said. "My bad."

She looked up at him, growing more thoughtful—looking at his eye. He knew the question before she put words to it, and shook his head, raising his hand to let his fingers hover near the bruise. "Just one of those things."

"It's spreading, you know," she said, although there was something in her tone that let him know she knew quite well he was just being evasive. And yet she let it be. "By tomorrow it'll be a black eye."

"Great. That'll be nice and subtle."

"Trust me. It's not *subtle* now."

"Here's the spot!" the photographer called to them from within the trees. He'd found the little clearing left by the removal of several drought-killed trees, a space large enough to provide the feel of the surrounding woods but still offer some light.

"So the question is," Dale said, staring through the trees at the reporter and her photographer, "if we refuse to go in there, will we just prolong their stomping around?"

Laura made a face he hadn't expected of her. A wrinkled nose, the slight tip of her head toward the trees. A private expression between the two of them. "I think we should get it over with."

Without thinking, Dale held out his hand to catch hers. The tug of Sully's leash made him realize what he'd done and he gathered up the leather instead, wondering if she'd noticed.

Not that she'd ever say.

I LIKE LAURA. she holds me like a hug to show off for the strangers, and then dale holds me. he knows he put me close enough to lick laura's ear. i like my dale's laugh, all deep and rumbly. wag! beagle woo! dale scrubs my ear. wag!

people smells come down from the clinic. i know some of them. i remember.

i'm glad we're down here.

"I DON'T GET IT," Dale grumbled, pretty much without thinking. He'd seen Amelia off without waving, feeling more like a rearguard than a host. The last thing he needed was for that woman to get inside the clinic with the terrier. Although come to think of it, it would serve her right.

Good grief. Either I'm losing it, or I'm truly starting to fit in here. He wasn't sure which possibility alarmed him the most.

"Don't get what?" Laura glanced up at him, those dark eyes in that quiet face and its clean, ethnic mix of features.

He admired the view for an unexpected moment, and shook himself out of it. *Get a grip, Kinsall.* But of course his mouth was set to babble, and he said, "I get the impression you usually already know the answers to the things you ask."

She only lifted a shoulder and let it settle back into place. "If that were true I wouldn't let on, would I?"

No. Of course not. Unfortunately, the more she didn't tell, the more he babbled. So he walked the edge of the parking lot so Sully could make himself feel important on the withering weeds and said, "The whole thing with the Ohio clinic. Why can't they just *let go?*"

Okay, that was definitely a smile. She asked, "Have you looked in a—" and then she gave him a little double take and said, "no, apparently not," as she pointed to her own dark layered bangs in a gesture Dale knew well. He finger-combed his hair back into a reasonable order, wondering how bad it had been for the photos. Laura nodded approval. "Of course they're interested. You're tall, dark, and—" she hesitated. "Mysterious. Rumors of heroic background. They can't resist."

Dale kicked at one of the many wild, roaming cinders that had come to rest by the roadside as they turned along it, almost duplicating their path from the night of the reception. "Damn it, I'm not mysterious. I'm just private. I came out here so I *could* be private." Well, that and the climate.

"It'll fade," she told him, and her dark eyes sparked as she added, "just don't find any more bodies."

Dale paused for a Sully moment at the sign to the clinic, letting Laura move to the outside so as to be politely out of the line of fire. Traffic zipped by in twos and threes, released from the single traffic light just down the highway, and then died away again. "Maybe I should just write a letter to the editor with a dull boring account of the details. No more mystery."

"Get Sheri to help you write it."

He turned to look at her, squinting down in an effort to see past that poker face. *She's kidding.* And then, isn't she? And he took his attention from the road to do it, except in that instant Sully stiffened. *daledaledale—*

And Dale sensed it more than saw it, heard the rattly acceleration of the engine, felt the push of displaced air, got only a glimpse of blotchy brown paint and young men in the back of an old pickup. He didn't think; he reacted. He grabbed Laura from the side of the road, closing down on the wiry lean strength of her upper arms to whirl her around, sheltering her with his own frame as something cold and wet striped across his back and Sully yelped in surprise and the young men whooped garbled words of triumph and sped away. Dale had just a moment to meet Laura's bewildered gaze, an acknowledgment that neither of them truly knew what had just happened—and then Sully started to cry in a confused, wounded way, a dog hurt who doesn't understand why. Dale's own reaction kicked in before he had it all figured out—eyes tearing, lungs seizing so tightly even coughing would have been an improvement, nose running fiercely.

Laura understood first. "Mace!" she choked, and then to his utter surprise, fumbled at his waist for his shirt, a navy cotton knit with the clinic's name embroidered on it and not quite big enough anyway. And then he recalled the cold stream across his back, knew he'd been soaked, and started tugging right along with her. He bent so she could pull the shirt off over his head, and through bleary, tearing eyes, he caught her fierce, furious expression as she flung the shirt away. Downwind, too, which impressed him in that instant he had to think about it before the coughing caught him again. Laura, too, choked and spat, wiping her eyes but not nearly as immersed in the fumes as he'd been.

And Sully cried, wailing as he rubbed his face against the harsh, dusty ground, frantic and blind in his pain. Lurching, Dale scooped him up and found the little hound beyond reason, flipping and flinging himself around—enough to stagger Dale down to his knees as he fought the coughing, in the back of his mind dreading what this would do to the damned asthma. And in the back of his mind, thinking about those phone calls. Thinking that someone had been watching after all. Just not knowing why.

BAWH! BAWH! eyeseyeseyeseyesnosenose bawh! daledaledale!

LAURA INTERVENED, body blocking Dale and sliding her arms beneath Sully's writhing form. "Let me," she said, persisting when Dale resisted out of dumb determination. "You kept me clear while you took a bath, damn it—now let me take care of him!"

Sully. Oblivious, innocent…he'd never known people could hurt him.

He knew now.

"Go," Dale said, words without actual voice behind them. *I'll be right behind you,* he couldn't say, not even with his eyes. Instead, he tore himself away, heard Laura shouting for help with her words distorted by her running, heard Sully's wails fade to a frantic whine. But Dale headed for the side of the clinic, stumbling down the hill, not sure if he was breathing or not but figuring he hadn't passed out yet. He grabbed the hose and with no regard whatsoever for even or odd, he cranked the newly repaired spigot on full blast and turned his face into the spray. His face and then his back, hosing off the remaining chemical as water sluiced down his torso and then his jeans. Terry came running out of the RoundUp and wrested the hose away, putting Dale up against the clinic wall with one strong hand to hose him off. Dale leaned there like a man in the world's strangest shower, shivering under the onslaught. In short order the water stopped and someone shoved a towel in his hands.

"—Saw the whole thing," Terry growled to someone else. "Those kids…they targeted Dale and Sully the moment they turned out of the lot."

"They came from your parking lot?" Dale gasped through chattering teeth.

"Damn sure did," Dru growled, revealing herself as the towel bearer. "What those fools thought they had to prove—" she snorted most expressively and then shoved something else into Dale's hands as well. Big Blue. "Use it."

"Sully—"

"You think that Dr. Nakai won't take care of him? Now use it. I don't care if you think you need it or not."

His lungs burned—of course they burned. Of course he coughed, and of course his chest was fast filling with gunk. An actual asthma attack it wasn't, and Dale thought to object again, to push his way through to the clinic door and then back to Sully—until through his still watering eyes he got a glimpse of Dru's face. Dru the motorcycle twelve-times granny with her spiky gray hair, cigarette voice, and narrow-eyed gaze. "Do it," she said, shifting her shoulders up into bulldog mode. "Or I'll sit on you and force the stuff down your throat myself."

"Oh, hey," Terry said, deceptively mild. "I get to watch if you do."

Dale waved them both off and brought the inhaler up for four quick puffs. He pulled the air in deep, held it against the agony of an impending cough, and released it as quietly as he could.

Then he jammed Big Blue in his wet back pocket, slung the towel around his shoulders, and gave Dru a good glare. "Got this from my desk, didn't you? And completely blew my cover, I'll bet."

"Depends," Dru said, unrepentant in her shrug. "Most everyone was watching the whole screaming beagle saga. Stay cool and you can probably get away with it. No one's gonna question why you needed a shower—everyone already knows you took a snort full of Mace. It's gonna take days to air out the clinic just from that dog of yours."

Sully. God, poor little fellow. Dale ran to the clinic entrance, wet jeans clinging, sneakers at full squish. He dodged an unfortunate cat-owner on her way out and—in spite of Sheri's frantic attempt to stop him—ran into the treatment room to find Sully in much the same shape as Dale himself—wet, shivering, curled up in towels on the grated surface of the sink-side counter they generally used to wash the blood and grime off injured animals. Sully's eyes gleamed with ointment; his teeth chattered. His frantic cries had died to an unsteady whine.

Only then did Dale realize that Laura, not so far away, had turned her back to him as she finished donning a scrub shirt. Sheri's protests suddenly made more sense. Ahh, damn.

But when she turned to face him he forgot the awkward moment, struck by the way she struggled to hide the feelings showing on her face. Deeply upset for Sully, her eyes and her warm skin flushed—and yet relief there, too. "You're okay."

He saw the hint of a question more on her face than heard it in her voice, even as she regained her composure to tuck a black strand of hair behind her ear, and he nodded. "Better than hoped. And very wet." That got a smile from her, one of those smiles that turns bigger than it's meant to just from the emotion of the moment; she looked away from him, frustrated with herself.

Dale turned back to Sully and scratched gently behind a wet ear. "His eyes?"

A deep breath and she was all business. "I haven't done a fluorescence test but I wanted to play it safe. Even if he didn't take a direct hit, he might have rubbed grime into them. They're flushed clean, but—"

"Yeah," Dale said. "But." But they weren't taking any chances. The antibiotic ophthalmic ointment would have been the treatment of choice given either grime or Mace, so there it was. Dale knuckled Sully's nose slightly. "You should have given me more warning."

"I don't know how you saw it coming at all," Laura said, for the first time reflecting some of the shock still reverberating through Dale.

Dale found a smile, wry as it was. "Just a collection of subliminal observations that added up."

"Ah." She nodded, a gesture meant to be wise but one that quite touchingly wobbled too much to succeed. "Do you suppose—" she started, and he shook his head gently, about to tell her he needed time to think about it all. Her hand seemed to hover on the edge of doing something—reaching for him, hitting him, petting Sully—but never had the chance to do anything more. Sheri burst through the door with one of Dale's scrub shirts. She threw it at him, hitting him in the chest.

"At *this* clinic," she said, "we wear clothes. You think you haven't given people enough to look at today?" Then she scowled, a more directed look. "And fix your hair. We've got people waiting." Then she turned on her heel and left.

Laura's hand dropped. But she smiled at Dale's befuddled expression, a real smile and not a facade of an expression, and she rubbed Sully's ear. Not pursuing what he was sure she'd gone back to…his black eye. She knew enough. She knew something wasn't right. "Could have been worse."

"And how," Dale said, struggling to pull the soft cotton over his still-damp skin, "is that?"

She waited for his head to pop out, for his hands to hesitate as he tugged the shirt down. "Amelia Dresser could have been right there in the parking lot, complete with photographer."

"Then I guess she's the only one we know for sure didn't have anything to do with it." Dale gathered up a few dry towels and replaced the damp ones shrouding Sully, then picked the dog up. Sully tucked his head under Dale's arm. "She'd still be here if she did. Taking pictures from the sidelines."

"Those boys," Laura said, and though her words were quiet,

her face gave away her anger with a deep flush. "No one got a plate number, you know. And they shouted something but no one understood it. The police won't be able to do much."

Dale remembered Jorge at the side of the clinic…remembered his little gaggle of friends. Jorge was right, it wasn't fair to target him for his age or because he liked loud music. But for the company he kept? Oh yeah. "I think I know someone I can talk to."

Sheri swept back in, gave the room a scowl that included everyone and everything in it, and said, "People waiting, you know? And fix your hair." Her gaze fastened on Sully; it softened a moment, then snapped back up to Dale. "You give that dog over here. I'll make sure he doesn't get in the way." And before Dale knew it, he had relinquished custody. Sheri swept out again, already cooing nonsense.

Dale looked at Laura and Laura looked at Dale, and she offered him one of her quietest smiles. "From what I've seen of Sheri, that little display must mean she's really worried."

"From what I've seen of Sheri," Dale said ruefully, "that little display means I've got clients stacked up several deep." But he didn't mean it. And the look he exchanged with Laura before he squished out to pick up the next client chart…

That was worried, too.

ELEVEN

DALE SLUMPED OVER his desk, resting his forehead on his arms. *Looong day*. His eyes still stung, as did his nose; repeated washings and another change of shirt hadn't gotten rid of the pepper spray aura. He sneaked a look at Sully with a shift of his head, finding the dog curled into a very tight beagle ball, the dark smudge of natural "mascara" around his closed eyes glistening with ointment. "You're okay," he said out loud, more for himself than for Sully.

Sully didn't so much as crack an eye. *woe*.

"Uh-huh." Dale returned his attention to the desktop mere fractions of an inch away and contemplated the day. Suddenly the interview gone sour seemed the best part of it. They'd sent the snake-bit dog home…that had been good. Otherwise, with Laura departed to take care of her own practice, Dale had somehow fumbled through the day, numbed by the attack and almost grateful Jorge had left before Dale had a moment to talk to him. Tomorrow, then, for that joyful confrontation.

He knew Jorge's crew had done this. He just didn't know why. Or how it fit—*if* it fit—with everything else going on around here. The three dogs had arrived here because of the murders, he was sure of it. Amelia had interviewed him because of the murders. Someone's attention had been drawn to him the moment he'd found that body.

And deep down, Dale feared the problems wouldn't stop until the murderer was found…even if he didn't know it for sure. Couldn't know it for sure without checking into it himself. Because hard experience told him the police wouldn't. Oh, they were hot on the murders, all right. But the clinic's woes... Dale's twilight missile with no evidence but the mutating bruise on his forehead...hang-up phone calls and a few vague warnings...

Next to the murders, those would rank somewhere in the "would you like to file a report so we can put it aside?" category. Dale knew that category well.

On the other hand, they might not know about the cut Glory Heissman's dog had sustained. And they probably didn't know about the dogs appearing at the clinic.

How could they?

Maybe he needed to give Rena Wells a call.

But the thought didn't dampen the little voice in his head. *Talk to Glory,* it told him. *She'll talk to you like she might not talk to the police.* And then maybe Dale himself could see how the string of madness fit in.

"Shut up," he told the little voice. "Aren't we in enough trouble already? Let's figure that out first."

"Yes," said a dry voice from the direction of the open office doorway. "Let's."

Dale lifted his head at the sound of Dr. Hogue's voice. A glance at the Sullybed showed that Sully was studiously not looking at anything or anyone. *Woe.*

Dr. Hogue invited himself into the office. His own office was situated on the second floor; Dale hadn't been up there more than twice, and briefly at that. It was not shared territory, no matter the decreasing hours for which Dr. Hogue occupied it.

Dale cleared his throat, hunted for safe conversation, and came out with, "We haven't crossed paths much lately. I hope you're enjoying your reduced hours."

Hogue stood before the desk with his hands propped on his

hips and Dale gave an inward wince. It wasn't a friendly stance. He'd always found Hogue to be a little reserved, a little stand-offish—a vet who'd let his office staff develop their own style for the office and who might not interfere…but he also didn't participate. But this wasn't reserved. This was…hostile. Dominance maneuvers.

"In fact," Hogue said, "I've been concerned about the state of this practice almost since your arrival. The vandalism, the notoriety, the lack of professionalism…I had expected better of you." There was no sign of the kindly older vet who had hired Dale. This, Dale thought, was the man who was capable of throwing away Laura's resume.

For a moment, Dale blinked at the older vet. His anger beat against him from the outside, overcoming fatigue. He fought to keep his voice level anyway. "I'm not sure what concerns you. The animals I see have received the highest standard of care."

"Jaunts to discover bodies—"

"That was on my own time—"

"But you still managed to draw the clinic into it. And you pulled Dru off work while you were at it—running some errand for you because the police delayed you."

If that was the common understanding of Dru's involvement, that was fine with Dale. Even now a cough lurked endlessly in his chest from the peppery spray. "It was an isolated incident."

"Hardly," Hogue snorted. He looked imposing enough, steely-eyed and commanding. Secure on his turf. "You invited another vet into a yearly interview I've carefully cultivated to highlight this clinic. And don't you think I haven't noticed the phone calls, or the vandalism. Or even your face."

Dale looked down at his scrub shirt, a replacement for the shirt with which he'd started this day. "You know, it seems to me that this could go the other way around. I was never Maced before I got here. My *dog* was never Maced."

Woe.

Dale somehow managed to avoid looking at curled-up Sully, a happy-go-lucky dog who until this day hadn't realized truly bad things could happen to him. He leaned back in his chair and crossed his arms, looking up at Hogue. He chose his words carefully. "It seems the things around here are happening *to* me, not because of me."

"Yes," Hogue said grimly. "Just as they happened to you in Ohio."

Dale's arms clenched into place; his jaw clenched, too. "That has nothing to do with this."

"Doesn't it?" Hogue didn't back down. If anything, he grew more imposing. "Can you be sure of that? Because I can't. And I want this stopped. All of it. The phone calls, the vandalism, the weird interludes with weird people. I want respect restored from the staff for the vets—and I want that terrier *out* of the clinic."

Dale almost brightened, almost asked, *Did you catch it?,* but caught himself in time. Heard the words behind the words. The threat that he hadn't seen coming. *Fix this, or hit the road.* And even deeper than that, a resentment at how quickly the staff had accepted Dale, how thoroughly they'd rallied behind him.

There was no way to fight that kind of resentment. If Hogue had thought Dale was the kind of man to follow Hogue's professional style, he'd been wrong all along.

But there was no point in saying so. Hogue either already realized it and was using the clinic trouble as an excuse for this conversation, or he didn't realize it and it was just as well that the other things kept him distracted. So Dale said, so evenly he felt a stranger's voice coming from his mouth, "I want those things to stop, too. The welfare of this clinic is foremost on my mind these days."

Hogue hesitated, eyes narrowing slightly as he parsed

through Dale's reaction, not quite sure if there was any hidden meaning there. In the end, he gave a short nod of his head. "Good," he said, dropping his hands by his sides. "Then things should go more smoothly from here on out."

Dale didn't voice his opinion that things wouldn't go smoothly at all until the killer was caught. No community would settle down with a murderer lurking in its midst, and the clinic in general didn't seem likely to settle down ever. No, he blinked his stinging eyes and found nothing else worth saying, and after Hogue left, trailing satisfaction behind him, Dale put his forehead back down on his arm.

From somewhere in the depths of the clinic came the first questing growl, *grff?* and Dale winced without looking up. No point in looking. He knew what was coming.

Grff-grff-grff-GRFFF—

Well. Laura had deserved the job in the first place.

EVENTUALLY SULLY CREPT from his bed and eased up to place a paw on Dale's leg. *food?*

"See, I told you you'd be all right," Dale said, aware of his own tentative appetite but still not quite ready to face the world. Another moment of quiet in the wake of echoing terrier nails on tile and he'd reach for his car keys, grab one of the turkey-Swiss subs Terry was learning to have on hand, and head for home. Tomorrow was an early shift of routine surgeries, and for once he hoped to finish out the day in his own shirt.

Out in the reception room, the phone rang.

Dale peered at the phone on his desk. Contemplated it. It might not be ringing, but it was set to line one. He could pick it up and answer all the same.

If he wanted to.

He scowled at the familiar tightening along his spine and sat up straight. "Not this time," he told it. "It's my clinic, and

I'll answer the damn phone without worrying who's on the other end. Hanging up is easy, you know."

Sully gave a low *woo* of agreement as Dale reached for the phone.

It was, of course, one of *those* calls. "I told you—" said the voice, and Dale hung up.

"See?" He looked down at Sully. "Right again. Hanging up *is* easy."

Except when he made it through his front door, dropping his backpack, toeing off his shoes, and tossing the supper sub onto the kitchen table, the answering machine on the counter blinked insistently at him. Menacingly, under the circumstances. Dale growled at it, startling Sully into an echoing growl. And then he very deliberately measured out Sully's meal, sprinkling a pinch of shredded cheddar over the kibble as a special treat. He popped the top off a cold Dos Equis and took himself out to the back patio chair, putting his feet up on the low adobe wall, the beer down on the flagstone tile, and the sub in his lap.

The sub took two beers to wash down. By then, he thought he'd listen to the machine, feeling more than a little foolish. Aunt Cily had his number; so did Laura. So did the answering service for that matter, but they would have tried his cell when they got the machine and Brad was taking tonight's calls anyway.

"You don't listen very well," said the answering machine when he pressed the button. A man—the *same* man. Impatient this time. "I told you I'd be watching. I saw you today. I saw what you did. You won't be the only one who pays the price if you don't shape up."

The hang-up click sounded loud in sudden silence of Dale's house. No refrigerator hum, no air-conditioning; the stereo was off and the television likewise. And Sully had slipped out when Dale came in, no doubt to knock over the empty beer bottle and lick the scant remaining drops from the flagstone.

If he'd been smart, Dale's heart would have beat faster with fear. He'd scour his every action, trying to understand what had upset his persistent caller. He'd hunker in and keep quiet, pleasing Dr. Hogue and his watcher alike.

But Dale didn't listen very well. Not any more.

VISINE IS your friend. Dale's eyes still burned, but his chest had eased more than expected. The rewards of being good with his inhaler. Dale tucked the eye drops into his backpack, jammed in the remains of his sub for lunch, and added a hunk of trail sausage for good measure. It was still too early for break-fast…but Dale had a young man to talk to.

For the first time ever he considered leaving Sully at home…but the yard beagle-proofing hadn't been fully tested and then again there was Sully, standing by the garage door with his tail in a jaunty position and yesterday apparently for-gotten.

Dale doubted that last, but filled his stainless steel travel mug full of coffee and released Sully into the garage to hunt down hapless stink beetles while Dale dumped his stuff into the Forester. They drove out into an early barely-dawn, and arrived at the clinic with enough time to walk quiet rounds and replace yesterday's drama with something closer to normal. Clean clinic, sleepy animals, Sheri's office space tidier than one would ever imagine from watching her at work, Dale's own office starting to feel like home and minus most of the packing boxes. Jorge's junk purgatory took up less space, but still remained.

Speaking of whom…

With Sully settled on his bed to possess his new flavored Nylabone and Dale's review of the scheduled surgeries com-pleted—a spay, a dental with some tooth-pulling, a neuter-ing—Dale wandered out toward the back of the building to hunt down Jorge.

He found the kid setting out food for what had to be the terrier, a shiny stainless bowl at the edge of the painted concrete feed and wash room floor. The block walls of this addition had dull industrial almost-white paint, sturdy shelves stacked with premium food for kennel and client use, and a neatly organized area for the specialized food and supplements. A huge double laundry tub lined the wall along with the raised bathtub, all so clean and neat as to make Dale skeptical…as though perhaps someone had come in early to make sure everything was irrefutably spiffy. And when Jorge glanced at him, his robust complexion paled noticeably…but other than that, he was cool. So cool. Dale asked, "I don't suppose you can actually catch him."

"Nah." Jorge stood, wiped his hands against his baggy pants. "He don't come out when anyone's here. Anyway, I kinda like him. He's a tough little guy. And he always does his business in the same corner."

"Dr. Hogue would be much happier if he weren't here."

Jorge grinned. "Yeah," he said, and then seemed to remember who he was talking to. "But he ain't gonna be easy to catch," he added quickly, reaching for the stack of pre-filled bowls Dru had left him the day before. "There's a hole in the wall, behind the sink. That's where he goes."

For an instant Dale forgot about his business with Jorge and lost himself in visions of the terrier slinking around inside the very walls of the clinic. Snickering, in its terrier way. Plotting. Lurking, waiting its chance to emerge and charge.

Or hey, maybe killing whatever mice this mature building might harbor.

And the terrier, from some indefinable somewhere, went, *"Grrf."*

"He knows I put the food down," Jorge said, and headed for the door to the long kennel runs and their healthy boarders.

Hearing the clink of bowls, the dogs exploded into enthusiastic barking. Healthy, all right.

"Not so fast," Dale said, coming back to his original purpose. Loudly.

Jorge rolled his eyes, then nodded at the kennel. "Let me shut 'em up, man. Gotta feed 'em."

Dale gave a short nod, but he went to the door to watch. So he saw when Jorge gave the rear exit a longing glance, but he also saw the kid turn around and head back up the long aisle. He caught Dale's eye and shrugged. "Gotta talk to you sooner or later, right?"

The background noise had turned into chomping and the scrape of bowl across concrete. Much better. Happy noises, even, except Dale was doing everything he could to keep the thought of Sully's cries from his mind and to keep his voice even as he said, "Tell me about yesterday."

"You were there," Jorge said sullenly, and shrugged again.

A tiny strand of temper snapped. "Don't make me dig for this." Dale straightened from the casual posture he'd worked so hard to maintain, knowing he'd only tower over the kid.

Sometimes towering was a good thing. "There are a whole lot of ways this could go right now, and losing your job isn't the worst of them. You're a smart guy, smart enough to get along with Dru. You know I saw you with the kids who Maced me yesterday. Me, and Laura Nakai, and *my dog*. You might not like me and I don't know how you get along with Laura, but anyone who didn't stop what happened to Sully yesterday doesn't deserve to work with dogs."

Jorge's mouth dropped open; true indignation crossed his features. "I didn't have nothing to do with that! I would never— not a *dog!*"

Dale's darkly humorous inner voice noted that Jorge didn't have any trouble with Macing Dale. Then again, he couldn't have known that Dale's lungs still burned…that he'd slept with Big Blue by the bed. "But you knew about it."

"No, man!" Jorge offered up a series of emphatic gestures.

Dale waited him out, waited for his attention, and then raised an eyebrow. That's all. *No more games, Jorge.*

Jorge's mouth tightened down. He palpably refused to look at Dale. "I don't wanna lose this job."

"I didn't want to get Maced." Dale gave him a moment to think about it. "Losing the job isn't in question, Jorge. This is about whether or not you can *save* it."

"You don't run this clinic." This from under lowered lashes…a testing volley.

Dale shrugged. "I can make it happen. My friend Deputy Rena Wells can do more than that."

Jorge mouthed a foul Spanish word he probably hoped Dale hadn't learned yet, then another. Finally, looking as cornered as anyone facing a firing squad, he let out a burst of words. "I know 'em, yeah. Who did it. We came by yesterday so I could get my paycheck, right? And yeah, we watched the reporter a while. But we were on our way *out,* man, just minding our own business, and this white dude turns to us and offers fifty bucks if we hang around and deliver his message…some garbage about watching you. He had the Mace and everything. I said no way, man. This is where I *work.* But they did it anyway. Not me." He lifted his gaze without lifting his chin and said, "I can't believe you're making me rat on my friends."

Dale shook his head, tightly. "I haven't asked for names yet." He might, but for now he had another shock to absorb. *It wasn't just a stupid prank. The phone calls…*

And still, the question was *why.*

Dale took a sharp, sudden breath, bringing himself back to Jorge. "Your so-called friends almost cost you your job. You might want to think about that."

"Almost?" Jorge's sudden hope was as palpable as his sullen avoidance tactics. "I need this job, Dr. Kinsall, I need it bad—"

Dale made a sharp gesture. "You might not have been in that truck, but you could have warned me. *You could have stopped it.* So what you *need* doesn't matter right now. What Dru needs does. And she doesn't need to break in new kennel help during the busy season." He took a step closer to Jorge. Towering. Looming. Mad. "Let's be clear on this, Jorge. This is me talking, not kindly Mr. Dr. Dale. Me, the guy who spent all day yesterday worrying about my dog. If I hear there's more to this, you'll be gone so fast the kibble will spin behind you. And Deputy Wells will have a little chat with you when I'm done."

Jorge swallowed. Old enough to act the part of a man, young enough so he was still only acting. "I hear you, man."

Dale stepped back. "Good. Now... I've got surgery. And I've got to take a moment to put on the kindly Dr. Dale face again. So I'm leaving—but don't mistake this as being off the hook. The hook is in deep. Way deep. You got that, right?"

Jorge nodded. Vigorously. And he let Dale reach the doorway before he said, most hesitantly, "The little dog…he's okay then?"

Dale should have relented. He should have given the kid a break. And then Sully's heartrending cries rang in his memory and he kept right on walking.

I'VE GOT TO WARN LAURA. She needed to know she might be tainted by association, that somehow the astonishing circumstances of Dale's arrival had mutated into threats…that the clinic vandalism hadn't been the least bit coincidental.

All the same, he didn't expect to look up at the end of the day and find her standing in his office. He especially hadn't expected to pop his head free of the scrub top he'd been changing out of and find her standing there.

He thought she was amused. It was hard to tell. He tugged vainly at the scrub shirt; his wrists were tangled at the sleeves. "Hey," he said, desperately trying for Joe Cool. Hadn't he just done this scene after the Macing the day before?

"Hey," she said, every bit as casual as he tried for as she dropped her hand to receive Sully's wagging assault, fending him off with expert gentleness. Sully snuck in a quick, neat kiss and bopped off to tend to beagle business, nose in the air. Laura said, "I think Sheri set me up. She had to have known…" She nodded at his shirt.

One hand popped free; he jerked the shirt away from the other. "Oh," he said, "I think Sheri set *me* up." He stuffed the shirt into his backpack and grabbed an L.L.Bean short-sleeved pullover he'd bought specifically because it was the same color as the soft Flagstaff dirt that clung to Sully's paws.

"I'll have to thank her," Laura said, as usual so deadpan he couldn't quite tell if she was serious and he stopped to do an expression check.

Okay. That was a smile.

He grinned back, tunneled into the shirt, and said from beneath the material, "I don't think I'll mention it to her. That should drive her nuts."

Laura didn't wait for him to reemerge. "Where'd Sully go?"

"Right here." Dale waved vaguely, popped his head through the shirt, and discovered no beagle within sight. *Fine time for a walkabout.* He tugged the shirt down into place, momentarily distant from Laura. Ah, yes. He held up a finger to excuse himself and walked swiftly down the hall to linen storage, the door to which wasn't quite latched. He pulled it open, found Sully rubbing a shoulder on a discarded scrub shirt in the dirty laundry nook on the floor, and scooped him up without comment, letting him dangle noodlishly from one hand snugged up against Dale's side as he returned to the office. "Did I mention he has a hair fetish?"

Sully beat his tail against the side of Dale's leg. *laura!*

"Not yet." Laura looked more bemused than anything. "How did you—" But she stopped, closed her mouth, and made an obvious determination not to go there. To stick to the matter at hand. "I called Sheri earlier today, actually. I wanted to get here when you were through for the day but not gone. We have to talk."

Dale put Sully down on his bed. "I'm not sure I like the sound of that." Not after the way he'd started the day.

"No. I'm afraid you won't." She hesitated, looking over her shoulder. Though there wasn't anything specific in her expression, Dale suddenly realized she was uncomfortable here. *Hogue.* Of course. The man's car was still parked at the side of the building; he was up in his office, packing away selected items in preparation for his retirement.

"Come to my place." He hadn't thought it through, just said it. Thinking it through made him realize there was nothing worth mentioning in the fridge but the other half of the trail sausage. "I have beer," he added, and then thought that through and groaned and rubbed a hand over his eyes and said, "I mean...we do need to talk. We can go for a walk. Or whatever." *God, this just gets worse.*

She said, so solemnly, "*Whatever* is just fine. I'll follow you out."

The back door. Definitely the back door.

Let Sheri wonder.

TWELVE

"YOU COULD HAVE CALLED," Dale realized out loud. Their walk on this dirt road near his house—*primitive road,* the sign warned—had been silent thus far, with Sully obediently at heel and the surrounding pine forests beckoning but forbidden. Rather than beer, they were equipped with sports bottles and water. The dying wind of the day teased dark hair loose from Laura's ponytail and left it to move whimsically around her face. To the north, the sun just barely slipped down beneath the notch where the peaks of Elden and Humphreys overlapped, and the sky started its slow fade from intense turquoise to star-studded indigo.

"I didn't think it was a phone-call kind of discussion," she said, futilely tucking an errant strand behind her ear. "I wanted to be able to see your face."

Dale winced. "You've figured it out already?"

"That you're no poker player? I'm afraid so."

"Then," Dale declared, "I can only hope for darkness to fall quickly." He tugged Sully back to heel as a foolish prairie dog shot up from its hole within whisker reach and then ducked away again.

poop.

Dale gave him a Look. "We don't need any more adventure right now, thank you."

Laura bent to pet Sully, who gave her his most martyred look, begging for rescue. "Responding to another collection of subliminal impressions?"

"I—what?" Oh yes. It had seemed like a glib line at the time. He cleared his throat of the cough lurking there and said, "Something like that," which meant precisely nothing but eased the conversation along. "Listen…about why I was going to call you…" Any excuse, that's why. Or at least this time he wished it were so, as he dragged the reluctant words along. "I've been getting calls lately. Not nice ones. I haven't been able to figure it out. Someone's been pissed at me since I found Mr. Corcoran, but I really don't know why. Last night I got another…and I'm almost certain it's related to the Macing. And that Macing was no coincidence. Someone paid those boys to do it. So I'm sorry…but it looks like you got caught up in something that was meant for me."

She listened in silence, as was her way; suddenly his throat was way too dry and he coughed sharply, lifting the sports bottle to squirt water exactly the wrong way down his throat. Still the cough. The climate had helped not at all.

Laura waited until the choking had subsided to the occasional irrepressible cough. "It won't get better unless you take it seriously."

Dale gave a sodden bark of laughter. "Good God, you can read my mind, too."

"No, just a collection of supraliminal impressions." And she said it with a straight face, too, leaving Dale awash in admiration, at least until he returned to the meaning of her words, the worry about his health.

"You and Cily," he sighed, and stopped to gaze at the volcanic mountain skyline as he worked his throat to squelch a lingering cough.

"She must care about you."

"She does, or she'd have given up by now." He looked down at her. "It's not a big deal. The coughing. It's just leftover from yesterday."

"Maybe you should respect it."

"I—" he started, and then stopped. No, of course he hadn't listened to his body's little signs of trouble. He'd come into work with burning lungs—lungs that had every right to protest after the previous day's assault. He'd done his surgeries, and he hadn't taken the extra midday inhaler dose his prescription allowed during times of stress. And then he'd come out here on this walk and Laura had quite perceptively recognized the persistent little cough as a warning.

Well, damn it, what was he supposed to do? He hadn't been about to leave the clinic on its own after a phone call like the one he'd received, never mind canceling all those surgeries. And why hadn't Laura reacted more to his news instead of to his remarkable ability to swallow water the wrong way down?

And damn it even more, why did she have to be right. He didn't even have Big Blue II on him, as much as he'd sworn to himself that he'd be prepared from now on.

He realized he still stood at the edge of the dirt road, the woods beside him and the Peaks in front of him and Sully sitting on his foot. And that she'd given him all the time he needed to think his thoughts through. She shifted and said, "I got a phone call last night, too."

"You *what?*" Under the circumstances, it was coherent enough. He understood the implications quickly enough. *More than just the clinic, now.* "Damn it, I'm sorry—"

She held up a hand; he wanted to put his own up to spread against it and didn't. "No," she said, "I'm not sure that's it. It wasn't just about you—or about my choice to spend time with you."

Oh. *My choice to spend time with you.* He liked the sound of that. Sully's tail beat against his ankle. "What did the guy say to you?"

"Guy?" She paused, giving him a curious look. "This was a woman. She said I should watch my step, that I'm making some bad choices."

"Sounds familiar. Except…"

"Your caller is a man?"

"Every time," Dale agreed. By unspoken accord, they turned around, walking a little more slowly now. Not far from here, the third victim had just been killed.

Laura tipped her head against the wind to free the hair that had caught at the corner of her lashes. "Has he ever said enough so you understand just what the problem is? What he wants you to stop doing?"

"No," Dale admitted. "I think…he thinks it's obvious. He clearly thinks I'm an idiot. And I have the feeling—" he hesitated. But she looked at him, slowing her pace even further, and he sighed. "I have the feeling that I disappointed him somehow. That he thought I was better than…than whatever it is I'm doing. I know that doesn't make sense—"

Her shrug was enough to interrupt him. "Maybe it'll make sense when we have more information," Laura said, though she still watched him as they walked, closely enough to make him wary of her next words. "Have you talked to the police about any of this?"

Dale couldn't help it, he snorted. "I've never found the police to be much interested in little portents of warning," he said. "A nice big domestic dispute, that's something they respond to. Or blood splashed around. But phone calls and *feelings*…not their best thing."

"I see." But she nodded as she said it and he suddenly realized he wasn't going to have to explain—that she'd put two and two together and knew he'd had no luck staving off the Ohio fire. At the same time, she wasn't the sort to roll over that easily…and she didn't. "You might call Rena Wells."

Dale made a scrunchy face. "Is there anything Sheri *hasn't* told you?"

"I don't know. I guess we'd have to compare notes." But Laura ducked her head for a brief smile. "Still. You might."

"That's easy for you to say," Dale muttered, thinking of the interest in Rena's eyes and thinking that he liked her well enough but… Just *but*.

"But you'll do it." Not a nag, not an order…just quiet concern.

"Yes." Sigh. "I'll call her."

Sully pulled his ears up to frame his face, an alto growl vibrating in his throat. *fierceness.*

Dale glanced down the side road they passed to discover the distant form of a cyclist exiting the path that led to the dry, shallow caves pocketing the side of the cinder hill that rose from this part of the forest and took the trees with it. Someone out in the forest in spite of the restrictions. Of course. "You tell him, Sullydog."

The cyclist turned away from them and Sully relaxed, confident he'd done his part to protect them. Laura looked on with a faint sadness, then turned her face away.

Dale distracted himself into other thoughts…though they typically didn't keep to themselves. "Three times we've walked together," he said. "And three times we've talked about me. You know my dog. You know where I live. You know I'm in denial about my asthma. You know why it came back. Do I have to go on, or have I made my point?"

She gave him that look, the one where he couldn't tell if she was angry or simply thoughtful or even very quietly amused. Or maybe…just being. She said, "Kachina Village. One small cat who likes to sleep in my shoes. Grew up in Tuba City, went to school here. Almost moved to New Mexico once, but that…didn't work out. And my Navajo rug collection rocks."

"Are you—?" he asked, not sure if it was a rudeness.

But Laura seemed capable of taking anything in the spirit in which it was given. "Half. My mother was Spanish. I speak both languages."

"Are they still here?"

This time she looked away, and after some moments she said, "My father's people don't like to speak of those who have passed."

Dale felt an absurd relief. She wouldn't ask him about his parents. She wouldn't want him to talk about that first fire—so many years ago, and yet the thing that had somehow shaped his whole life. And he suddenly realized how uncomfortable it must have been for Laura, any discussion of George Corcoran.

There'd been plenty of that.

"The Navajo are matrilinear," she offered, changing the subject without skipping away from it completely. "I could have been more a part of that community, but I guess I never quite felt part of it." This, he knew, was personal—more personal than formulaic answers about siblings and childhood pets. "My own fault…perhaps a reflection of the way my mother felt. But the Diné are an inclusive people. Family is everything. In the end I guess it was my choice to stand apart."

"Could you change that?" he asked, taken with an unaccountable desire to heal a breach that obviously disturbed her. "If you wanted to?"

"I expect so." But she didn't offer anything else.

He didn't push. He also squelched a terrible joke that would compare her rug collection with etchings, scraping up the rare wisdom to keep his mouth shut. Left to silence, broken only by the intrusive remnants of his cough, his thoughts slipped right back to where they'd started. The phone calls. The vandalism. The way it had all started when he'd found that body. First the clinic under threat, now Sully and even Laura.

He'd talk to Rena Wells, all right. But he'd also talk to Glory Heissman.

NO SECOND THOUGHTS NOW. He might not learn anything here, in George Corcoran's neighborhood, days after determining to return. Or he might at that. Either way, he had to try. To see if there was any hint of a connection between George Corcoran's death and the events at the clinic.

There was a *For Sale* sign in front of Corcoran's house. The yard no longer had its impeccable demeanor. The grass had browned and the windows failed to sparkle; the front edge of the property held a profound number of small, mummified dog droppings. A piece of yellow crime scene tape fluttered from the edge of the house, fraying in the intense spring winds and snapping hard enough to crack if Dale had been able to hear it above the bluster in his ears. He'd given up on the baseball cap he'd been wearing to shade his eyes from the sun and stuffed it into his back pocket where it wouldn't get blown away.

But he was still riding the high of virtue—he'd remembered his midday inhaler before leaving on this lunchtime walk, and he had a peanut butter and honey sandwich in his stomach and a water bottle in his hand. Sully's leash looped around his other wrist, a lazy man's hold, and Sully squinted into the wind as his ears flapped out. Every now and then he glanced up at Dale.

poopy wind.

"They say it gets better about the time we hit summer," Dale told him. "But that's about when the monsoon starts up."

Squint. *don't hear you.*

George Corcoran's yard wasn't the only one to bear signs of intrusion. Several houses down on a sparser lawn of native

grasses, a stooped older man bent even further as he worked
with a dog scoop arrangement of rake and pan. Sully started
wagging a whole yard away, and the man straightened, more
or less, as he spotted the greeting. His own wasn't quite as wel-
coming. "I hope you're going to pick up after him."

Dale tugged a neon blue corner of thin plastic bag from his
jeans watch pocket, the fold of a commercial product for just
that purpose, and the man nodded. "Okay, then. I like beagles.
Good honest dog. Used to have one myself."

Dale didn't hesitate to go for the opening. "What kind of dog
do you have now?"

The man straightened even more in surprise, though it didn't
last. His spine subsided back to its hunch as he said, "Don't
have a dog. Wouldn't be fair, a yard this small." He gestured
at his backyard and the chain link fence. "A dog should have
room to run, I always say." He caught on to Dale's puzzled look
at his scooping tools and said, "Ah. No, I got this because of
that damned woman down the street."

Dale made a not-so-wild guess. "Glory Heissman?"

The man gave a juicy snort, then had to clear his lungs. "Of
course, Glory Heissman. Is there anyone else in this neighborhood who runs around with fuzzy rats on leashes?" He cocked
his head to look up at Dale. "But you're not from around here.
How'd you—oh. You're that vet fellow, aren't you? Front page
of the paper yesterday morning, everybody's darling. Found old
George, did you?"

Dale pointed a thumb at Sully, who stood with tail solemnly
wagging, quite sure the conversation was about him. "He did.
I batted cleanup."

"And you're back because…?"

A shrug hid Dale's uncertain manner. How did one interro-
gate an elderly man about his neighbor's death without being
overt? There was no point in making waves, not when Hogue

wanted him out of the news and some unknown caller who'd suddenly become two callers, male and female...

Well, who knew what he and she wanted. That had been the problem from the start.

But Dale suddenly found it easy enough to say, "Lunch time walk. Pretty much what got us into trouble in the first place."

This seemed to make sense enough, for the man only nodded. "I used to walk around this whole area," he said. "Then my knee got too bad. Now this is my exercise...every few days I come out and clean up this dog crap. Sad state of affairs."

"Mr. Corcoran's house went up for sale pretty quickly." Wow. Very smooth. Nancy Drew in jeans and testosterone.

But the man didn't seem to notice, not when he was so ready to expostulate on George Corcoran's part. "And he'd be damned sorry if he could see how that son of his has let it go. Stupid young man, Aaron is—never had any use for his father when he was alive. Except for George's money, of course. George had finally cut him off and now look what happened—that jackass has it all anyway." He peered up at Dale. "Pardon my blunt speaking," he said. "It just twists my knickers to see the place like that. George was a damn sight more fastidious with that lawn than made good sense, but it was a harmless quirk. He didn't drink overmuch, didn't make any kind of ruckus, and was a fine fellow to everyone but that Heissman woman—and she deserved every curse he threw at her." He gave a small chunk of mummified poop a sullen kick with his toe. "I should have gone before George. Hell, *Aaron* should have gone before George. Some things just aren't right."

Dale had plenty of reason to agree. And not much more time if he was going to get a look at Glory's place before he had to turn back and head for the clinic. He said as much, inserting "walk further" for "Glory's place," and the old man left him with a warning. "Watch yourself if you head down much further. That woman forgets to close her gate sometimes. Or so she says. *I* think she does it on purpose."

"Thanks." Dale let Sully linger so the old man could tweak his ears and Sully, much satisfied, was then happy to go trotting down the street slightly ahead of Dale, his tail set to *cocky* and a bounce in his gait.

Glory's home was evident upon approach. Aside from the truck and its gingham-lettered camper shell in the driveway, there were the short sections of fake picket fence before the dried-up flowerbeds in front of the house. And the requisite little old lady bending over with her petticoats showing. And off at the corner, an incongruous, miniature dog sled. And even as Dale pondered the existence of George's son Aaron, the gaggle of little dogs in the barely visible backyard spotted Sully and threw themselves at the chain link in a veritable frenzy of offence. Sully froze in surprise and then gave an abrupt and puzzled bawl.

Dale contrived to drop the leash. *It got me into this; it can help get me out of it.* Sully looked back in disbelief. "Now you hesitate?" Dale made sure no one peered from the house windows and wiggled his fingers in a *go on* gesture. "Go. Stir up a fuss. I'm right behind you."

Sully, doggy partner in mayhem, needed no second urging. He bounded away at top speed, tail flagging. Dale immediate trotted after him, hoping his expression captured the appropriate annoyed and embarrassed demeanor. He'd certainly had a lot of practice with that one lately.

By the time he reached the fence, Sully had added his frustrated bawl to the sharp barking of the little dogs; he pressed his nose through the chain link and then jerked back in wounded surprise when tiny little teeth closed on it, leaving bright red needle scrapes. *mean!*

"Let's not take this too far," Dale told him, capturing the leash. He took the dog's face in his hands, rubbed a thumb across the scratches, and deposited an unmanly kiss between Sully's eyes. "There. You're fine."

This, of course, was the moment that Glory Heissman descended. She came marching out the back of the house with a purpose Dale couldn't blame, and he pre-empted her harassed demand as to his presence there by standing and smiling and saying over the ruckus of the dogs, "Hi. I'm sorry. He got away from me when he saw your dogs. Just wanted to say hello, I guess."

Her eyes narrowed. She looked him head to toe and back again and then her eyes narrowed more. "You're the new vet." She turned to the little creatures ponging off her calves and knees and the fence in front of her and notched her voice up to an impressive level. "SHUT UP!"

Amazingly, they did. Not without resentment, cat-like stares that promised sullen behavior in the immediate future, but the noise cut off like a faucet.

Not an inappropriate image.

Glory repeated, "You're the vet. The new one at Foothills. I saw you in the paper yesterday."

"I had no idea they'd put that story on the front page."

"Don't let it go to your head," she said, a little more acerbically than seemed polite. "Earlier this spring the front page story was about a family who keeps a skunk as a pet."

"Ah." Dale nodded. "That certainly puts things in perspective."

"What are you doing here?"

No beating around the bush for this woman. "Walking," Dale said, ignoring the sharpness of her tone. Or rather, pretending to ignore. "He's a good office dog. In return, he gets lunch walks. We try to vary the scenery. That's why we were here the first time."

She made a little face, a visual haughty sniff. "That's right. That's when you found Corcoran, then."

He winced. "I'm afraid so. Not one of our better days. Worse for Mr. Corcoran, I expect."

"Don't go wasting any sympathy on that forty-something goat," she snorted. Sully gave her a puzzled look and sat on Dale's foot, his *protect-my-dale* posture. "No one here is sorry to see him go."

Dale couldn't help but raise an eyebrow.

"Oh, don't look at me like that. Of course I didn't want him dead, but I didn't want him here, either. He was rude to me every chance he got."

Imagine that.

"Fuss, fuss, fuss. He even made trouble for me after he was killed—can you *believe* the police came to talk to me?"

"That…" Dale hunted furiously for noncommittal words. "That must have been difficult."

"Now they're talking to his son." Her voice took on a smug tone. "As they should. It's always a family member, you know."

"Is it?" Dale asked blankly, caught off guard by her attitude more than her words. Of course the police were looking at the son—bad blood between them, money involved, easy access…he couldn't help but wonder if considering Aaron Corcoran a suspect had distracted them from the bigger picture. *Talk to Rena…*

She might not talk back, of course. At least, not about official police business.

"Of course," Glory had been saying. "And if Corcoran was a pain in the ass, that son of his is ten times worse. I'm glad he's not keeping the house."

"Actually," Dale said, beginning to realize he was completely outmatched by Powerhouse Glory, "I'm surprised you didn't find him first. All the paw prints around the body…they were the right size for your…your…" he couldn't quite make himself say it.

"Toy Huskies," Glory declared. "And I wasn't outside that afternoon. In fact, I had a sick headache, and I accidentally left the gate open. They had quite an adventure that day, I'm sure! Poor Nanookita came back with a terrible cut on his foot."

Which she hadn't had treated for days. Poor Nanookita indeed.

"I told the police that," she added. "But they wanted to hear it over and over. And had anyone spoken to me on the phone during that time, or been in the house with me? How stupid can you get? When you've got a sick headache, you don't answer the phone. Besides, you'd think they'd have better things to think about. Fire season is on top of us and there are *still* people going into the woods." She aimed a sly look at him. "You were in the woods, in that newspaper photograph."

"That was private property," Dale lied blandly, finding something of a poker face after all.

She narrowed her eyes at him and he'd suddenly had enough of her. He'd gotten what he'd come for, more or less—to get a better idea of who she was. To get a feel of whether she was the kind of person who'd kill and then calmly cover her tracks, even if she hadn't covered the tracks of her dogs. *An open gate.* Hard to disprove that one…there was only the question of why she waited so long to have the injured dog treated.

Maybe she was scared. She'd known the dogs had been out; she had to have heard about the broken glass.

Except Dale doubted this woman was truly scared of anyone. She'd probably spoken to the police just like she spoke to everyone else. And though there'd been bad blood between Glory and George, aside from her own pain-in-the-ass nature, what motive did she have for killing the other two? What motive for hassling Dale?

But he looked back at her narrowed eyes and knew he wouldn't want his own life to depend on this woman's good heart. Knew it the same way he sometimes glanced at a dog and diagnosed it...and then had to perform the tests to prove it.

The police weren't assuming the murders were related either. They were questioning Aaron Corcoran. Maybe whoever killed George was simply...inspired by the bizarre nature of the first killing. They certainly didn't have any details in common.

At least not that the police had released.

Talk to Rena.

It would be better than going around in circles in his head.

It would be *much* better than standing in front of this woman, a mean and scheming woman hidden in a cloaking device of country cute.

Dale scrubbed Sully's ears, gave Glory an unconvincing smile, and apologized again for causing the doggy uproar. The dogs stalked back and forth behind her in stiff-legged outrage, their continued silence proving she was quite capable of controlling their behavior when she chose to. And Sully, confused by the silent undercurrent of distrust running between the humans, trotted at Dale's heels in a most subdued manner as they headed back to the clinic.

THIRTEEN

HE'D ALMOST FORGOTTEN the Environmental Fair. For all he owed it to Laura, he almost forgot it anyway.

A day of working side-by-side, vaccinating dogs and cats in the little C-class RV provided by the third vet, narrowly avoiding each other's elbows and feet and the bump of hip and knee…an intimate little dance made somewhat awkward by Dale's inability to stand up straight in the trailer.

Midway through the afternoon, he walked out of the RV and stood up straight—truly straight—for the first time in way too long, his hands kneading at the small of his back as he breathed deeply of the fresh air. The fair had caught some luck with the weather—the wind offered up the random blustery moment but was otherwise less frenetic than in recent days. In front of the RV, a white paper tablecloth remained secured to a card table by I-mean-business bungee cords, and the paperwork piles sat under rocks big enough to make the table sag. The fairgrounds activity area was lined with shade shelters—canopies flapping, corners weighed down with sandbags and water jugs and staked to boot.

The people here were used to preparing for the worst when it came to seasonal wind.

Laura arrived at his side, offering an uncharacteristic stretch. "What do you think?"

"Of the fair?" Dale crouched by the side of the RV, where Sully's portable fabric crate sat snugged out of the way and

Sully curled up with his latest favorite blanket, a bandana he'd snagged from Dale, and a no-spill water dish. Unfazed by the surrounding chaos, he slept deeply, and only blinked sleepily when Dale unzipped the crate door.

"Of the fair," Laura confirmed.

Dale slipped Sully's collar over his head and coaxed him out of the crate, staggering and yawning. "Gray water reclamation, solar heat, wood stoves, forest thinning…they're all here. But I think the beef barbecue is the biggest draw, if you want to know the truth." Sully gave the card table leg an inquisitive eye and Dale said, "Excuse me, but I've told everyone you're civilized," and drew him around the backside of the trailer.

Upon return he spotted a familiar lanky figure across the broad grassy aisle between the rows of shelters. Rena Wells wore a heather gray T-shirt with SECURITY printed on the front in block letters and black jeans, and Sully wagged his tail at the scent of her.

know her.

Not well, but he knew her indeed. "Rena!" Dale called, and then realized she was already on her way over. A rising murmur of conversation behind him as the volunteer receptionist instructed a dog owner on filling out the rabies forms inspired Dale to head out and meet her in the middle of the grassy area. Some of this conversation, he didn't want overheard—not even if he didn't learn anything. Just asking the questions would be enough to set Dr. Hogue off. Or perhaps his nameless watchers, considering he still had no idea why he'd ruffled their feathers.

"Hi," Rena said, her eyes a little more alight than Dale had expected. "I didn't know you'd be here. Nice shiner."

"Neither did I," Dale said. "I mean…know that you'd be here. I knew I'd be here. And it's almost gone."

"Huh," Rena said, mock thoughtfulness on her brow but that

light still in her eyes. "At Corcoran's house, I thought maybe it was just the shock. But it's not. You just talk that way."

"More's the pity, I think that way too," Dale said, mournful enough. "Laura thought this would be a good way to introduce me to the community. I think she was just rounding up help, but it worked." Because she'd had to work so hard to talk him into it. Uh huh. But he grew more serious and said, "You know…that thing with Mr. Corcoran…does it bother you…?"

"That someone's dead?" She looked startled. "Of course it bothers me. I wouldn't wear the uniform if it didn't."

Dale shifted uncomfortably. "I mean, *really* bother you."

"Ohh," she said, sudden understanding crossing her face. "As in 'thinking about it too much' bothering you?"

"Yeah," Dale said. "Like that. I keep seeing that moment I turned him over—"

And it was true. It was all true. Just like he kept reliving the sound of Sully's cries, and older but still vivid images from the clinic fire. From the house fire. George Corcoran, rolling over and gurgling in the dry desert air of a Flagstaff spring.

But he wouldn't have mentioned it to Rena if he wasn't heading for territory he probably shouldn't be exploring at all.

"Maybe you should talk to someone." Her spare features softened with concern. "I can probably get a recommendation from the department shrink, if you don't know anyone around here yet."

He didn't want to tackle that train of thought. Maybe something in him recognized the rightness of what she said…that he'd piled up enough events in his life to let them drive him. It could be time to let go.

And what? Stop caring? Not a chance. Dale said, "I haven't seen anything in the news about it lately. I wondered if you knew anything."

Reluctant and short, she shook her head. "Nothing I can tell you," she said. "Just that it's still in active investigation, along with the—" and she stopped short, self-annoyance on her face. "Don't take that wrong," she told him, responding to the tilt of his head. "No one's sure the three…*events*…are actually related. They don't have anything in common. But we don't know that they aren't, either. It's not a good time to make assumptions."

Until now he'd only been guessing on that last—that they weren't certain if the murders were related. There'd been the chance that the police had been holding back some crucial piece of information, something only the murderer would know. They probably still were…but nothing, apparently, that clearly tied the killings together.

The question was, were they tied to the clinic? Were they tied to Dale? He considered telling Rena about the injured Nanookita but instead blurted, "Do you know if anyone connected to any of the murders is being harassed?"

Rena stiffened; her face turned into a cop face. Alert. Not giving anything away, not now. "Connected? Connected how?"

And because it felt too silly to say out loud, Dale hesitated.

Rena didn't. "You? What's going on?" Her gaze narrowed to his fading black eye. "Talk to me, Dale." Pure cop.

And looking at her, Dale was abruptly sorry to have mentioned it. The past turned loose a swamp of emotions—futility foremost. He tried to remember her as she'd been at the murder scene— showing a balance of procedure and concern. "It's just—"

"Dale!" Everyone at the fair suddenly swooped down upon him.

Upon second glance, it was only Sheri, her son, and her mother. They were enough. "Dr. Dale!" Sheri said. "This is my mom, but don't you go getting any ideas. You're too young for her. Did you hear about Jorge?"

Dale swallowed his surprise. Sheri, he had learned, would always manage to surprise him. Or embarrass him. Or, if she had her way, possibly both at once. He greeted Sheri's mother, a woman who had clearly taught Sheri how to dress. Sheri wore purple calf-length slacks and her mother's were screaming lime; Sheri's African print shirt bounced off her mother's giant floral motif. Together they might as well have been sisters— robust, giant smiles, elaborately coiffed and patterned hair…and wicked eyes.

Dale felt like running.

Rena did pretty much just that. "Later," she told Dale. "I mean it." But she left him to his fate readily enough.

Between them, Sheri's young son dressed somberly in navy blue. He looked resigned. But he and Sully embraced each other like long-lost friends, leaving Dale trapped in a conversation that bounced between Sheri and her mother so quickly that Dale could do nothing but breathe. Just *breathing* gave him the chance to realize that several days of attentiveness had made a difference. Not a bit of tightness in his chest. *What about Jorge?*

"Isn't that right?" Sheri asked him, snatching his attention back like a kid caught daydreaming in school. Fortunately Sheri's mother immediately filled in the gap.

"And is it true you have a stray living in the walls of that place?" she demanded. "I think Sheri should get hazard pay."

Dale shifted uneasily. "He's never actually bitten anyone." He gave Sheri a meaningful look. "I thought we'd just keep that one under wraps."

"Sure," Sheri agreed. "But I had to tell my mom. And she's got to tell her friends, of course. Tremayne, honey, don't lick the dog's face."

"He licked *me*," the young boy said, most reasonably. "Why can't I lick him?"

"You'll get a hairball," Sheri told him. "You'll get a hairball and you'll hack it up just like a cat—"

"*Well,* Mr. Dr. Dale, aren't you looking fine today," Dru said, joining the discussion with her usual hurricane force. She, too, had a child in tow, no more than a toddler. Someone had stuck a small, square "Waste-Not, Water-Not" bumper sticker to the back of the child's shirt, and someone else had given up on obvious efforts to remove it. "No paw prints, no bloodstains, no unusual hairstyles, no unseemly ruckus. How'd you manage that? You hear about Jorge?"

"You know," Dale said to the air over all their heads, "I used to have *quiet* days. Not a lot of them, but every now and then…" He took a deep breath and said brightly, "What about Jorge?"

"*Tsk!*" Sheri said, and Dru snorted dismissively.

"He got caught," Tremayne announced loudly, removing his face from Sully's ear for a brief moment.

Dale sent a startled glance at Dru, who nodded. "Fool child got caught wrecking other people's yards," she said. "Slashing hoses, trashing landscaping…damn, I'm gonna have to break in new help. And who's gonna help me till we find someone?"

Slashing hoses?

The hubbub of the fair receded for a strange instant, as Dale absorbed all the implications. Yard vandalism…slashed hoses. How much more entertaining to weld a faucet? And if Jorge had lied about that…had he lied about the Macing? About the man who supposedly paid his friends to do it?

Whatever Dale thought he'd known about the events bedeviling the clinic, he could no longer be certain of any of it. Jorge had lied, and Dale had believed him. Whatever he'd learned—from Glory, or Rena, from George Corcoran's cranky old neighbor— there was no telling what had been fact, what had been implication, what had been wishful thinking…and what had been lies. All he knew for sure was what he'd seen with his own eyes.

He'd best stick with animals. They never lied to him—or if they did, he always knew.

And suddenly Laura was beside him, arriving so quietly that the others barely noticed. Dale looked down, pulling himself out of his reeling thoughts, and gave her a feeble smile in response to her questioning look. She didn't buy it, but she nodded back to the RV anyway. Several people in bright turquoise shirts waited, watching them while pretending not to. Each had a dog in hand, a mixed crew of basset and Bernese Mountain Dog and Pembroke Welsh Corgi and All-American. The dogs wore matching turquoise bandanas, and unlike most of the animals congregating around the rabies clinic, they sat quietly, looking amused at the commotion. "The local kennel club always does a breed parade at these things—it's part of their educational outreach. At the end they'll give a little talk, but you don't have to do that part."

"I don't?" he said, startled. "What part *am* I doing?"

She scruffled Sully's ears. "The breed parade, if you want to. It's very informal. You won't be the only one they've picked up here on the grounds—remember the wolfhound from this morning? He'll be there, too. And I think a sheltie. But they don't have any other beagles."

"So they asked you to ask me?"

"I think," Laura said, quite solemnly and not at all affected by the lively discussion between Sheri and Dru in regard to the stowaway terrier, "your recent notoriety has intimidated them."

"If they ask about my eye," Dale muttered, "I'm going to tell them I got it in a biker bar. Starting a fight. Yep, I went into a biker bar and started dissing Harleys. That's how intimidating I am. And I'll do the parade if you come with me."

"The clinic—"

"—hours were over fifteen minutes ago." Dale stuck out his elbow in invitation. "Take it or leave it."

She looked more taken aback than he expected, and he realized that she wasn't used to diving in. That she lived her life on the fringes, watching the parades and not joining them. He nodded at his arm and after the barest moment, she slipped her hand through the crook of his elbow. Answer enough.

The parade, Dale quickly gathered, was calculated to attract attention, drawing people down to the end of the booth row where the kennel club drill team members would pull away to present a quick performance before those who wanted to stepped up to a microphone to discuss the physical character- istics and personality traits of their breeds. The group as a whole welcomed him with cheer, much surreptitious gazing, a little too much giggling among the women, and the air of having accomplished something.

Dale simply took pleasure from the gentle feel of Laura's hand on his arm, and would have been up for making another circuit of the booths just to keep it there—except near the end of the parade he nearly brought the whole thing to a crashing halt when they reached the Waste-Not Water-Not booth. Win-Win. Sure.

Because there was the man who'd accosted him about sluicing off the sidewalk on the wrong water day. And there was the woman from the reception who'd found his green eyes to be worthy of such discussion. Marcia Roth.

They saw Dale the very moment he saw them, and turned upon him such expressions of intensity, of inspection, that he lost his step. If not for Laura, who smoothly steered him out of the parade to stand at the sales booth for composting toilets, there would have been a doggy pileup.

Dale spared a startled glance at the half-size composting outhouse model, just enough to make sure he didn't knock it over. Laura, her hand slipping away from his arm, nonetheless leaned closer to say softly, "You certainly got their attention."

"And they've got mine." He had no idea they knew each other, that the flirtatious Marcia had any association with the biker. Dale thought about walking right on by…but no. Spotted, fair and square. That's what he got for putting his unmistakably tall self into a parade of any sort, especially when he was being his vet self and not his hanging-out self. He put a smile on his face and went to make nice.

"A VET SHOULD HAVE a friendly dog." Marcia regarded Sully with some disapproval as the beagle lurked behind Dale's legs.

"Why?" Dale squelched his impulse to defend Sully, as surprised as he was at Sully's reticence. *He* didn't think much of Marcia's perfume…a scent hound must find it downright painful. He coughed as his lungs took a hit, then managed to step aside from being directly downwind.

To judge from the tone of the pamphlets on the table beside her, Marcia was used to making righteous pronouncements. To judge from the look on her face, she wasn't used to having them challenged. She closed her mouth abruptly, stepped back, and finally said, "Because!" And quite abruptly and visibly decided to chance the subject. "Those two poor dogs you took in…did they find good homes?"

On a hunch, Dale said, "The first two. We're still working on the third."

Her eyebrows went up high enough for Dale to suspect lingering results of plastic surgery. "Three?"

"We had another show up on the porch the other day…I thought you might have heard. You seem to know what goes on around here."

It had been blatant flattery, but Marcia accepted it, smiling prettily. "I've been busy getting ready for the fair."

Right. Pamphlets to print, small children to sticker…

Dale gave an easy shrug, finding himself oddly unconvinced. In the background, bad speakers blurted out the music for the kennel club drill team routine. "I guess we've got someone else helping out. This one's fine, though—just homeless, I gather. As soon as we—" *catch him* "—get him squared away, I'm sure we can find him a home." He picked up a pamphlet, discovered strident conservationist rhetoric, and put it back down again. "You feel strongly about the environment, I gather."

"Don't you?" Marcia said. "This area is a bundle of fragile ecosystems, and humans go stomping through every one of them as though it makes no difference at all. We're in a drought worse than that which caused the Dust Bowl years, and yet we still have to create restrictions to prevent people from washing their *driveways?*"

"Whoa," Dale said. "You don't have to convince me. It never occurred to me to wash my driveway in a desert climate." Or, half the time, even his dishes…

"No?" the bicycle man asked sharply, disbelieving.

"No." And Dale cast a sharp eye back at him, and then did an internal double take at a sudden thought. "Though I wonder how far you'd go to convince me if you thought it needed to be done." Say…with phone calls. "If you thought, for instance, that I wasn't setting a good example. Like I'm not setting a good example with my dog." For Sully hadn't yet made any of his usual friendly overtures. Maybe the Macing had affected him more than Dale originally thought. Plus, of course…the perfume. Dale had to shift again as Marcia moved herself directly upwind, laughing at his comment.

"As far as we'd go to convince anyone," she said. "Pamphlets under your windshield wiper."

In this wind? Instant litter.

The bicycle guy might have read his mind. "It's recycled paper," he said. "It breaks down pretty quickly under this sun. It's worth it, to get the word out."

Yeah, Dale thought, meeting the man's zealously bright eyes and thinking about how he'd come down off the road to accost

Dale in front of the clinic. *You'd make phone calls. You probably spend all evening making phone calls. Scolding.* He was surprised to realize the thought let relief ooze into the background of tension he'd been carrying. *Not that big a deal after all.*

In the background hubbub of noise as the drill team music faltered, Sheri's voice came through loud and clear. And her mother. Dale glanced over his shoulder, then nodded back at the family. "My receptionist," he said. "She could probably use some environmental education. I don't think she's got a single natural fiber anywhere in that outfit." And if they took him up on it, they deserved what they got...

Marcia eyed Sheri doubtfully. "I think she's beyond hope."

"Nonsense." Bicycle guy thumbed the top layer from the pamphlets, the stickers, and several educational flyers. Dale prepared to flee. A glance at Laura showed that she had followed the exchange, and that she, too, prepared to flee.

Someone would have to warn the drill team to turn their music up.

Sully was eager to trot away from the booth—only to skitter aside in surprise as Alfred Ledbetter came up from behind. "I heard that whole thing." And while Dale was still caught up in exchanging a surprised glance with Laura—*no, she hadn't seen the man coming, either*—Ledbetter barged ahead as though they'd already been in conversation. "They don't know dogs very well. If I were your beagle I wouldn't have gotten any closer to Marcia Roth, either. Not with that perfume of hers!"

Dale nodded in wary agreement. "You know her, then?"

"Of course," Ledbetter snorted. "She gets in the way of my own work. She wants me to join their group. I don't *think* so. I accomplish more on my own. You think any *group* brought those dogs in to you?"

Dale might have pointed out that a *group* paid for most of the treatment, but Ledbetter wasn't done yet. "That reminds me…that old blanket of mine—you threw it away?"

And once again, Dale felt his new poker face slide right into place. "I'm afraid so…it's too late to get it back if you've changed your mind." He didn't even know why he lied—or thought he lied, because in truth he wasn't sure—only that Ledbetter's manner felt abruptly odd. And who cared about the disposition of a gross old blanket he'd left behind along the way?

Then again, it wasn't as though anything else around here made any sense. Dale worked at a clinic where the mailman was an object of obsession; he'd moved to an area where drought-stricken residents washed their driveways. Glory Heissman bred caricature teacup versions of a breed with a working temperament, and his own once-respected boss had overlooked the skills of the very fine veterinarian beside him simply because she was a woman. Or maybe because she was a Navajo woman.

Ledbetter nodded, fading away without any further social niceties, typical enough. Dale found himself shaking his head…and found Laura watching him with an expression he didn't recognize.

She said, "I wasn't expecting that."

"What?" And then he got it. "The blanket thing? You could tell I was…well. It *might* be the truth. I'll have to check. I don't even know why I—" He stopped, made a face at himself, and finally said, "Well, I'll toss it out if I find it. Then it'll be true."

She cleared her throat. "I barely caught it. Maybe I underestimated your poker playing capabilities."

Dale shook his head, a rueful gesture. "Wouldn't worry about that. It's just…I've recently discovered I do that with people I don't particularly like. And I don't think I particularly like that."

She cocked her head, regarding him thoughtfully. "Lie to me, then."

"What?" Taken off guard, Dale turned to instant fluster. "*Lie* to you? You're kidding, right?"

She gave him one of those barely-there smiles. One of the ones that gave him a little kick in the…yeah, in the gut. "Just checking."

In return he offered her a sour glance, making her laugh outright. They moved back toward the mobile vet unit, easing away from the growing Clash of the Titans encounter between Sheri, Win-Win and the speaker system for the drill team. None of it could distract him completely from what had happened with Win-Win. "I think I was wrong."

"How so?" And she slipped her hand around his elbow of her own accord, rendering him speechless for a long, noticeable moment.

Finally he managed, "About the phone calls. And George Corcoran. And the vandalism. I thought they had to be related somehow. But any group that stickers small children is probably capable of making nasty phone calls for the cause."

"And that lump on the side of your face?"

He shrugged, careful not to dislodge her hand. "It could have been an accident. Weed whackers fling stones."

"And the Macing?"

"I've only got Jorge's word on what happened, and he's trying to save his ass. Er, I mean save his job."

"Close enough," she murmured. "He's got reason to lie. To blame it on someone else even if he wasn't actually in the truck."

"And he hasn't been happy with me from the start." Without thinking it much through, he added, "I've got a bad feeling about that biker. He probably *liked* making those calls."

"A bad feeling," Laura repeated carefully. She didn't say anything about a collection of subliminal impressions, even though the moment called for it. Dale admired her restraint. Laura Nakai, small self-contained woman of neat habits and a love for precise beauty in her rug collection; a woman of keen observation who seemed to see Dale well enough without the hunches he relied on.

Not that they always worked so well with people. Okay, with people he was generally clueless. Jorge proved that. But now and then…

He'd had a bad feeling about Ohio. He'd thought the phone calls more than just pranks; he'd tried to tell the cops. They hadn't listened—not hard enough. They'd tried to make up for it…but the arson was still unsolved. Maybe one day.

Not soon enough.

Dale realized they'd been walking in thoughtful silence a few comfortable moments, approaching the mobile vet unit to find it in the process of being broken down for travel. Sully spotted his crate where it had been moved off to the side and made straight for it, straining at the leash. *my crate.* Dale dropped the lead and let Sully pop inside to possess the crate for a few moments before folding it up and heading for the car. He was more than ready for a shower, a few good beers, and quiet time with the latest puzzle and a swing singer or two turned low. The last he'd heard of the drill team music was "It's a Small World After All," and it had started up an evil running hum in the background of his thoughts. He could only hope that Sully had been spared.

"You know," Laura said, restarting the conversation in the middle of a silence, "I'm not sure you're the kind of person who should find bodies."

Dale grabbed his backpack, looking up at her. "What's that supposed to mean?"

"Just that some people would…walk away."

"Let it go," he supplied for her, as Rena Wells had said earlier. She nodded. "Let it go. Not let it change them."

"Would that be a good thing, then? To see someone like that

and walk away unchanged in any way?" He knew he sounded defensive. He couldn't help it. Not when he'd counted on Laura to understand—counted on it more than he'd actually realized.

The glance she gave him was understanding. "That's not what I mean. Of course it changes a person. Any profound thing in our lives changes us. But we integrate those moments. We move on. How we move on might be affected by what we saw, but we still move on."

"Not my best thing," Dale said, and knew it for the truth. He'd never moved on from that first fire. He'd had to run across the country in an effort to move on from the second. And now this…

She was right. Rena Wells was right. He needed to let go and just plain have a life.

FOURTEEN

DALE SLOWED THE Forester at the dirt road turnoff, his house practically in sight. Sully's head popped up in the back seat, tipping up to sniff the cool twilight air coming in through the front vents. "Smell like home?" Dale asked him, finding the dark shape of Sully's head in the rearview mirror.

dinner.

But Dale didn't make the turn. Almost without conscious decision, he returned pressure to the accelerator, driving on. Sully shifted uneasily. *food!*

"Won't be long," Dale told him. "You can munch while I check something at work."

Because there was paperwork to do. Right, that was it. Paperwork. And he could check the clinic while he was there—in lieu of the security guard he wished they had on hand these days.

He snorted into the falling darkness at the thought, pulling up to the light that emptied this back road onto Route 89. Just the thought of a guard in this tiny satellite town of Flagstaff—a place where people rarely locked their doors at night. Where they really didn't need to.

But they hadn't been getting those phone calls. They hadn't been welded and Maced. So when Dale pulled into the parking lot, he switched off the headlights and sat there a moment in the near darkness—sat long enough for Sully to remind him, with a whine and a paw on Dale's arm, that they had indeed arrived. He sat a moment longer yet, listening to the engine

ping, looking at the lights in the living quarters behind the
RoundUp Café. For that moment it only made him feel more
alone, but Sully didn't allow him the illusion for very long.

we're heeeere… He made a gargling whine deep in his throat.

"Yeah, yeah." Dale unbuckled his seat belt and fished in his
backpack for the clinic keys. "Hold on."

He climbed out of the vehicle and extricated Sully from the
back seat. No reason to feel watched. No reason at all. *Right,
except for the constant reminders.* He stopped himself from
running his fingertips over the soreness along the side of his
eye, up into the brow. Nope, nothing strange going on in Dale
Kinsall's life.

We'll talk later, Rena had told him. Not the Rena who talked
about her kids or greeted him with a wide smile on her freckled
face. The one who meant business. He felt a faint unaccus-
tomed flicker of relief. She hadn't just brushed him off. She
might still, but she hadn't yet. That was a nice change.

But she had told him to get a life. Laura had told him to
get a life.

*So here I am, following up on a whim that has nothing to
do with getting a life.*

Because never mind the paperwork and the clinic check—
now, he, too, wondered about Ledbetter's blanket. It'd come
back once and then he'd never rummaged in Jorge's stuff again.
Was it still jammed in the corner of his office after all?

More than that. He couldn't imagine Ledbetter wanting the
blanket back. He couldn't quite wrap his head around the
notion that the man cared what happened to the thing once
he'd given it up.

So Dale fumbled with the keys to the front door, let Sully
in and dropped his leash, and locked the door behind him
before hunting for the light switch.

"Grr!" The terrier's offended warning echoed through the

empty clinic; its nails skittered across the tile and retreated into the back. When the lights flickered on, Sully squinted back at Dale, caught in his hesitation with one front foot in the air and not willing to take that next step closer to the terrier's turf.

"Don't be embarrassed," Dale said. "Others more manly than you have declined to face that beastie boy." He gestured in a gentle shooing motion. "Hit the Sullybed. I'll be in with your dinner in a moment."

Not quite convinced, Sully nonetheless headed for the relative safety of Dale's office, casting backwards looks the whole way. Dale snagged the day's paper from the recycle pile behind Sheri's desk, checked the NOSE FOR TROUBLE tally—nearly seventy, though the new ones only came in a trickle anymore—and discovered the front section was missing.

He didn't have a good feeling about it. Not with Amelia's interview due to hit print any day now. Back in his office, he approached his desk with as much wariness as he would the terrier's turf. Not much could have pulled his attention away from the paper sitting on top of his unwieldy IN and OUT stacks on the desk. Nothing except his quick glance at the corner. At the Mess. He'd had to rescue his dead plant from it once. He liked the pot, a dated ceramic thing of bright yellow, endowed with the ubiquitous smiley face of the 70s. It was back in the window under the listing blinds, and the wet dirt had even produced a tiny nub of green peeking up to see if it had a chance.

In the corner, where the plant had once been, the blanket remained.

"Guess we didn't get rid of it after all."

Sully barked, more sharply than his wont. *dinner!* And then waited with his ears pulled forward and his brow wrinkled, worried about Dale's priorities.

"Yeah, yeah." Dale held the blanket up for a moment. *Yuck.* Old beyond old, a surplus olive wool square with ragged edges and thin spots, some of it deeply crusted with blood. Definitely covered with hair. Probably not washable at that, even if someone must have had hopes. "New policy," he said out loud, dropping the blanket with no regret. "My office is no longer the Repository of Used-Up Things. Used-Up Things can go in one of the dog kennels. Or they can sit outside at the corners of the building to give our visitors something to pee upon other than the corners of said building. And—*hey!*" He rediscovered the paper and snatched it up to stare at his likeness covering the top half of the first page. Well, there was Laura, too—smiling her quiet smile, the one that said she probably knew more than you probably thought. Yeah, a nice picture of her fine features, cheekbones a monument to her heritage on both sides, heart-shaped face tipped up slightly to glance at—

Yeah. At big, clunky Dale Kinsall with a bruise dappling his eye and black hair sticking up kind of funny and a distracted grin aimed more at his companion than the photographer. Sully was, as had been intended, aiming to nuzzle Laura's ear.

Bigger than life.

"In spite of Kinsall's checkered past regarding fires, he seemed comfortable and casual while discussing drought issues with colleague Laura Nakai of Pine Country Clinic—including the dangers from fire."

"Aurgh!" Dale said out loud, just like Charlie Brown.

"Grrr!" The terrier replied from its lurking safety, muffled but still emphatic. The overnighters in the kennel heard and responded, turning a single growl into a bark fest.

food! Sully retreated into a tight beagle ball on his bed, eyeing Dale reproachfully over his paws.

With perfect choreography, the phone rang.

"Aurgh!"

Dale let the phone ring through to the machine message with the answering service number. He stalked through to the kennel and closed the door out to the runs, and then the door to the feed room—but not before he snatched up the bag he kept for Sully. Sully's bowl came off the shelf behind his desk. Sully was no longer anywhere to be seen. Dale portioned out the meal anyway, putting it down by the water bistro-bowl.

No magically appearing beagle.

Then a particular groan of bliss filtered through the diminishing barking, and Dale twisted around his heel to discover what he should have known from the start…Sully had been obsessed with that blanket from the moment he'd scented it. And Dale had carelessly dropped it on the floor, where Sully now found the very best spot to roll his shoulder, compulsively rubbing his face and ears and neck into the wool.

The phone rang again; Dale let it ring through again. If it was important, Brad would hear about it. If not, then Sheri would check the machine in the morning.

They'd gotten into the habit of keeping the machine turned down. No more heavy breathers during lunch.

"Hey," Dale told Sully, tugging gently on the blanket. "Your dinner's waiting. Go for it."

Sully considered his options for a moment, frozen in the decision process. When dinner finally won, he leapt for it with uncoordinated enthusiasm, pouncing right on top of the bowl.

Dale looked at the blanket. "Food always wins," he told it. "Ugh. What a mess." And then he looked closer, for Sully had no special affection for wool. He'd never shown anything but a normal interest in the smell of blood, either.

It was hair that drove his little fetish. Not cat or dog or, for all he knew, moose hair. Sully was forever stealing caps and hats and rolling ecstatically on pillowcases.

Human hair.

Dale held the blanket up, making the same face that also occurred naturally any time he had to squish a spider. Oh yeah, plenty of blood, enough to make the material stiffly unyielding. And short, fine Dane hairs scattered throughout, as made perfect sense. But not enough to trigger a Sully-fetish. Dale glanced down at the beagle, who—with his usual perfect timing—looked up from his empty bowl to belch most earnestly. "Tell me I'm not really giving this so much thought."

full now. nap time.

Except he was. Giving it plenty of thought.

He closed his eyes tightly, squinching. *And was this the connection?* The reason he and the clinic had drawn such trouble?

He really wanted to believe that Jorge had been lying, had been involved after all. That the biker had made his righteous nagging calls. That it really didn't add up to anything at all.

Abruptly, Dale took the blanket into the treatment room, turning off the constant questions in his brain. *Just make like Sully.* With Sully, the nose was all. And right now…Dale would follow his. He flattened the blanket out over the metal table, taking advantage of the excellent light to stand back and consider it. Dirty. Redolent of dog and dried blood. Crusted thickly in spots. And there…a chunk of hair, held in a clump by a dried, stringy piece of flesh.

Dale hunted up a pair of tweezers, plucked a single hair free, and quickly prepared a slide. *Not thinking. Just doing.* He inserted the slide under the microscope at the end of the room, took a deep breath, and bent to the eyepiece.

It wasn't dog hair.

Not even short Dane hair. This hair was cut at the end. There was no thin medulla, no pigment reaching down the shaft to the root. Not cat hair, with its thicker medulla. Not even deer, with repeating patterns of spherical cells filling the medulla.

Human hair. Light Caucasian hair, if he didn't miss his bet. Fine, light hair with the pigment distributed evenly throughout.

And it had been attached to skin. To skin, glued to the blanket with blood.

Time to think about it after all.

But not to make any sense of it.

Alfred Ledbetter had left this blanket here. He'd brought in a Great Dane who'd lived one yard away from the first gruesome murder, and he'd left this blanket here with its human hair. Its human…scalp. Ledbetter had said to throw it out; he'd cared enough to check on it, however casually.

And yet Ledbetter had been in a public forum during the time of the murder. Captured for posterity in the *Flagstaff Post*, just like Dale in today's edition. Happened across the dog more than a day later, he said.

Yeah. Make sense of all that. Add in some prank phone calls, a few nasty incidents, and stir. Add in two more dogs, one confirmed from the second murder scene, one suspected to be from the third. *Make sense of it if you can.*

Dale couldn't. He turned his back to the counter, sitting against it. "That," he said out loud, "is because you're a vet." When he played detective, it was to discover what ailed the animals who couldn't speak for themselves. And if he'd once hoped at least to determine whether the recent unpleasantries were connected to his discovery of George Corcoran, he quite suddenly knew when he was in over his head. Connected? Yes. But he'd be damned if he could sort out just how or why. Not with Ledbetter clear of the first murder and Glory Heissman most definitely at the scene of the second murder and Jorge suddenly tied to the very kinds of pranks that had beset the clinic. Not a single one of them connected the dots to the recent events in Dale's life.

It was time to let someone else sort out the hows and the whys. To take all his hunches and questions and the little things that Rena Wells waited to hear, and to hand them over along with this blanket and its blood—*human?*—and its definite crusty chunk of scalp. *Sitting in his office...how long?*

Too long.

He reached for the phone. On second thought, he patted all his pockets, digging deep past the accumulated coins, lint, and a half-wrapped peppermint to pull out the already tattered card she'd given him earlier in the day. A little determined squinting deciphered her cell phone number and he punched the numbers, putting the phone to his ear.

A few rings gave him a bad feeling. Sure enough, in another ring he ended up in voice mail. "It's Dale," he said. "I've...found something I think could be important. Call me— it doesn't matter when." He gave her his number and hung up to give the phone a disgruntled glare. "It's the age of technology," he said. "I should be able to talk to whoever I want, whenever I want, wherever. Your commercials say so."

But the phone remained unapologetic.

"Fine," he told it. "Be that way." He'd call Rena in the morning. She'd listen. *This time, someone has to listen.*

For now...he found a garbage bag, pulled on some gloves, and tucked the blanket away. After he took the gloves off, he had to wash his hands a couple of times anyway, just knowing he'd handled the blanket. And then came the hand lotion— couldn't forget that, not in this climate. Unless, of course, you wanted your skin to crack and bleed. Sometimes, Dale had discovered, it did that regardless of the lotion.

When Dale turned away from the sink along the back wall, he found himself under the studious scrutiny of the terrier. It sat primly on its bottom, looking more like a football with legs than ever. It tipped its head in thought—an angle which only brought out the thinly sporadic nature of the wiry hair sticking out all over its body and especially its face—and seemed to come to some conclusion.

Something involving disdain.

"Yeah, well there's not much hope for you, either," Dale told it. "You ever see a live trap? Because I'm going to talk to Animal Control about borrowing one. Just in your size, too."

Unimpressed, it rose and left the room with an unhurried stride that showed its waddling gait to full advantage.

Fine by Dale. It cleared the way back to his office. There, Sully lifted his head in greeting, pretending with some fair success that he hadn't noticed the terrier incursion down the hall. *sleepy.*

"At least you've had your dinner." Dale grabbed the paper for a more thorough reading at home—or not, but at least it wouldn't be hanging around the office—grabbed his keys, and snagged the leash he'd never taken off Sully. "It's my turn. I'm headed for pizza."

And on the way down the hall, Dale grabbed the garbage bag with what now suddenly seemed like it might be evidence. A faint *grr!* followed him down the hallway as he switched off the lights. "Live trap!" he called back down the hall. "I mean it!"

The dark hallway remained unimpressed. Silent.

And Dale, tossing the garbage bag into the back of the Forester, suddenly felt like he was bringing the darkness with him.

FIFTEEN

DALE OPENED HIS EYES to the lazy ceiling fan, finding himself already tense, already in race-the-clock mode. For a moment he didn't know why.

Then he remembered the garbage bag. He remembered the human hair, the bit of scalp, and the now familiar feeling of being watched. He remembered that none of it made any sense, not even the fact that he'd probably managed to tie himself—and the clinic—to the first murder. *Because why would anyone have left behind a blanket with all that evidence on it? And how had it gotten all that evidence on it when Ledbetter couldn't possibly have been at the murder?*

And he remembered his wise decision that this particular puzzle wasn't his to piece together. He glanced over at the cell phone on the upturned box currently serving as a bedside table. It hadn't woken him. A quick, half-focused glance revealed no messages at all, never mind the one he wanted from Rena Wells. So…he'd call her again.

Beside him, Sully stretched, opening his eyes just enough to make it clear he wasn't opening them any further. *early.*

Dale rubbed enough sleep out of one eye to read his watch. Six o'clock in the morning. Was the sun even supposed to be up at this time of day? Maybe he'd wait just a little longer before calling Rena. She had his message; she'd call as soon as she was ready to deal with the phone. He'd sounded dramatic enough in the message he'd left the night before to raise the interest of a jaded short-timer, and Rena seemed to be anything but that.

Until he'd stumbled over the blanket, he'd intended for this to be a slow morning. A Dale-drinks-coffee-over-a-puzzle morning. Extras bonus, cold pizza for breakfast. His clinic shift didn't start till noon, and no errands loomed. His refrigerator was as full as it ever got, and he'd picked up his new inhaler on the way home from the fair the previous evening.

New plan. Get up early. Throw Sully out into the backyard. Turn on the soaker hose so he could work on beagle-proofing the fence for a while. He thought to double-check the day—odd or even—and confirm that he could turn on the hose at all. No soaker hose, no fencing work…the ground was rock hard from the drought. But he was in luck, if one could call it that. His turn for a little water. He went out to his back patio in his ragged gym shorts, cranked the faucet on, and watched Sully startle away in offense as tiny sprays of water appeared. A cup of coffee, a long-sleeved shirt against the leftover chill, and he could pound a few sod staples, extending chicken wire across the ground and up the bottom foot of the fence. The sun spiked across the eastern horizon, blinding but not yet offering any warmth. Dale pulled on a pair of jeans as well.

For a few distracted moments he wrestled with the coffee machine, weighing just how early he could call Rena. He had her cell number…would the call go through once she hit the street, or would he have to wait until she took a break? Maybe he should chance waking her. Maybe he should have just called the police last night and turned over the blanket…

Except he had far too much reason to know how things could get lost in the system when they had no context.

Outside, a truck rumbled down the street…someone else getting an early start. Dale scrubbed his hands over his face, decided the coffee wouldn't process any faster just because he was watching, and went off to apply soap and water to his face instead. He eyed his toothbrush, but…nah. Not with impending coffee. He'd have a cup and then use the inhaler; he'd have to brush his teeth at that point anyway, just to avoid having the charming fungal infections that occurred if one didn't.

Dull, boring morning thoughts. He let himself linger in his low-key state, grabbing up the tools by the back door—sod staples, hammer, hog rings, clenchers—to lay another twenty feet of chicken wire along the back of the yard. One foot along the ground and secured with the staples, another foot reaching up the chain-link with hog rings holding it in place. Not that Sully was a digger…but there was no way he'd get under this fence when Dale was done. And then he could spend all the time out here that he wanted.

Sully helped, of course. He sat on the unrolled chicken wire directly in Dale's way, staring solemnly at the box of staples as though he could change the contents into something edible. When he thought Dale wasn't looking, he made a grab for the box, dragging it a foot and spilling staples out behind it. Dale resorted to scruffing up the hair on Sully's head until the dog was so offended he moved a few feet off to stare thoughtfully at the hog rings. "I see you," Dale told him, delaying another grab.

Just past seven, brain still half on automatic, he went in to wash up and consider the prospect of breakfast, the other half of his brain still spinning over the contradictions and confusions recent days had presented. He stuck a granola bar in his mouth as though it were a cigar, chewing the first bite while he held the remainder with his lips, and headed to the dog food bin to measure out Sully's breakfast, waiting for the beagle to come charging in from the yard—his super-beagle senses alert at the prospect of food.

Dale knew one thing for sure in that half of his brain now

functioning. Whatever was going on around here, he wanted an end to it. He wanted normal days where his concerns were limited to getting those last boxes unpacked and mulling another excuse to call Laura. Hmm. Yeah. *Because you've been so subtle already.* Cool and suave, always his style. Uh-huh.

SOMETHING SMELLS GOOD. better than good. over there. better than breakfast. i hear dale and breakfast, but this…wag! very smellsome. but…outside the yard. poop.

look! there's a new way under the fence! easy! here i come! smellsome! here i come!

hey! who are you?

smells familiar.

bad familiar. when dale's face bled. when the stinging stuff hit my eyes. way before, before laura first scratched my ear.

hey! no! no, not yours! leave me here. dale! mmphgphh hand on my face!

woe.

COFFEE MUG IN HAND—Tigger from Winnie the Pooh, and one mug Sheri would *never* get to see—he cracked the door to the backyard and called Sully, whose favorite morning sunshine spot was up against the outside of the low adobe wall that partially lined the patio. "Hey, sleepyhead," he called, keeping his voice low in growing awareness of how easily sound carried in these still, quiet desert mornings. "Food is happening." And he waited for the scrabble of feet against hard-packed dirt, traveling the trail Sully had already worn along the outside of the partial wall.

Huh. Silence. A thrasher, boldly warbling through the songs of other birds in a limited playlist that didn't fool anyone. A Western meadowlark, ignoring the thrasher to sing its own liquid notes, perched at the very tip of the looming ponderosa pine at the corner of the fence. A very distant dog, barking so faintly as to be a mere watermark of noise.

"Sully?" Dale slid the door aside to step out in his bare feet—only to be called back by the ring of the phone. *Damned early.* Too early to leave Sully out there if he was on the trail of a stink beetle or night-cold horny toad, when his triumphantly ringing bark would inevitably follow. Yeah, the neighbors would love that, even if they were few and far between. He stretched for the cordless he'd left on the kitchen counter and snuck a sip of hot coffee before he answered. "This is Dale's mouth. Dale's brain isn't awake yet, so leave a message—"

"Very cute." The man's voice was brusque and familiar. Familiar enough to make Dale stiffen, reaching blindly to set his coffee on the counter, all his attention diverted to the voice at his ear.

"Look," he said, finding a balance between desperate and furious, "I don't know what I've done to get your attention, but—"

The man interrupted him, gruff in a way that didn't sound quite natural. "Too late for that now. You should have just stayed out of it. You should have tried to fit in, paid attention to what's important here. Dr. Hogue would never have caused so much trouble, and you've even dragged that pretty little Laura Nakai into it. Now you'll both have to pay."

"Too late?" Dale repeated, argument rising in his voice. "How can it—" *click* "—be too late when I haven't done anything?" He finished his words over the flat bleat of the dial tone. He scowled at the phone. "Whatever you wanted, you should have just come out and said it." All the previous threats and implications and indications that he'd displeased someone…even with the blanket in hand, it didn't entirely make sense.

Belatedly, the man's last words trickled into his awareness.... *You'll both have to pay.*

Pay, how? Pay, *why?* And did Laura—

Dale didn't even finish his own internal question; he dialed Laura's clinic, not quite sure when he'd memorized the number and only belatedly checking his watch; it wasn't yet seven thirty. They might not even answer the—

But no. The pigtailed receptionist picked up the phone, and her voice went from pleasantly business-like to...was that a giggle?...when she recognized his voice. "It's all quiet here," she said. "We just got here...we're doing a cleanup day before the early drop-offs come in. But oh. You probably want to talk to Laura? She's reviewing charts."

"Everything's okay there?" Dale asked cautiously, wary of inspiring a plethora of questions, but equally reluctant to interrupt Laura's work if he was overreacting, his mind too full of the bloody blanket stashed in his car. In the background, someone else fired up a noisy diesel and drove off to get on with their day.

"Sure," the receptionist said, surprised—and taking a breath for what was sure to be a puzzled question.

Dale forestalled it. "Don't interrupt her," he said. "Just...tell her to call me if...well, she'll know."

A pregnant pause from the other end of the line. "That," said the girl, "is a really strange message."

"Yeah. I worked hard on it." Another silence, this one not likely to end soon. Dale said, "Just tell her, okay? Thanks," and cut the connection.

And then what? Still too early to call Rena.

Not too early to call Foothills, just barely. Sheri might not be there yet. Isaac was back at work after several days off with a spring cold and he might or might not pick up the phone. But still.

Dale hit the auto-dial for Foothills and was startled when

Isaac snatched the phone up right away, his normally deep voice hitting an octave higher than it should. "It's Dale," Dale told him. "What's—"

From a man who spoke deliberately and never babbled, Isaac blurted into a pretty good imitation. "I'm waiting for the police," he said. "Did you know there's a stray dog in here? Ugly one. The door was open when I got here. Your office is trashed, man. The dog's looking kind of rough, too. He's got material stuck in his teeth."

"He bit you?"

"He bit *someone*. But he got clobbered. Kicked around. I don't think anything's broken but—"

"You *caught* him?"

"Not hard, under the circumstances," Isaac said, finally calming enough to insert a dry tone into his words. "Look, I talked to Sheri. She said you'd said something at the fair, about finishing up some paperwork."

The whole fair had probably known...

And he'd left the paperwork untouched at that.

"I locked the door," Dale told him, his words uncertain as he suddenly realized someone might have expected to find him there. Had actually been looking for him, and settled for bashing the place around. "I'm sure I—Jorge never had a key, did he?"

"He has a key," Isaac admitted. "But he'd never kick a dog around."

"He's got friends who don't have such a good record."

"I think they're still in jail. Or just got out. How stupid would they have to be to come here and—" Isaac moved the phone away from his mouth and said distantly, "Hey, Dru. Got Dale on the phone now. Better not touch anything till the cops get here."

Dru's answer came clearly through the earpiece, and did

not include words she would use in front of any of those grandchildren.

"Isaac!" Dale said, voice raised, waiting for Isaac's grunt of acknowledgment. "When the cops get there, tell them I'm on the way. I've got..." Well, it would have been nice if he'd been able to talk to Rena. But he couldn't keep things to himself until he connected with her, not under the circumstances. *Another threat. Another attack on the clinic. God.* "I need to talk to them."

"Okay," Isaac said, clearly mystified by the intensity that had crept into Dale's voice. "Hey!"

Scuffling noises assaulted Dale's ear; he held it away from his head until Dru's demanding voice came through. "What's going on, Dale?"

No Mr. Dr. Dale. Dale was just as glad to be here if she was in *that* mood. "I'm not sure," he said, bluntly honest. "We may have gotten tangled up in the murders."

"Besides finding Mr. Drowned-in-the-desert?"

"Besides that," Dale confirmed. He groped for the Tigger mug. A sip proved the coffee gone cooler than to his taste. He drank it anyway. He had the feeling he'd need that caffeine really soon now. *Already* needed it. "Look, I'll be in as soon as I get Sully rounded up. Just make sure the police know I'm coming...and that I need to talk to them. Okay?"

"What about that ugly pig dog?"

Dale blinked. The terrier. Right. Isaac had actually caught it. "I'll check it out when I get there. Just don't let it get away from you. And Dru..." He hesitated, picking his words carefully, and then gave up. "I've got enough to deal with. Don't make my life miserable by giving Sheri the idea I've told you more than you're going to tell her. The last thing I need this morning is Hurricane Sheri."

"Hmph," Dru said, and there was no promise in the sound.

Dale sent a stern look through the phone, little good as it would do. "Be good, or I'll find sly ways to feed you disinformation and Sheri will laugh her head off when she finds out you were taken."

Dru emitted an offended noise. "You wouldn't!"

Dale said nothing, letting her think about it. And think.

"This once," she said in a burst of words. "Just this once." And then, "Looks like the cops are pulling in. Might even be that Wells woman. You want I should tell them you'll be in as soon as you finish picking up beagle poop?"

"Rena's heard you use that one before," Dale said, not biting. Not until after he hung up and realized she'd probably do it anyway. *Too late to do anything about it now*. The cost of keeping Hurricane Sheri at bay. He downed half a mug of lukewarm coffee in one gulp, heading for a change of clothes— at least until he caught sight of Sully's waiting breakfast.

No way.

And no hesitating this time; Dale strode straight out to the backyard, past the patio and the low wall, out to the middle of the yard where he had a complete view of the yard.

The empty yard.

"Sully!" he called, short and sharp. Surely Sully hadn't dug his way out, not after all this time and only a few lackadaisical experiments with the notion. The dig-proofing was only precaution, not immediate necessity…wasn't it?

Dale ran to Sully's favorite corner by the ponderosas, the first area in which he'd installed the fencing. Undisturbed. He hastened along the fence line, hunting clues, hunting—

Hunting *that*. Disturbed dirt, slightly darker soil spilling across the dusty ground, a barely noticeable ditch beneath an already high spot along the bottom of the chain link.

Now? After all these weeks here, Sully had dug his way out? During breakfast, no less. *Sully. Gone.*

Dale stood frozen with the immediacy of everything to be done at once. *Follow any signs of Sully, of the characteristically cat-like paw print. Call Animal Control. Call the clinic, let the cops know he'd be delayed. Call—*

Call Laura.

You'll both have to pay. Sully, gone in the wake of the latest threat. Couldn't be coincidence…could it? And if not…Laura had to know. Had to watch her own back.

Dale crouched by the little burrow, looking more closely. Not wanting to see it, and then being unable to deny it.

It had been dug from the outside.

No longer frozen, Dale ran for the house. He grabbed the phone, auto-dialing the clinic and not pausing as he pulled a water bottle from the fridge, clipping it to his belt. Finding a billed cap to shade his eyes, jamming it on as Isaac picked up the phone. "I'm gonna be a little late," he said. "Someone's…let Sully out of the yard." Might be the truth. Sully might well be lurking around the edges of the property, trotting down the dirt road…off for an adventure. A cruel trick, but one that still left him a chance, even a slim chance, of grabbing up the little hound before he wandered too far.

"The cops *really* want to talk to you—"

"And I want to talk to them." Dale grabbed his inhaler, stuck it in his back pocket. Some men had little round butt circles from snuff cans. Dale's pocket wear-spots were more creative. "But they'll have to come here if they want it to be now." Part of him wanted that to happen. Part of him wanted to hand this whole thing over to the cops right now—whichever batch had responded to the break-in. County, probably; the one-man shift for West Winona tried hard to be everywhere, every when, but rarely managed.

But the other part of him wanted nothing to do with that which would delay him from searching for Sully.

Isaac's voice stopped him as Dale headed for a hang-up. "Dr. Dale! I meant to tell you, before—when Dru grabbed the phone—"

"What?" Dale demanded, in a voice for which he'd have to apologize later.

"That little dog. He's one of ours. Once a year, for spring shots and such. I even double-checked to make sure I remembered right."

"One of our patients?" Dale said, still impatient, not getting the significance of it at all.

"Right. And I thought…so I looked—"

"Isaac."

"And I was right! You know that guy who just got killed? The matchsticks guy? This was his dog. And then Sheri—she's here now—remembered that the Dane came from—"

"I know," Dale interrupted—even though he hadn't been sure about the third dog, not until this moment. He'd suspected. He hadn't understood how it all tied in, and he still didn't. But somehow…

Dogs at the clinic. Blanket at the clinic. Ledbetter with a picture-perfect alibi.

Never mind motive, which Glory Heissman had. Which Aaron Corcoran had. Which someone must have had for victims number one and three. Dale cared squat for motive. He knew only that those important to his life had somehow once again become a target.

He couldn't let it happen twice.

SIXTEEN

PICK UP THE PHONE. *Someone, pick up the phone.* Dale edged for the back door, wondering how far he could get from the house and still maintain the connection through the cordless phone. It felt like he'd been on the damn thing all morning, what with the good morning threats and the clinic drama and—

"Laura," he demanded when the receptionist answered, not even waiting for the whole introductory spiel, not willing to chance one being put on hold.

"She's—"

"I don't care. Get her. It's Dale."

"I guessed," the young woman said dryly. "On your head be it, Dr. Kinsall." She put him on hold after all, one of those silent holds that didn't even have a little click from the blinking light, and Dale sweated an agonizing moment or two wondering if she'd managed to hang up on him and any second the dial tone would kick in and—

"Dale." Laura might have sounded peeved; she didn't. "What's wrong? What was that earlier call all about?"

"I heard from our mystery friends this morning," he said, his mouth feeling dry just at the thought of the moments passed since he'd discovered Sully missing. And how long before that had the dog actually made his way out of the yard? "Not a nice call. You were mentioned…and last night the clinic had a break-in. I don't know that you're safe. And—" He had to swallow to get the rest of it out. "Sully's gone from the yard. I just realized it. I don't think it's coincidence."

"Okay." Her voice tightened. "I hear you. I just don't understand how it all comes together."

"Neither do I. But Laura—" He took a breath, lowered his voice. "I was going to call Rena Wells this morning. I've had this wreck of a blanket sitting in my office for weeks. Ledbetter brought one of the rescue dogs in with it. You know, the first time I came to talk to you? That dog. There's a lot of blood, Laura. A hell of a lot of blood. And…there's human hair."

"Human—" she stopped, baffled and frustrated by it. "Dale, I don't—that is, you've said that Ledbetter was at that trail use meeting—"

"Yes." Dale couldn't stop himself from interrupting, and took a deep breath. Rubbed his thumb and fingers over his eyes. "I don't *know*, Laura. I can't figure it out. But this blanket…the hair is attached to skin. To *scalp*."

Her abrupt silence might as well have been distinct words. *That can't be good.* When she spoke, she chose her words. "And you think the caller took Sully?"

"Or gave him a way out that wouldn't be obvious—under the fence. If he—if they—" for Laura had heard from a woman "—want to use him as another warning…well, turning him loose would do it. If they know dogs, they know that. He's a beagle…he took off after the first trail he scented. No one to point fingers." He abruptly remembered, "There was a truck. A diesel. I heard it out there…I didn't go to check."

"There's no way he dug his way out." She posed it as a cautious question.

He made an abrupt, exasperated noise. It was possible. He had to admit it was possible. "I don't *know*," he repeated. "I just don't think it's coincidence…it's too much for coincidence. I—" He couldn't bring himself to say the words.

Laura said them for him. "You have a feeling."

He didn't respond directly. "I don't think we can afford to take this lightly. They threatened you. They threatened me, and they may well have followed through on it. You should check your house. Don't do it alone, though. And damn it, be caref—"

"I'm coming over," Laura said, quite calmly. "If someone's been to my house, it's already done. My cat gets outside all the time anyway. We'll look for Sully. We'll find him, too. *You'll* find him."

DALE HUNTED THE AREA outside his yard, skulking around the prairie dog holes in the empty lot next to his, checking out the gopher mounds with the soft, disturbed dirt. Crouched, his knee coming through the hole in his jeans, his fingers barely brushing the gopher dirt.

No Sully tracks.

Microchip, he reminded himself. The small chip under the skin of Sully's shoulder blades would identify him to any agency with a scanner, and they all had scanners these days. *Supposing someone takes him to one of those agencies. Supposing he doesn't encounter a car first—*

No. Dale blinked, startled by the ache of clenching his jaw. His knuckles stung. He looked down at his hand, turning it over to discover embedded grit and grime…minor road rash. He'd slammed his fist into the ground.

Great. That accomplished a lot.

Or maybe it had. Because he'd gone beyond mad; he'd gone beyond simply reacting to the things happening around him— beyond reacting, observing, believing nothing could be done because nothing had worked the last time.

Last time, he'd played the game—played by everyone's rules. Played nice.

No more nice.

He left the empty lot, went back around to check the outside of the fence where it seemed Sully had made his escape.

Footprints. Oh yeah. He backed away; he wouldn't disturb them. It wasn't hard to pick up Sully's tracks, heading for the road; the disorganized tracks of an uncertain dog.

They'd probably had food.

At the dirt road, Dale lost the tracks again. Dale Kinsall, professional tracker. Not. But as he puzzled out the road, he realized there were fresh tire tracks laid down. Big tires. The truck he'd heard. Even under these conditions the tires made their mark on the road, more as a change in the way the light hit the compressed areas than actual impressions. Someone had pulled to the side of the road here, then backed up slightly to get a better angle on the way out.

Down the road, a limp collar lay in the weeds. Dale jogged to it with a sudden spurt of fear. Not Sully's collar…but one freshly deposited. A taunt of sorts. He picked it up, turning it over in his hands.

He couldn't assume anything. Someone—his mysterious scolding caller—might have taken Sully as seemed likely. Or maybe it'd been enough to lure Sully from the yard and let his beagle nature take over. A warning in the form of disaster. Dale didn't dare hesitate in his search, no matter the chances that Sully was driving down a road somewhere. If the dog was afoot, he'd become so lost, so fast…

He walked down the road, calling for Sully, stopping to peer down long driveways and make sure the landscaping wasn't hiding a small curious beagle.

He met Laura at the end of the road, where she pulled in to block the entrance with a rattly old Toyota pickup, rolling her window down all the way. Dust coated the vehicle, inside and out. "Any sign?"

Dale shook his head, his voice rough with simmering anger. "Not enough. I know he's out. He may have ended up in someone's truck. He might still be on the loose."

She tipped her head slightly, looking at him. "You okay?"

Dale snorted. "Hell, no, I'm not okay. I'm mad. I'm tired of coy phone calls, and I'm tired of taking grief when I don't even know why. I'm tired of worrying about the clinic. And I'm damned sure going to get my dog back."

"All right then," Laura said. She jerked her head at the passenger side door. "Get in. We'll cover more ground this way." She waited for Dale to jog around the front of the pickup, strong-arming his way past a reluctant door and slamming it just as hard as it needed to be slammed. "Which way?"

She looked at him as though he should know. "What," he said, the simmering anger overriding his usual hunt for the right words, "*now* you think I should have a feeling?"

She shrugged, noncommittal and unconcerned that they blocked the road; with three houses on it, traffic wasn't likely to pile up.

Aw, hell. Now was not the time to go hunting hunches.

Except hunches were all he had to go on. *Thinking* about things hadn't gotten him anywhere but trouble. No answers, no decisions…just confusion and hesitation.

"Down the street," he told her. "The same route we walked the other night." Familiar ground to Sully, when nothing else was. Just in case he was on his own…in case he'd dug out by himself…

Laura glanced into her rearview mirror and pulled smoothly out onto the asphalt, hanging below the speed limit so they could inspect the browned growth at the side of the road along the way. Soon enough the asphalt ran out; she slowed even further as they drove along national forest land, the trees rising up around them. Looking in silence; seeing nothing but drought stressed ponderosas and brown needle-covered ground.

"Left," Dale said suddenly, barely in time for Laura to make the turn. She glanced at him, her mouth opening—and then closing again. Left it was, leaving the route they'd followed on their walk to reach the pullover by the one of the area's many trails. Just enough room to park a vehicle or two. Laura slid the pickup into place but left it running, looking at Dale.

But Dale was twisting back to look at the roadside they'd just passed, at what might have passed for a dead snake.

A leash, coiled at the side of the road.

Taunting.

Laura glanced into her side view mirror. He knew when she saw the leash; she stiffened slightly. *"Bitsiighaa' chaa',"* she muttered, and then shook her head slightly at Dale's tensely inquiring glance. "A personal disparagement." It was all she'd say.

And by then Dale had looked ahead and discovered another truck, a full-sized pickup. Not so much further, even if partly obscured by a slight curve in the road and by the crop of roadside trees. He nodded at it. "Why not park here?" More than that, he wondered if they had a diesel engine. An engine like the one he'd heard in his neighborhood this morning. Like the one that had rumbled in the clinic parking lot while the faucet had been vandalized.

If you're going to follow your nose, there's no halfway. "C'mon." He unfolded his legs from beneath the small truck's dash area, and when it came time to slam the door, he caught himself short. No use in making that much noise. The door settled into place slightly ajar, but he only leaned his weight against it, letting it latch just enough to turn the cab light off. By then Laura waited for him on the other side and they took off down the road together, Dale with long strides and Laura nearly jogging to keep up. But she didn't question his haste or his direction; her only hesitation came as they approached the truck and her hand settled on his arm.

She'd seen it, too. That the truck was a diesel. A Dodge, with its characteristically loud thrumming engine, the kind of engine Terry had heard the morning the faucet had been welded, the kind of engine rumbling outside the clinic the day Ledbetter brought in the second dog…and most importantly, the kind of engine Dale had heard rumbling through the early morning of his neighborhood. Not once but twice. In, then out. And after the second time, Sully failed to show for breakfast.

Dale found the doors locked, the interior murky through tinted windows. The pickup bed held a storage bin—nothing inside but the usual assortment of trunk items—and a tool box, snugged with bungee cords to the inside panel, a little bigger than the norm but nothing special. Dedicated peering into the half-cab backseat netted him a limited view of a five-gallon bucket filled with tools he couldn't identify—tools he'd never seen before. If he could figure them out, he might get some idea who owned the truck…who'd taken his Sullydog…

But whoever had taken Sully…whatever reason he'd been taken…why bring him *here?*

And then what? Let Dale stew for a while and then return Sully pet as slyly as he'd taken him, probably with a dramatic warning tied to his neck. If he was lucky, this time the warnings would specify Dale's transgressions.

"Dale," Laura said, and he realized that although she'd been with him at the start of his inspection, she'd moved away at some point.

Dale didn't stop to sort his questions out. *Find Sully*—then they'd know. Meanwhile Laura still beckoned him to the woods, a gesture with her chin to the spot where she'd been a moment before. "Come look at this." She led the way, and knelt at the side of a faintly established trail to point at the dry, crumbly soil and obscuring brown pine needles. Not the rock-hard dirt of a packed trail, but impressionable ground. Ground that held an unmistakable paw print—and the cat-like print of a beagle at that.

Dale started forward, an instant reaction. The trail was faint, but he could still pick it out, winding among the trees and heading uphill. He could lope along and still find his way…but while his body could lope and his eyes could find the trail, his lungs weren't likely to keep up with any of the rest of him.

Run, then. Run until he felt the first of the exercise-induced asthma, suck down on Big Blue, and work his way through to the other side—where he'd actually function for a while. Athletes did it all the time…had it down to a science. Dale had never tried, knew it only as theory. Following the first attack, he'd have a window of opportunity. Theoretically. And with his maintenance regimen in good shape and Big Blue in his pocket, he had what he needed to get through it. *Theoretically*.

And then he'd find Sully.

"Dale—"

He looked back to find himself yards ahead of Laura, who seemed to hesitate out of concern rather than an inability to keep up. "It's okay," he said. "I've got it under control." And when his lungs tightened down—after a long upward slope and a little level ground, the trail waxing and waning before him but always that scuff of a heel print or slip of a toe to confirm their way—he put a hand up at Laura's concern and pulled out Big Blue. She waited, face flushed—and then she gave a little nod to herself and instead of hovering, ranged away from him, examining the ground ahead.

Breathe. Relax. Believe.

And it worked.

It didn't take all that long. Not even when it felt like forever—not even when it gave Dale just enough time to wonder what he was doing—whether he'd taken the wrong path after all, whether he'd done the wrong thing to go looking rather than heading straight for the police at the clinic and to the phone, calling every animal management agency and shelter he could find in the phone book.

Maybe his heavy-breathing friends had taken Sully. Maybe it had something to do with the blanket, with the murders, with whoever had been watching him.

Maybe not.

Should have called Sheri. No matter what had happened to Sully, she could spread the news of his disappearance faster than any other single person in all of Flagstaff. He had his cell. He could still—

A ringing bark sounded through the woods. A bark meant to carry distances while on the hunt. Beagle. *Sully.* Dale came to attention so abruptly something in his back creaked, and Laura froze, crouched over the trail. When she looked back at him he nodded. "That's him." Relief flooded through him. *We're in the right place.*

But they didn't have him yet. Not by far. Dale took a breath, testing his lungs.

Laura came back to stand by him, her eyes worried. "Someone does have him," she said. "The hiking boot treads, the paw prints…they're all fresh. If this were an official trail…if the woods were actually open…"

"Yeah," Dale said, his voice a little hoarse. He coughed, short and sharp, but took an unrestricted breath of air in the aftermath. "A little too much coincidence there. Someone's got him. Has to be whoever called me this morning. As for just *why*…" He gave her a grim look. "That's something we'll have to ask when we get there." He swiped a grimy hand over the thin, worn material of his jeans and squinted at the slope ahead of them. "I could call him, but…I'd rather not give our *someone* that much warning."

Laura nodded absently, her own attention on the territory ahead. "Ready?"

Damned if he wasn't. Damned if he hadn't actually thought ahead, proactive instead of reactive. Damned if this time, he hadn't made it work.

Well. For now.

He dropped a hand to her shoulder and gave a squeeze, affirmation and connection and shared determination. This time they moved out together, a forced but more moderate pace. They traveled in silence broken only by Dale's little telltale coughs, pointing out the trail sign as they spotted it. As they were about to crest the long, steep slope, they hesitated in tacit accord. Dale wiped sweat from his brow with a wrist as Laura pulled her clinic polo shirt up to wipe her own face. She unclipped her water bottle from her braided belt and offered it to Dale, who thought to refuse and then thought twice. If he'd managed to break a sweat up here in the high desert climate, he'd need more than a few swigs of water before the afternoon was over. He took the bottle, nodded his thanks, and swallowed deeply before returning it.

Laura drank, nearly emptying the bottle. She kept her voice low as she returned the bottle to her belt. "I don't think we're far."

Dale nodded agreement. "I feel skulky suggesting this, but…maybe we should stick behind the trees. It'd be nice to see them before they see us." He took a deep breath, clearing his throat deep and as quiet as possible…and getting a hold on his rising temper. "Besides, if there are trees between us, I can't lose my mind and go rushing down to grab Sully before we figure out what's going on."

"There's always that," Laura agreed dryly…but her face held complete understanding and Dale suddenly wondered if she'd let down her guard with him or if he'd just learned to read the subtleties of Laura somewhere along the way.

Maybe a little of both.

"Ready?" he murmured, unable to suppress another little

rush of fury that someone had taken Sully, that they'd taken him *here*. Unable to suppress a little shiver of the absurd that any of this was happening at all.

From below—distinctly below, as though the ground dropped much more rapidly than it had risen once beyond this crest—a dog yelped in confusion and fear. Human voices rose, angry and contentious. Voices. More than one. And that yelp had been *Sully*—

Dale jerked forward, a funny gray edge turning his view to tunnel vision, and at first didn't recognize the strong grip on his arm, or hear the low alto of Laura's warning. "Dale," she said. "*Dale.*"

Right. Caution. At least two of them. Careful approach, not stupid cave man charge-and-screw-up. Dale took a deep breath, tensed every muscle in his body, and forced himself to relax. "Yeah," he said. "I'm okay." But someone…

Someone was going to hurt. Even if it meant acting like a cave man.

Laura nodded at a stout ponderosa, and took his hand to lead him that way. She led the way to the next, and then—

Then they were looking down an astonishing craggy drop, the footholds made obvious where volcanic rock had been cleared of scraggly vegetation and fallen pine needles. The trail cut abruptly right, slipping through two giant rock formations so tightly that Dale would have doubted it was possible to get through if he couldn't still hear voices, now muted.

"That's good," Laura murmured, close to his shoulder. "If we can't see them…they can't see us while we manage this climb."

Dale peered down the rough track, automatically checking the ease of his breath. Still in that grace period…how long, he didn't know. But that first drop… "Can you?"

"With help." Laura turned around and dropped to her knees, feeling behind her for the drop to the first foothold—the one that was longer than she was tall. When she reached that point of commitment, she held out both hands and Dale took them, warm and strong and just as grimy as his. He lay flat-out, his head and shoulders hanging over the edge as their heads brushed and arms tangled and untangled and down she went, slow and careful and finally murmuring, "Got it." He released first one arm and then the other, making sure she'd found handholds and then watching—as though he could do anything about it if she fell—to see that she made it to the bottom. Then he backed up to the drop himself and thought he'd best not be the one to fall after all that.

But his height gave him an easy time of it and within moments he stood beside her, wiping his hands on his jeans as she shook her failing braid free and recaptured the hair in a thick, sleek ponytail. No words, now—she just nodded at the narrow crack between the harsh surface of the volcanic formations, and he scraped his way between them, trusting he could make it and not entirely sure his height would indeed serve him well this time. Maybe Laura should have gone first—

And be stuck facing Sully's kidnappers on the other side alone?

Then again, no.

With daylight in sight and a plethora of cinder rock roadrash on his arms and one cheek, Dale hesitated…listening. Checking the breeze to see if Sully would know Dale had arrived, would give him away with wagging. And he couldn't tell…but he could hear the voices clearly, so he held his ground to listen. On the other side he heard Laura's breathing, a little fast with effort; he couldn't easily turn his head but he extended an arm back and she took his hand, just long enough to squeeze it briefly in reassurance. She was okay; she was waiting.

"This is crazy." It was a voice that Dale should know but couldn't place. Not a happy voice. "I'm telling you, he doesn't know anything. If you'd left him alone, he never would have suspected that there might be something to figure out. But no, you had to leave phone calls and then that whole Mace thing—and what the hell was it with his eye? I saw that in the newspaper photo. I know you were hanging out around his place. Don't tell me you didn't have something to—"

"Shut up." Another voice Dale should know, strained and angry. "You seem to think he's some kind of good guy just because he takes the damn dogs. You think he's on our side? He doesn't obey the water restrictions. He went into the forest for the sake of a stupid photo. He's no better than the others."

The first voice grew into a matching anger. "Yeah? I'm not so sure about them, either. Do you really think you're making some sort of point? Because you might not have noticed, but no one's getting it!"

"Boys, boys."

Dale stiffened at this third voice.

This voice, he knew.

Marcia Roth.

What the hell?

"Al, you know we tried to keep tabs on the good doc in other ways, but they didn't work."

"You mean he didn't fall for your *charms*," Al said. *Alfred Ledbetter?* How did that make sense?

"Don't get rude. He's all big cow eyes over that scanty little vet from across town. Don't ask me what he sees in her. I'm *glad* I called her the other day. I hope she's been sweating."

Dale could almost forget that Laura was hearing this, too. Almost.

Until he realized she'd deal with it in her own way…that she wouldn't make it into a big deal no matter how she felt about it.

But Marcia wasn't done. "What I *don't* get," she said, "is why the hell you had to break into the clinic. Now you not only don't have the blanket, but the cops are officially involved."

"He was talking to Rena Wells yesterday at the fair," argued the second man's voice. Not-Al. "The cops were about to be in the middle of it anyway."

"Only because you went too far—" Alfred Ledbetter, more exasperated than ever. "Do you even understand the position you've put us in?"

"Nothing that's new to us," Marcia said coldly. "New to *you,* maybe. It's about time you were in as deep as the rest of us."

"Look," the third voice said—though there was only one man it could be. Laura's sudden intake of breath told him she'd identified the voice as well as he. *Yeah.* Those had been *bike* tools jammed in the back of the pickup cab. And the voice…belonged to the wild-eyed Waste Not-Water Not biker.

And it looked like Ledbetter had learned to play nice—sort of—with others after all. He'd done a fine job of pretending otherwise at the fair, but Dale suddenly remembered the rumble of a truck as Ledbetter dropped off the second dog. An impatient driver, revving the engine. The biker's truck.

"*Look,*" the man repeated, a little louder, and then a pause as if he were checking for the others' attention, grunting approval when he had it. "We'll take care of this, and then we'll go to the house and find that blanket. There's nothing else to tie us to anything that's happened—if there were, we'd have heard about it. But we haven't been so much as interviewed by the cops, have we?"

If Dale had had the patience, he'd have stayed hidden. He might have heard more…specifics and details about what these three were trying to hide, even though he already knew. Because though Ledbetter had had an alibi for the first killing…what about the biker? What about Marcia Roth? Ledbetter had gone back for the dog, that's all…no alibi necessary. Just as he'd gone back for the shepherd mix; just as he'd dropped off the beastly terrier. And other than that…he'd never been in "as deep as the rest of us." As deep as the biker; as deep as Marcia Roth.

Marcia Roth, who'd shuddered dramatically at the thought of finding George Corcoran in a neighborhood she sometimes walked now that the forests were closed. *Nice touch.*

If Dale had had the patience, he'd have stayed hidden. But Dale didn't have any patience at all. He wanted Sully, and he wanted to end this ridiculous episode. He let out all the air in his lungs, flattening himself for easy movement, then stopped short at the biker's next scornful comment. "How do you even know he'll come for the dog? That he can even *find* us here?"

Ledbetter snorted. "Didn't you hear his voice when he was calling for this little guy? He'll look hard enough to find your breadcrumbs. And if he wasn't the sort to find us, then you wouldn't be so worried about him in the first place, would you?"

And Dale found himself saying flatly, "Guess what. He found you." He slipped out from between the rocks—and then stood directly in front of the opening, blocking Laura. Her hand settled on his damp shirt over his back, but she didn't push. Not quite.

And just as well, because what the hell was that—a *gun?* It was the first thing to catch Dale's eye, some sort of big clunky automatic, the operative term being BIG. The biker held it, squatting up on a rock to freeze in mid-gesture as Dale burst on to the scene and likewise froze—not only at the sight of the gun, but with the desperate attempt to take in the unexpected scene before him.

Because…

Was that a damp spot on the ground? A *spring,* seeping out from under a big rock, surrounded by a cathedral of even bigger rocks that left only this small arena for four humble humans and one not-so-big dog?

Sully stood on one of those tall rocks, making throat noises at Dale, too huddled in on himself even to wag. *woe. most woeful ever.*

The leash wasn't one Dale had seen before; the choke chain hung loose around Sully's neck and the flat nylon leash secured him to a struggling juniper. Plenty of room for Sully to jump off the rock; plenty of length on which to hang himself if he did. "Stay!" Dale said instantly. "Stay right there!" But when he put out a hand signal to reinforce the command, the biker quickly brought his gun up.

Dale pressed back against the rough rock, but his voice stayed even. "You won't find the blanket. I turned it into the cops late last night. I found human hair on it and they know it." He spread his hands wide. "If that's what this is about, it's too late."

"You *checked* the blanket?" Marcia said in disbelief.

The biker firmly shook his head. "You didn't have the time," he said. "I picked you up in Cinder Hills not long after you left the clinic."

Dale shrugged. *Poker face, poker face…please be there.* "Not as fast as if I'd gone straight home."

And since that was true enough, given Dale's pizza run, the biker hesitated. Dale turned to Ledbetter. "Who is this guy?" he said. "He's at the clinic during the day, he skulks around my yard in the evening—" He turned to the man, getting a perfect view of an inexpertly bandaged ankle. Puffy, more bruising than blood…dog bite. *Thank you, ugly terrier.* "That was a Win-Win button Sully found that evening, wasn't it? That's why you had to clobber me—so you could get it back. Don't you have a *life?*"

"Not to speak of," Ledbetter answered for the biker, and smiled—if ever so briefly, an expression that didn't look quite natural on his scarecrow's face. "Family fortune, black sheep, blah blah blah. Spends his time spotting people who don't take environmental protection as seriously as they should. Soldering the odd faucet or two. Paying off money-hungry kids to do his dirty work now and then."

Jorge. Desperate to keep his job, sorting and reclaiming things from the clinic toss-pile…he'd been involved after all. He just hadn't known *how* involved.

Ledbetter didn't pause for Dale's internal revelations. "Gabe Karn, meet Dale Kinsall. It's beginning to look like you should have left him alone like I said you should, isn't it?"

"You damn sure should have left my dog alone," Dale growled, and Ledbetter turned to Karn with an I-told-you-so shrug. Sully inched toward the edge of the rock with hope on his face and Dale pointed a finger at him. Stay.

"Don't be so smug," Marcia said. "You think you won't do serious jail time for your part in this?"

Ledbetter snorted. "I didn't do anything but follow in your footsteps."

"Bringing in those strays," Marcia said bitterly. "Did you think it wouldn't be obvious? But no, you couldn't just leave them—"

Another snort. "Stray dogs. They didn't mean anything to—"

Dale endeavored to look as neutral as possible, but his new poker face must have failed him, for Ledbetter looked Dale's way, cut himself off in mid-word, and muttered, "Ah, hell."

"Only because I saw the shepherd mix next to Corcoran's." Dale blinked, gave Karn an incredulous look. "You caught him watering his lawn, didn't you?"

"I *warned* him," Karn said, oblivious to Dale's aghast reaction. "And Marcia warned him before that."

"And the first one? What—" Dale thought of the toothpicks Sheri had stuck in the John-doll's chest and couldn't quite come up with the words. Both of Laura's hands were on his back now; he could feel the hint of a tremble there. He leaned back against her, not so subtly suggesting that she get herself to safety.

Except, of course, that she couldn't get back up that cliff.

"He was planting water hog landscaping," Ledbetter supplied, and looked at Karn with some annoyance. "I never would have mentioned it to you if I'd had any idea—"

"Doesn't matter," Marcia said shortly. "You told him about it and that made you an accomplice."

Dale squeezed his eyes shut. So that's how Ledbetter had ended up in the middle of this, the man who otherwise kept to himself.

It wasn't even true. Maybe Ledbetter had figured that out. His face twisted with scorn as he said, "I should have turned him in anyway. I would have, if I'd known you'd take a turn at killing next."

"The hose was my idea, that's all. In a way he died by his own hand. By his own disregard." Marcia smoothed her tight sports tank over her breasts, as if the material wasn't already stretched to the max.

"But people still aren't getting the point!" Karn snapped, and his eyes had a wild look that spoke of a lot more than *black sheep* to Dale. "They're still watering when they shouldn't, still washing their damned cars, still walking closed trails, tossing cigarette butts into the dry forest—"

dale! dale—

Cigarettes. *Amos, the terrier's owner.* "But if you saw him, that meant you were on the trails, too—"

"That's different!" Karn drew himself up, pushing off against his knees to loom over Dale. "I protect them." On his bike, no doubt. Probably the same man Dale and Laura had seen only days earlier, exiting the woods on his bike. At the time, he hadn't looked quite so maniacal. Or menacing. Or capable of pulling a trigger.

dale! dale—

"Look," Dale said, and suddenly he didn't want to know any

more. Not about this woman who'd flirted with him at the reception and the environmental fair, and not about the wild-eyed man who'd once accosted Dale for being odd. Definitely not about a man for whom he'd gained some respect, but who had protected and aided two killers with more annoyance than remorse. "I came for my dog. If you'll untie him, I'll leave."

daaaaale!

"This is where we meet," Marcia said, a surprisingly vapid non sequitur. "At this spring. No one else knows about it. We make sure it stays that way. The terrier's owner was headed in this direction, you know."

Maybe not so much of a non sequitur after all.

She looked wisely at Dale. "We're making a difference. *I'm* making a difference. I like the way it feels. No one's ignoring me now. Now I listen to people talk about me and they don't even know it. I like that, too. I don't want it to change."

Dale found it hard to believe anyone had ever ignored Marcia Roth. But what he thought most definitely didn't matter. "Marcia—"

"You ignored me at the reception, didn't you?"

"I didn't mean to." *I* meant *to run away just as fast as I could.* "Look. You're all annoyed with me. I get that." *I get that you lured me out here with my own dog so you could kill me.* Dale swallowed hard, and this time when he leaned back on Laura's hands, he wasn't trying to push her away. Two small hands against the muscle of his back…the pressure increased slightly. Support and encouragement. *Or else a demand that he let her out…* "But the cops have the blanket. They know. Anything you do now will only make things worse—"

"*If* you handed over the blanket." Karn shrugged, the gun waving a little too freely. Dale flinched as he looked down the barrel. "Even so…we don't have so much to lose."

"*I* do," Ledbetter said. "It's too late! You said he hadn't handed over the blanket—well, you were wrong! So put that gun down—" He reached up for the weapon, hopping slightly to match Karn's level. "Give it—"

Karn met him with a sweep of the gun, pistol-whipping Ledbetter across the forehead. Ledbetter reeled back, tripped on the uneven ground, and pitched forward, arms windmilling uselessly, falling in the sort of slow motion that gave Dale time to wince, to see it coming as Ledbetter hit his head on the rock next to the spring, clunking it hard. He went instantly limp, slumping face down in the tiny puddle. Bubbles rose in the water.

For a moment, there was silence—barely even a gasp of horror, just startled silence. Then Karn turned to Dale and Marcia shrilled, "Just shoot him!"

daaale! dale—

Dale saw it coming. Sully, frightened and hunched in for the long haul with nowhere to crawl under, into, or behind, reached his limit. Sully, sitting on his rock and nearly level with Karn's head, a modestly sized dog in everything but voice—

"BAWHH!"

Karn startled wildly—and Dale was already moving, using his height to grab the gun where Ledbetter had missed, grappling with the other hand to bring Karn down off the rock altogether, one part of his mind resonating with *are you a complete idiot?* and the other part full of the determination that had been building for weeks without outlet.

This time, stop the fire.

"BAWHH!" Sully sounded off again, furious beyond endurance and dancing at the edge of his rock. Something slammed into Dale's back, something with elbows and spandex and wicked fake nails clawing for his eyes from behind. He'd forgotten about Marcia, and now he staggered to stay on his feet, still clinging to Karn. The gun went off and the bullet went who knows where, and then Dale took a second impact and he did go down.

He took Karn with him. He twisted at the man's wrist and hand even as they fell; the gun went off again. But amidst it all he heard a growl like a small wildcat, had a glimpse of the movement behind him and an even quicker glimpse of Laura's furious expression as she burst out from her hiding place. Marcia suddenly shrieked, her weight lifting from Dale's back. She swung wildly around as though she were the last skater on the end of a whip, headed for—

Klunk!

Right for the narrow channel between the rocks.

She jammed into place like a cork.

Karn saw it, too—and in that instant of distraction Dale pulled back enough to sling a wild punch, one with all his anger and fears and frustrations loading his fist, heading for nice crunchy nose. Karn jerked away and the blow landed just over his eye.

Something crunched, all right.

"Damn!" Dale yelped. "Damn, damn, *damn!*"

"BAWH!"

SEVENTEEN

"WHO'DA THUNK IT?" Sheri shook her head in wonder, making it quite clear *she* never would have thunk it, no sirree. And then she took another swig of beer and genteelly covered her mouth with two fingers when she commenced to belch. "Thanks, Mr. Dr. Dale. This is mighty fine."

"I think Doctor Hogue would have preferred champagne." Dale gave his own beer a rueful glance and then finished off the last two inches. He'd tried but been unable to find a way to thread the bottle through the cast that covered his wrist and the palm of his hand, and then left his two outside fingers bent at the bottom knuckle to stick straight out.

He tried again, just to be sure, then put the bottle on the floor next to the waiting area seat he'd taken. Sully promptly grabbed the bottle and made off with it. "Nothing but fumes," Dale called after him, as though it would make a difference.

It didn't.

"I don't think Dr. Hogue would have stuck around even if we'd had champagne," Sheri announced. She looked at his legs, which were in the way as usual. "Boy, you got long legs, don't you?" She looked around the after-hours waiting room for those who might support this statement—but among Jade and Isaac and Dru and Brad Stanfill and Terry from the diner, the giggling and snorting and popcorn throwing had reached epidemic proportions. No doubt the real reason Dr. Hogue had left his own retirement party so soon.

Unless, looking at what Dale had wrought of the clinic, he'd simply thrown in the towel on all counts.

More likely than Dale wanted to admit. He hadn't been what Hogue expected, not after all. He'd been on the verge of losing this job. And then he'd become the hometown hero, and Hogue had done some out-loud thinking on the virtues of sending Dale on his way versus the annoyance of delaying his own retirement…and had retired on the spot. No more reduced hours, no more extended packing of the office. No lurking around to exert his influence and keep things running "as they should." He had a financial interest in the place, but other than that…

It was all Dale's.

Hmm. He could make changes in the decor if he wanted. Dale thought about Sheri's observation and gazed at his legs, extended into the waiting area as they were. "Taller chairs," he declared experimentally.

"Figures," Dru said out of the blue, "that old man would finally decide to retire, as in actually *leave,* and he waits till you're one-handed. And me without kennel help! That damned kid. Stupid."

Damned kid. He'd told the truth about the Macing. He'd made some wrong choices…but not with the intent to harm anyone. Dale wondered if Jorge had the guts to come back looking for his old job once he got free of his legal tangle—and now that he was reportedly offering up details of Gabe Karn's previous payoffs for vandalism, that might happen sooner rather than later. *Make it sooner, kid, and you might just have a chance.*

Especially if it took Dale out of the target zone of that particular expression on Dru's face. Dale solemnly examined the cast, trying to feel remorseful about his one-handedness. Nope. No, that punch had been worth every moment of inconvenience from the boxer's fractures. All he'd had to do after that was sit on the smaller man, watching as quiet, reserved Laura plucked Marcia from the rock channel and flung her to the ground. She'd been ready to pounce, too—except Marcia put her hands in front of her face and squalled surrender so pathetically that Laura's attacking fury had faded to rolling eyes.

Seeing Ledbetter dead beside her probably hadn't helped Marcia's morale. Not from the blow to the head, but drowned in the tiny spring he'd helped to protect, an end every bit as bizarre as the other three murders.

But the spring was no longer a secret. Two gunshots had been enough to draw attention, and before too long Dale had eagerly turned Karn over to the authorities, all the while holding one wiggly beagle who couldn't get enough of licking the underside of Dale's jaw.

"Earth to Mr. Dr. Dale," Dru said. She took the chair next to him, nudging Sheri out. Sheri seemed just as happy to check out the recently delivered pizza. "You paying any attention? I'm bitching here. You're the boss, and I'm bitching. I want some help in those kennels!"

"Mmm." Dale tried on one of Dr. Hogue's disinterested expressions, but to judge by Dru's reaction he needed practice before a mirror.

"Oh, please," she said, entirely unconvinced. "Look. I can't do all that stuff by myself. I'm an old lady, you know."

Dale snorted uncontrollably, deeply grateful he'd already swallowed the beer. Then he stuck his cast out in front of Dru. "Here, sign this. And Isaac will help until you find someone who passes your stringent requirements."

Isaac heard his name from across the room, where he and Sheri had been huddled over the pizza but now huddled over the white board beside Sheri's desk, looking as though they couldn't possibly be up to any good. He looked up, nodded at Dru, and then nudged Sheri, grinning.

Sheri's return grin was a frightening thing. Dale decided to pretend he hadn't seen it. And Dru, mollified, was settling back into her own chair, clutching the can of ginger ale she'd chosen over beer. "Oh," she said. "All right then. I can see you've got your priorities straight."

"No doubt you'll sort me out if I get off track. Are you going to sign this?"

Dru pulled a pen out of the front pocket of her balloon-covered scrub shirt and absently scrawled something illegible. "But what about the clinic?" she asked. "Given you're short-handed and all. So to speak."

"Ha, and ha again. Don't you worry about—"

Sully came charging out from the back, skittering around the corner with that claws-on-linoleum sound. He reached the entry door just as Hank the mailman stuck his head in. "I'm not too late? I got hung up on a package delivery. Whole buncha loose dogs, and they…well…" he shook his leg in an unconscious gesture, as though freeing himself of remembered attention. Sully watched with some intent, his head bobbing with the motion of the leg.

"Nope, not too late," Jade said. "Have some pizza, I'll get him."

"I brought by that little carrier thing earlier—you still got that back there?"

Straight-faced, Jade said, "Ready and waiting." She headed off to the patient kennel room.

"Huh," Hank said. "Pizza, huh? I don't mind if I do." He patted his round, low potbelly and picked himself out a small slice. "So you got the bad guys, huh? Environmental vigilantes, the paper's calling it. You know, that Dresser woman who writes local interest stuff. She's sure grabbed onto this story."

"So I noticed," Dale said. He had an interview with her the next day…one Amelia Dresser had secured only by offering a written, notarized agreement that if she ever pursued his past, with research or in interviews or even by sending another staff reporter in the right direction, she'd owe the clinic free ad space for as long as Dale worked there. Every week. Quarter page. Whatever Dale wanted to print, he could print.

Since he suspected her editor knew nothing of it—and that she wanted things to remain that way—he thought he'd be pretty safe. He'd been certain of it at her expression when he specified the bit about sending another reporter after him. Thwarted resignation.

"Aw!" Hank said, loud over the general background noise of pizza chewing. "Aw, c'mon now!"

"Sully!" Dale stood, the voice of doom ready for use.

But Sully was already backing away from Hank, looking a little baffled and embarrassed, as though his misbehavior had just...*happened*...quite apart from what he'd intended to do. Dale tapped his leg and Sully hastened to his side, sheepish for only a few steps before he decided to forget all about it. He sat at Dale's feet with the look of a Very Good Dog and turned his attention to engine noise of the arriving car.

"Lookie that!" Hank said, delight replacing the chagrin in his voice as he put the remains of his pizza back in the box and reached for the burden that Jade brought out—a semi-rigid dog carrier with the top unzipped, revealing the battered, scruffy terrier mix enthroned within.

"Punk dog," Dru muttered.

Hank looked down at his new burden with a big grin plastered on his face and a piece of pepperoni stuck at the corner of his mouth. "Lookie that!" he said. "And none of the family wants him, for sure? He's mine?"

Jade exchanged a glance with Dru. "Trust me, he's all yours."

"Aww!" Hank said, an entirely different tone of voice, reaching in to pet the dog. The terrier nuzzled his hand weakly.

Unless it was just trying to bite.

"Ggrr," it whispered.

Definitely trying to bite.

"Just as personable as ever!" Hank exclaimed. "Now I gotta think of a name for you."

As darkly as anyone ever could, Dru said, "You'll think of something."

Then she turned back to Dale and said, "I guess I'll worry about this place if I want to. There's no way you can cover surgeries with that hand—"

Dale smiled. It felt beatific. He wondered if it looked beatific. He'd recognized that rattly engine. And he'd been right. When the door opened, Laura peered around it and might have been about to ask if the coast was clear if a chorus of voices hadn't cried, "Laura!" before falling into separate exhortations to come in, to eat pizza, to tell them all about the big fight. Dale looked at Dru with his beatific smile and she raised one expressive grizzled eyebrow. "Uh huh," she said. That was all. And then again. "Uh-huh." And Laura, beset by offers of pizza and Hank's proud presentation of the enthroned terrier and demands for details, looked through a gap in the chaos and smiled at Dale, and then startled him with an outright wink.

He did, somehow, restrain himself from going "Bawh!"

WITH THE PIZZA GONE and the accompanying bread sticks gone stale and Sully sitting imperiously on one of the too-short chairs waiting for Dale to finish cleaning up before making a last round of the hospital crates, Dale finally took a deep breath and contemplated the surrealistic nature of his life since arrival here. Since before his arrival here, in truth…except now…

Damned if it wasn't beginning to feel like home.

He stuffed everything into the half-filled trash bag Sheri had left by her wastebasket and leaned against the interior counter, using the lower level work area as a seat and crossing his arms to survey all with an unexpected air of satisfaction.

Then his gaze fell on the whiteboard, which had been of such interest to Sheri and Isaac earlier in the evening.

Never a good sign, that kind of interest.

DALE KINSALL, it read.

And

NOSE FOR TROUBLE: INFINITE

Definitely felt like home.